PRIZE SURPRISE SWEEPSTAKES!

This month's prize:

A FABULOUS SHARP VIEWCAM!

This month, as a special surprise, we're giving away a Sharp ViewCam**, the big-screen camcorder that has revolutionized home videos!

This is the camcorder everyone's talking about! Sharp's new ViewCam has a big 3" full-color viewing screen with 180° swivel action that lets you control everything you record—and watch it at the same time! Features include a remote control (so you can get into the picture yourself), 8 power zoom, full-range auto focus, battery pack, recharger and more!

The next page contains two Entry Coupons (as does every book you received this shipment). Complete and return *all* the entry coupons; **the more times you enter, the better your chances of winning!**

Then keep your fingers crossed, because you'll find out by November 15, 1995 if you're the winner!

Remember: The more times you enter, the better your chances of winning!*

*NO PURCHASE OR OBLIGATION TO CONTINUE BEING A SUBSCRIBER NECESSARY TO ENTER. SEE THE BACK PAGE FOR ALTERNATE MEANS OF ENTRY, AND RULES.

**THE PROPRIETORS OF THE TRADEMARK ARE NOT ASSOCIATED WITH THIS PROMOTION.

PVC KAL

PRIZE SURPRISE
SWEEPSTAKES

OFFICIAL ENTRY COUPON

This entry must be received by: OCTOBER 30, 1995
This month's winner will be notified by: NOVEMBER 15, 1995

YES, I want to win the Sharp ViewCam! Please enter me in the drawing and let me know if I've won!

Name_____

Address _____ Apt. _____

City   State/Prov.   Zip/Postal Code

Account #_____

Return entry with invoice in reply envelope.

© 1995 HARLEQUIN ENTERPRISES LTD.   CVC KAL

PRIZE SURPRISE
SWEEPSTAKES

OFFICIAL ENTRY COUPON

This entry must be received by: OCTOBER 30, 1995
This month's winner will be notified by: NOVEMBER 15, 1995

YES, I want to win the Sharp ViewCam! Please enter me in the drawing and let me know if I've won!

Name_____

Address _____ Apt. _____

City   State/Prov.   Zip/Postal Code

Account #_____

Return entry with invoice in reply envelope.

© 1995 HARLEQUIN ENTERPRISES LTD.   CVC KAL

I don't think I'm going to like this time period...

Not after that brief conversation I heard about witches and trials. Being a rather handsome black cat with the name Familiar, no less, I definitely don't want to be in Salem Village, home of the infamous witch trials.

What's the deal here? I get a little bump on the noggin and I wake up in "The Twilight Zone" in the company of this ravishing creature named Abigail West. But what's she doing all dressed up like a pilgrim and flirting with Samuel Truesdale, the driver of the car that hit me? He's dressed like Halloween's right around the corner, too. And I think he's smitten with Abigail.

Trouble is, we're in danger—and neither of these two lovebirds seems to notice that we're in some kind of time warp....

Dear Reader,

What can be more romantic *and* more mysterious than traveling through time to meet the man who was destined to share your life? We're especially proud to present TIMELESS LOVE, a unique program in Harlequin Intrigue that will showcase these much-loved time-travel stories.

So journey back with Caroline Burnes and the crime-solving cat, Familiar. The idea of time travel has always fascinated Caroline. Some of her favorite books involve that theme, but if she had the chance to travel around in time, the witch trials would not be her destination. Caroline would prefer the days of Robin Hood or perhaps the wild, wild West, where she is positive, in either time, she'd be an outlaw who specialized in tormenting people who mistreated animals. As always, her final words are to urge pet owners to spay and neuter to help prevent the flood of unwanted animals.

We hope you enjoy *Bewitching Familiar*...and all the special books coming to you in the months ahead in TIMELESS LOVE.

Sincerely,

Debra Matteucci
Senior Editor and Editorial Coodinator
Harlequin Books
300 East 42nd Street, Sixth Floor
New York, New York 10017

Bewitching Familiar

Caroline Burnes

Harlequin Books

TORONTO • NEW YORK • LONDON
AMSTERDAM • PARIS • SYDNEY • HAMBURG
STOCKHOLM • ATHENS • TOKYO • MILAN
MADRID • WARSAW • BUDAPEST • AUCKLAND

This book is dedicated to Ron and Ashley Emrich and
Chad. I could travel backward or forward in time three
hundred years and never find better neighbors.

ISBN 0-373-22343-9

BEWITCHING FAMILIAR

Copyright © 1995 by Carolyn Haines

A NOTE FROM CAROLINE BURNES:

This book in no way attempts to pretend to be an accurate account of the Salem witch trials. I have used a liberal dose of "poetic license" to create my story.

In the summer of 1692, the witch frenzy was at its peak in the small town of Salem Village. The initial spark for the ensuing panic was brought about by a slave from Barbados, Tituba, who belonged to Reverend Samuel Parrish.

According to the accounts of the witch trials that I've read, Tituba innocently enough began to tell some of the young maids of Salem Village about her childhood in the islands. Captivated by Tituba's stories of magic and wonder, the girls were strongly drawn into Tituba's tales.

At the same time, the girls were also influenced by the strong Puritan beliefs that every bad thing that happened in the village—a sick cow or a bad harvest—was the work of Satan and his imps. The prevailing religious belief at that time was that God provided all good things, and that all hardship was the work of the devil.

The young girls, caught in the guilt brought about by their "secret sessions" with Tituba, were smitten by a plague of bad consciences. The conflict was so severe that one young girl began to show physical symptoms of her "guilt." The rest is history.

Rather than confess to the fact that they were actually taking part in magic rituals—harmless as they were—the girls began to claim they were bewitched. And they began to name names.

While most of the accusations were made in innocence, there is no doubt some were maliciously made.

All in all, nineteen people were hanged in Salem Village, and hundreds imprisoned before Governor Phips ordered the trials halted.

The history of the Massachusetts Bay Colony has always intrigued me, and after a trip to Salem, I couldn't resist the idea of my friend Familiar making a trip to a time and place where his intelligence and wit would surely have marked him as a witch's sidekick.

I hope you enjoy my version of the Salem witch trials.

Best Wishes,

Caroline Burnes

CAST OF CHARACTERS

Familiar—Does the magnificent feline detective actually travel back to the witch trials of 1692, or is this all a dream, à la "Dallas"?

Abigail West—Has she been sent back in time to serve a purpose, and will she be able to survive long enough to figure out her goal?

Samuel Truesdale—Can he save Abigail from the fate she brings down upon her own head?

Caleb Hawthorne—Is Hawthorne part of a conspiracy of greed using the fear of witchcraft to an ambitious end?

Jonathan Appleton—Spineless and filled with power, is he merely greedy, or is he a calculating murderer?

Silas Grayson—What master does he serve?

Brianna and Georgianna March—Are the March twins victims, players or both?

Tituba—Spinning tales of fancy for bored young girls, Tituba got far more than she bargained for.

Elizabeth Adams—She knows the healing properties of many herbs. Is she a witch?

Sanshu—The settlers have brought famine to his people. Is he out for revenge?

Hester Prynne—Will she abandon Abigail to the hangman's noose, or will she return in time?

Prologue

Ah, the first full day of summer, the solstice, as it were, when the buds have reached full, lush bloom, and a handsome cat's thoughts turn to... check out the gams on the walking piece of artwork.

Tall, elegant, and with a definite air of mystery, aided by that sexy little black shawl that's draped so dramatically around her head.

Must be a movie star. Let's see, maybe Michelle Pfeiffer in disguise. Or Ingrid Bergman's interesting daughter, Isabella Something or other.

I can't say much for the choice of a black dress on such a summer day, but those witchy, little black leather boots are the perfect selection for those long, shapely stems. And, brother, can she walk. She's going across Pennsylvania Avenue like she's got a hitch in her get-along.

Hey, hey, it's my lucky day. That shawl has slipped off her head and she's got a mane of hair that catches every highlight in the sun and shoots it back. And that style, all long and curly, with those sexy, dark tendrils hiding her face. An air of real mystery. Reminds me of one of those old movies—mysterious woman walking along a street with great purpose. You just know she's on some errand with a sinister twist, maybe to pay the ransom. This gal looks like she's got a secret. Or maybe a secret assignation. Yes, a meeting with a man.

Check it out. She just looked over her shoulder—and her eyes! One's gray and one's green. Only a Trained Observer like yours truly would notice such a thing at a distance, but it is startling. But there goes the headgear, and she's crossing the street away from me, a woman of mystery continuing toward her destiny.

It's one of the pleasures of Washington, to look up from the bustle of a busy day for a little glimpse of intrigue. A cat's thoughts turn to flights of fancy, and let me say that this little episode is pure, visual dessert.

Hmm, speaking of dessert, I could go for a little taste of Sarah's cheesecake. Her shop is just around the corner. Traffic's a bit thick now.... Hey, Madame Mysterious, that car's not going to slow down!

Hey! Take a look to your right, woman! That bumper's got your name on it! Hey! Somebody, get her attention!

Holy moley, no time for human intervention—their reactions are too slow. I've got to do something and fast.

The best I can do is try to knock her out of the way!

ABIGAIL FELT the sharp pain in her back, right between her shoulder blades just as she heard the squeal of tires. The momentum of the punch threw her forward, hands breaking her fall into the gritty Washington street. Chaos erupted around her as tires squalled and horns honked. Several people on the street screamed, and Abigail concentrated on not rolling under the tires of oncoming traffic.

From somewhere behind her she heard several screams and the sound of a woman's sharp cry of horror. "He hit the cat!"

Abigail West forgot the confusion around her as her body began to register the sharp, painful sensations that come with a tumble into unforgiving asphalt. It was only a matter of seconds later that she struggled to her knees and saw the still form of the black cat lying just inches away from the car tire.

The commotion around her was disorienting. People were talking, pointing at her and the cat and the now-motionless car. The driver's door was open, but there was no sign of the driver.

In an instant Abigail knew what had happened. Caught in the tangle of her own thoughts, she'd walked directly into the path of a car. The cat had launched himself at her and pushed her to safety, but he hadn't been as lucky. The bumper of the car had caught him as he'd fallen back.

Crawling over to the prone body, she looked into the crowd for someone who might be able to help her. There were only dozens of strangers, all staring back at her. She saw the range of emotions from mild interest to genuine concern. "Someone, please call a veterinarian!" She made eye contact with a woman who ran immediately toward one of the shops.

Abigail bent over the motionless cat. He was still breathing, his lungs moving too fast and too shallow. There was a tiny trickle of blood by his mouth, and Abigail lightly stroked his body, feeling for broken bones. "You saved my life," she whispered. "You came out of nowhere and saved my life." She slipped the silk shawl from where it had fallen around her shoulders and eased it under the cat's head.

"I tried to stop." A tall, slender man in a dark gray suit knelt beside her. "I went over to the drugstore and called the Pet Unit. They're sending a vet right away. They said not to move him."

"He saved my life." Abigail repeated the phrase again and again, chanting it like a prayer. "We've got to do something." She didn't look up, but her long, slender fingers continued to move gently over the cat's body. "What could have possessed him to risk his own life to save mine?" She leaned over farther and a crystal pendant slipped free of her black silk blouse. The elongated crystal swung on the end of a silver chain, catching the light in a rainbow of shimmering patterns that danced over the cat's sleek black coat.

For the first time, Abigail West looked up at the man who hovered beside her. His eyes were a solemn gray, a gray as troubled as the dark Atlantic waters, and as stormy. His hand reached out and caught the pendant of the necklace. In that split second their eyes held and Abigail caught the scent of something burning and found herself falling, falling into a dark, black hole where the last pinpoint of light disappeared.

Chapter One

The ground was rocky, harsh, a physical symbol of the life of the people around her, and Abigail hurried down the narrow cow path that sloped toward the summery rush of the small creek. She moved as swiftly as possible in the thick, ungainly folds of the dress she wore, a dress she had put on as if it were her own.

Only it wasn't.

She couldn't say how she knew that it was not her dress—it fit her perfectly—but it was not hers.

Just as the house she lived in was not hers. Yet she knew where every pan, every crude wooden spoon, every sewing needle and spool was supposed to be. Just as her hands knew to mix the coarsely ground flour and salt with lard for biscuits. It was her house, and yet not her house. Her clothes, and yet she could not shake the feeling that she'd never worn them before this very week.

The situation was maddening, and frightening, and she sought the solitude of the thick woods, for Abigail West feared she was losing her mind.

Only seated beside the swiftly running stream could she find any comfort at all. In the desperate community of Salem Village, she was a relatively wealthy woman. Her twenty acres of farmland were rich, the grass, green and plentiful for her sheep and cattle. Her house was secure and warm, the planks fitted and the fireplace large and useful with a good draft. Her clothes were neatly tailored and showed signs of much work and skill. All of this was in contrast to those who still suffered from the harsh winter of 1691-92 and the effects of lingering Indian unrest brought on by a smallpox epidemic. For all appearances, God had turned his back on the majority of the villagers. All except Abigail and one or two others.

And yet . . .

Yet there were her dreams.

And in those dreams there were many frightening things. Machines that fairly flew down the streets of hard rock. Women who laughed and worked, wearing strange clothes. A sense of accomplishment and satisfaction, and a place where light sparkled into a million facets from tiny drops of liquid color. A strange place of silver and gold with jewels as red as blood.

Her fingers went to the pendant hanging around her neck. She felt it beneath the layers of her shift, her dress and collar, and the light cloak. She did not dare bring the ornament out into the sunlight, no matter that it was the only proof that perhaps her dreams had some weight in reality.

Sitting on the banks of the stream she hugged her knees to herself and fought against the memory of the dreams, against the reality of the beautiful crystal pendant that shattered light into all of the colors in the world.

Surely she was possessed. Where had she ever heard of such riches and magical goings-on? There were wondrous things in her dreams—machines that went faster than the fastest horse—with men and women sitting inside them and laughing, their eyes concealed by dark glasses.

It was surely a warning from God. Or a temptation from Satan.

She hugged her knees tighter.

If any single person in Salem Village had the faintest hint of what was going through her mind, she'd find herself hanging from the closest tree.

Hanged as a witch.

Abigail leaned her head on her knees and tried to calm the beating of her heart. How had she come to be in such a predicament? Nothing in her life made sense. Nothing at all.

The sound of the rippling water soothed her and she took several calming breaths. The people of Salem Village accepted her. They knew her name and, strangely enough, she knew theirs. She could call to them in passing, and know the names of their children and the number of sheep or cattle they herded.

She could also read a certain calculation on their faces as she passed. She was a woman living alone. A prosperous woman. In the three short days that she'd "awakened" to find herself in Salem Village, she'd learned how extraordinarily dangerous it was for a woman to do anything out of the ordinary, especially prosper.

"How did I get here?" She asked the question of a small gray squirrel that had come up to watch her from the safety of a tall beech tree. For answer the squirrel twitched his tail and scampered away. "Where are my parents? My family?"

There was no answer save the murmur of the stream.

With a sigh she forced herself to her feet. Another trial was scheduled for the next day. Already one woman had been hanged. A woman that Abigail believed was innocent of any wrongdoing.

She straightened the white collar that covered her shoulders and made sure that her long, dark auburn hair was bound beneath the white cap that was the ordained clothing of women in the year 1692. For a split second the numerals of the year jumbled in her head. It was 1962. Wasn't it?

Looking around her at the dark forest, she could only shake her head and rush back to her house. That was all she'd done for three days—rush to the woods and back, trying to return some sanity to a life that was completely foreign to her.

With a firm resolve to try to figure out her feelings of disorientation—and the strange crystal pendant that hung around her neck—Abigail left the woods behind her. At the edge of her pasture she stopped beside the road to examine a place where the stones had been loosened in her fence. She'd heard that several solitary women were experiencing troubles such as knocked-down fences and the loss of their stock. Some of the villagers blamed it on witchcraft, but Abigail clearly saw the footprints in the soft, damp soil beside the fence. It was no devil or imp at work, but rather a large man with cobbled shoes. As she bent to pick up some of the smaller stones to restack them, she saw the unmoving black form stretched beside the fence.

"Oh, my." She hesitated. The animal looked dead, and if it was a black cat, as she thought it might be, she knew she had to somehow dispose of the body. She didn't own any cats, especially not a black one, but if the animal was found dead on her property... Her heart fairly hammered with sudden fear. It would be enough to bring her to trial as a witch. Enough to convict her.

Stepping over the stones, she went to the animal and knelt beside it, using the thick folds of her cumbersome dress to shield her knees from the rocks.

Her touch was gentle as she stroked the sleek black fur. At one time this cat had been treasured and well cared for. Beneath her fingers she felt the beating of a heart, and the small body twitched.

"Kitty, kitty." She stroked the cat, willing him to remain still and unafraid. There was no telling what atrocities the animal had suffered.

Great golden eyes opened and looked at her. The cat glanced around, then returned to stare at her with a look of bewilderment that brought a tiny smile to her full, generous lips.

"So, you've awakened in a strange land, have you?" She scratched his ears and earned a purr. "I know the feeling." Instantly Abigail felt a kinship with the cat. "Let's see what's afflicted you."

Her fingers pressed and felt, moving over his body and finding nothing except tenderness on his left shoulder. "It would seem you've taken a nasty bump."

She lifted the cat to his feet and allowed him to stand. He staggered briefly, then seemed to regain his balance. "Meow." He looked up at her as if he waited for some action.

Glancing around, Abigail found the footpath empty of all traffic, but soon several of the village men would be walking past on their way to supper. If the cat remained near the road, they would kill him without hesitation. The stupid fools would think he was a familiar.

"You're far too well fed to be a familiar."

At the last word the cat put both front paws on her dress and meowed.

She tilted her head and looked at him. "Fed."

The cat made no response.

"Well fed."

He watched with a golden gaze.

"Familiar."

"Meow." He put his paws on her.

For a moment the insanity of the past few weeks of accusations and witchcraft hearings made Abigail want to bolt. But as she stared at the handsome black cat she lost her fear. "Familiar."

"Meow."

A deep chuckle slipped from her. "So, you're a fine black fellow with a moniker that would drive these bumpkins into a lather." She shut her mouth. Where had that language come from? She'd never heard such words. Was she possessed?

"Meow." The cat brushed against her gown, rubbing with a sudden affection.

"If you're Satan, you've come to a poor place to do your dirty work. I'm already half-mad." She bent and scooped the cat into her arms. "But Satan or not, I won't leave you here for the men to stone you to death. Or worse. In case you haven't heard, my fine fellow, black cats aren't faring well in Salem Village these days. White cats are not having a pleasant time of it, either, but you black ones are special targets. Now, you can stay in my cottage for a few days, until I think of something to do with you. But you have to stay inside, and you have to stay quiet. I'm risking my neck for you."

The cat's gaze never wavered. Very carefully he put a paw on her chin. "Meow." It was a solemn vow.

"Mistress West?"

The shock in the man's voice made Abigail whirl around to face the path, the black cat still clutched in her arms. Standing in front of her was Samuel Truesdale, all six feet, four inches of him. His salt-and-pepper hair was free of any hat, and his gray eyes were furrowed. "What is that animal doing in your arms?"

Abigail's hold on the cat tightened a fraction. "I'm taking him home. I found him injured, here, by my fence." She'd seen Samuel Truesdale on his way to the trial, but this sudden face-to-face confrontation left her shaken. There was something about the man, something that called up a sense of disaster.

Samuel saw the lift of her shoulders and her chin and he felt a sudden admiration for the woman who stood in front of him, the cat now shielded by her arms. But for all of her courage, she was also very foolish.

"I thought a woman who managed a farm as well as you would have more common sense." He waited for his words to sink in, and when she didn't respond he stepped closer. "If the cat is found on your property, dead or alive, it could bring serious trouble down on your head."

"And you'd be just the man to bring it to my door, wouldn't you?" Abigail couldn't contain the sudden anger that made her cheeks flame with color. Samuel Truesdale had been sent from Boston to make sure the rights of the people accused of witchcraft were protected. A fine job he'd done, too. One innocent woman hanged and another fighting for her life while with each passing day the dungeons of Salem Village filled faster and faster with the accused.

"I bring no charges against anyone." He spoke softly in contrast to her angry tone. His thoughts were distracted by the tiny pulse that he could clearly see at the base of her neck where the cloak had come untied and her collar was slightly askew. He could almost feel that pulse, so warm against his fingers.... He looked up at her, startled that he had not heard her response.

"And you bring no defense for the innocent, either." She spoke boldly, even though the cat made an attempt to struggle free of her arms. She dodged his paw as it aimed, claws sheathed, to cover her mouth.

"There is little I can do to protect those charged with witchcraft, whether they be innocent or guilty. The village is mad with fear. Those young girls have stirred the people to acts..."

"Of savagery." Abigail shut her mouth then, knowing that it was too late. But instead of anger, she saw something else in the dark gray eyes of the man who stood on the road in front of her property. Exactly what, she couldn't say. The sense of tragedy touched her again, a chilling sweep that moved down her back.

"Guard your tongue, Mistress West."

The sympathy she thought she'd seen had disappeared. In its place was a cool exterior of stormy gray eyes and a generous mouth hardened into a thin line.

"Or what? You'll charge me with speaking the truth?"

Samuel felt a sudden impulse to step across the half-destroyed fence and grab the woman by the shoulders. She spoke too boldly, and too often. And it mattered not if she spoke the truth. No one in Salem Village was safe saying such things. And Abigail West least of all. Her name had already come up twice in the recent trial of a witch.

"I would charge you with nothing except reckless disregard for your own safety, Mistress West." He spoke softly, but there was a hard edge of warning beneath his words. "It is not I who brings the charges of witchcraft, though. It is the young girls of the village, and now some of the men. As you know, it is my duty to try to defend those who are accused." He pointed to the cat. "If you're caught with a cat, you will be accused. It will not matter how I defend you. You will hang."

Beneath the ugliness of his words she saw something flicker in his eyes. Was it sorrow? Regret? She couldn't be certain. But she'd suddenly lost her desire to argue with him.

"I can't leave the cat out here. Someone will kill him." She looked around. A feral animal might have a chance, but the cat she held in her arms was used to being fed and petted. He'd never survive in the woods.

Samuel stepped closer to the fence.

"Meow." Familiar spoke directly to him.

"You know your business better than I do, but I urge you to use caution. Protect yourself from accusations, Mistress West. Once the charges are made, there is little you can do to save yourself, or the cat. Good day." He turned away from her before she could see the mounting horror that he felt. He'd sat through the trial of one woman who'd been accused by several young girls of sending spirits to pinch and torment them.

In the span of a week a roomful of grown men and women had decreed that the accused woman should die of hanging. Samuel still didn't believe that such a thing had happened. And was going to happen again unless he thought of a way to stop it.

He had walked a hundred yards down the road before he turned back to look. With a shake of his head he continued down the road. Abigail West had disappeared, along with the cat.

"God protect her," he whispered as he increased his pace, but he knew without a doubt that if the villagers found the black cat in her home, not even God would be able to do a single thing to save her.

WHAT'S THE DEAL HERE? I get a little bump on the old noggin and I wake up in "The Twilight Zone" in the company of this ravishing creature with the mismatched eyes. I mean, where's Rod and the gang? How come there's no theme music? And what's Madame Mysterious doing all dressed up like a pilgrim and talking with the driver of the car that hit me, who's also dressed up as though Halloween is just around the corner.

And where the heck am I? What happened to Pennsylvania Avenue and the parade of babes? I was celebrating the first day of summer and, bam! I'm in some kind of time warp.

Trouble is, I'm not sure anyone else recognizes the fact that we're living in the past. And somehow I get the feeling that I'm not going to like this time period—not after that brief conversation I heard about witches and trials. Being a rather handsome black cat, with the name Familiar, no less, I don't think this is going to be a very good trip.

The question is, how do we get back to Kansas? Or Washington? Or anywhere in the year of our Lord, 1995. At this particular moment in time, though, life could be worse. I'm nestled securely against the swelling breasts of one of the most extraordinary women I've ever seen. A nice moment, but I sense it isn't going to last. Why is it that I think I'm at Salem Village—home of the infamous witch trials? And what the heck am I doing here?

Ah, here's home sweet home. We're inside, and I'm impressed with the size of the fireplace. There's some serious cooking done on that hearth. But... no! I can't believe it. There's no refrigerator. There's not even any electricity. What am I going to do for food?

And, brother, am I famished. This time travel business has given me a ravenous appetite. I hope there's something good for dinner tonight. And I hope Mistress West, as the gentleman called her, understands the needs of a very finicky familiar—hey, hey, no pun intended.

Well, first things first. Some chow and then a little look-see around so that I can figure out how I got here and, more important, how I'm going to get home!

ABIGAIL SAT by the hearth watching the cat devour the lobster she'd placed in front of him. Lobster was one of the most plentiful foods in Salem Village, with the community so close to the water and Salem Town. She'd heard that the prisoners awaiting trial were served lobster three meals a day—if they had money to pay for food. Those who did not, starved.

The thought drove her from her seat and she went to the window to look out upon the fading summer day. How had she come to live in this house in this village? She had no answers to those questions, and truth be told, she was afraid to ask anyone for fear they'd take it as some type of omen that she was bewitched. She ran her fingers down the thick glass that distorted her view. Had she shared this house with a husband? She didn't think so. There was no memory of a man, or a family. No lingering sensations of time shared around the kitchen table with a loved one. What had happened to those moments in time that should have been part of the fabric of her life?

A sharp knock on her door made her bite back an exclamation of surprise. Her nerves were frayed. Knowing that whatever else she did, she had to show a strong front, she gathered up the bowls of food for the cat, hid them, and then opened the door. A tall woman dressed in the gray and white of the day stood with a tentative smile on her face. Even the layers of clothing could not completely cover her attractive figure. Though her face showed a few lines and crow's-feet, she was young and attractive.

"Abigail, I've just come from town to warn you. The village is abuzz with talk about you." She wrung her hands. "I fear for you."

"Thank you, Georgianna. Please, come in." Abigail recognized the woman as her nearest neighbor, though her farm was a distance of half a mile away.

Georgianna March shook her head. "Nay, I'll not visit. I've been to the merchants in town and my chores remain at home. Since we are both women alone, you know better than anyone how much there is to do." She reached out and touched Abigail's cheek. "Be careful, lovely one. The talk is vague, but it has a tendency to grow in Salem Village."

Abigail nodded, her dread increasing twofold. "Thank you." She was careful to lock and bolt the door as soon as her neighbor left.

Abigail returned to the table. Her legs were weak with the jolt of anxiety that struck her. She was in a place she didn't know and two people had told her that she was being talked about—with the clear implication that the talk involved accusations of witchcraft. Unable to sit still, she got up and went to the window.

A long sigh escaped her and she pressed her forehead against the cool glass. The meeting with Samuel Truesdale had unnerved her. She'd spoken too boldly to the man. What if he repeated her words or her actions? Nervously she glanced out the window to the darkening road. She could almost imagine the mob coming for her, dragging her to the dungeons to await a trial, or the mockery of a trial. She had not left her small farm in the past three days—the last days she clearly remembered. Yet the panic of the town was tangible.

A movement in the stand of plane trees on the far side of the road caught her attention and she froze at the window. Shifting ever so casually, she tried to get a better look. Day was fading into night, but there was still an afterglow, enough to highlight the difference between the trees and the road. The movement came again, the gentle swaying of branches revealing a flash of white.

Someone was watching her!

Beside her the cat inched to the window. A low growl slipped from his throat as he, too, stared out the window.

With a quick movement she pushed him away, removing him from sight. "Stay down," she admonished him.

Her shawl had fallen from the chair where she'd thrown it upon entering the house, and she didn't bother to reach for it as she opened the door and stepped into the gray of twilight.

The idea that she was being spied upon sent a jolt of fury through her and she started running toward the road. Ahead, the trees shimmered and there was the distinct sound of branches snapping underfoot.

"Halt!" She called the command knowing that it would not be heeded. Whoever was watching her did not intend to be caught. She could hear the person crashing through the underbrush now, heedless of noise in their flight.

"Halt!" She raced after them.

When she reached the edge of the woods she stopped. Her heart was pounding with anger and fear. "Damn them to hell," she whispered. As she turned to go home, accepting defeat, her heart nearly burst.

Standing at the edge of the road was the black cat, and he was staring at the woods where the watcher had been secluded. Every hair on his body was bristled out. His golden eyes glowed in the light of the newly risen moon.

Chapter Two

Samuel Truesdale sat on the hard wooden bench, his elbows propped on a roughly hewn table. He watched Goodwife Sarah Grayson maneuver her long skirt with admirable dexterity around the three fires that burned in her hearth. But his thoughts were not on her domestic finesse nor the bubbling kettles where she made supper for him and her family.

Instead his mind wandered back to his encounter with the striking woman, Abigail West, and the strange black cat. As he thought her name he had the strongest memory of the tiny pulse of life at her throat. He'd never before felt such desire to touch a woman.

Was it possible that she'd bewitched him?

"Your thoughts are grave, Samuel Truesdale. Can you speak of what troubles you?"

Sarah's question startled him, and he looked away before her sharp eyes could detect his guilt.

"The trials of those accused of witchcraft trouble me, Goodwife Grayson."

"That they will not admit their guilt is a sign of how deeply the Dark One holds them in the palm of his hand."

He bit back his sharp reply. He was a stranger in Salem Village, and a guest in the Grayson home. Sarah Grayson was cut from the same cloth as most of the villagers—so afraid of the idea of the devil among them that she wouldn't willingly say his name out loud. And that fear pushed her to demand harsh punishment for those accused. In his three days in Salem, Samuel had determined that many of the accused also happened to be those who had a measure of common sense.

"The job you've been sent to do is not a pleasant one. It would be so much better for the guilty to confess and save themselves the torture of the examinations."

"Indeed. At least death would be final. Their torment goes on endlessly." He couldn't help the sharpness in his tone. There were times, when he'd be in the middle of a sentence, when he found his tongue knotted by the strange syntax that was so appropriate to everyone around him.

"As do the torments of those they afflict. I've heard those children screaming and writhing on the floor. The good reverend has prayed over his daughter, but the witches hold that girl tight."

"I believe it is her imag—" He cut himself off, aware that he was about to accuse one of the star witnesses of making up tales, or insanity.

He rose from the table, unable to share the room any longer with Sarah Grayson. She was generous to take a stranger into her home, even though he was paying for his room and board, but he didn't have to sit in her kitchen and listen to her narrow, fearful views.

"I had thought to send a message to Boston. I think I'll look into it."

"If you can find a messenger. The woods are treacherous with the bloody red savages."

He looked at Sarah and saw the hardness lined in her face. She was not an old woman, but she looked it. Life was hard for the settlers. If the Indians were not a threat, then the weather or disease did their worst.

"I think I'll walk toward the township and see if there's any news of ships arriving. Perhaps I can find one that will go down the coast to Boston Harbor from here."

"That's the only way you'll get a message to the magistrate there." Sarah's smile was calculating and slightly angry. It only heightened the harshness of her features.

He left the house immediately and began to walk, his feet unerringly finding the narrow lane of the road even though the light continued to fade from the sky. His anger followed close behind him, and he walked fast, hoping to clear his emotions.

It struck him suddenly that it was no wonder Abigail West's name had been linked more than once with witchcraft. He had no way of knowing her age. He'd heard it rumored, though, that she was thirty. A crone by most standards. Yet he'd seen her, and her beauty was impossible to ignore. Her dark hair, an astonishing shade of deepest auburn tucked modestly beneath her cap, still caught and trapped the light of the sun. And her eyes. No one could miss that odd combination of one gray and one green. That in itself was enough to mark her. Add a milky complexion that showed no traces of the wear of time or bad disposition, and it was no wonder she stirred talk. Many of the women of Salem Village would delight in a witch trial for a woman whose only apparent sin was her beauty.

And many of the men would gladly see her tried—for different reasons. Covetousness and greed among them. He'd heard the whispered remarks. Abigail's farm prospered while theirs did not. Her land was better. None of the fools considered that the way she cared for her animals, just as she'd displayed concern for the injured cat, was the possible reason for her success.

At the thought of the cat, he felt a knot of anxiety. There was something about the animal, a look in its eyes. If Samuel was not mistaken, the creature had made a move to put its paw on Abigail's lips, as if to stop her from talking. Almost as if it wanted to restrain her tongue—a tongue that needed some discipline.

At the oddity of his thoughts he felt a smile creep to his lips. It had been so long since he'd smiled that his facial muscles actually felt strange. He'd been in Salem three days—an eternity. He'd come to take over a position from Jonathan Guise, after he'd taken ill with the pox. Samuel suspected that his predecessor had been sick during most of the previous trial, but it had not stopped the speedy process of what passed for justice in Salem Village.

He, Samuel Truesdale, was fit and healthy, yet his questions and doubts about the charges of witchcraft provoked only suspicions about his character when he attempted to raise the flag of reason. As short as his stay in Salem was, he found it impossible to recollect his life before. He'd gone to school in England and returned to the New World and lived in Boston for several months. He had documents to prove it, but no strong memories. Strange that he had no real friends or...

He was drawing close to Abigail's house, and he realized suddenly that if his mind was not interested in recalling his past, it was very interested in providing him an opportunity to see the woman again. He slowed, moving off the road to stand beneath a magnificent old oak at the edge of her front yard. The deep shade cast by the tree, his dark clothing and the fading light combined to make him impossible to see from the road. He had no wish to startle the woman. He only wanted to look at her.

Because?

Because in a place where nothing gave him comfort or pleasure, the sight of her did. There was also a niggling worry for her safety.

The paned windows of her house, another flagrant sign of her prosperity, did not give a clear view inside, but he saw movement. A slender form passed by the front window. It would be the kitchen, he knew. All of the houses of Salem

Village were similar in design. The front door opened into a small hallway that divided the family room and the kitchen. There were two bedrooms behind those rooms, and more small bedrooms upstairs for those who could afford the upper addition. The steep slope of the roof made the upstairs difficult for a tall man—he knew from personal experience. The Grayson home had an upper story, where he was staying. So did Abigail's home.

All of that space for a woman who lived alone.

He shifted his weight and leaned back against the trunk of the tree. She was as much a mystery to the town as he was. She lived and worked, minding her own affairs. It should be enough to guarantee her safety from her peers.

The sun was sinking rapidly, and he knew he should walk back to the Graysons'. Sarah would be putting food on the table, and Silas Grayson did not like to wait to eat.

Especially not after a day spent in the arduous pursuit of justice.

At that thought Samuel winced. Silas Grayson was deeply involved in the witch trials. To the total neglect of his farm, he had maneuvered himself into an almost-official capacity, attending the questioning of the accused, sitting at the table where the magistrate, the corpulent Jonathan Appleton, made his decision, whispering his questions and recommendations to the prosecutor, Caleb Hawthorne, and the other men who decided the fate of some hapless victim. Silas Grayson performed his voluntary duties with great energy. If he tended his farm with such zeal perhaps he wouldn't always be unfavorably comparing his lot to others.

Samuel watched a moment longer, hoping that Abigail would step outside her door for some small errand. As he waited, the golden scythe of a new moon edged over the dark trees, casting a beautiful, glittering light on the road.

There was much of beauty in the new frontier of Salem Village. The land could be hard, but it could also be breathtaking. With the proper leadership, it could be a land of opportunity, not of persecution. But as June of 1692 eased to a close, Samuel was not certain which path the small village would take.

A movement at the window caught his eye, and he thought for a second he could see Abigail leaning her forehead against the wavery glass. Perhaps it was he who was imagining now. Again he smiled, and as he started to turn he heard the crackle of a limb in the deep underbrush across the road.

Though he had spent time in London learning the law, he had not forgotten the hard lessons of the wilderness. Instantly he moved to cling more closely to the protection of the big tree while his gaze pierced the darkness.

Someone was in the bushes. Someone was watching Abigail's house.

The knife of fear touched his heart. He knew from past testimony that it was often the word of spies, those who took everyday movements and twisted them into suspicious behavior, that brought ruin down on those accused of witchcraft. Who was watching Abigail?

The creak of hinges made him turn back to the house.

Abigail West, without benefit of her cloak, had stepped into the doorway. "Halt!" she called into the night. Then she started forward, running as fast as her multitude of skirts would allow.

"Holy Christ!" Samuel muttered to himself as he started forward, then stopped. His behavior and his language shocked him. Where had he learned such a blasphemous phrase? And what would he do—grab the woman and prevent her from entering the woods? How would he explain his presence there? Was he not spying, as well?

The questions worked as an effective hamstring, giving the watcher the time to flee. Samuel heard the crackle of branches and the sound of a body moving rapidly through the underbrush. Though his impulse was to give pursuit, he lingered in the protection of the tree. Clenching his fists in frustration, he reminded himself that it would do Abigail no good for him to rush out of her yard in the dead of the night. In fact, that could prove extremely damaging—to them both. Conduct between the sexes was severely regulated.

His attention was focused on the figure of the woman standing in the road when another noise caught his attention.

The black cat appeared beside Abigail.

Unable to look away, he saw the creature swell and puff to twice its normal size. It stopped right at Abigail's feet and stared into the woods. The most incredible sound—that of an angry snake—came from its distended throat.

Samuel watched as Abigail, ignorant of his presence, stood in the road, her chest heaving with exertion and anger. "Damn idiots," she whispered. "Stupid, moronic asses." She bent down to the cat. "I wonder what they hoped to see?"

"Meow." The cat started toward the woods and Abigail scooped him into her arms. "Not so fast, my little Familiar. You've got to stay in the house."

From behind the tree, Samuel could clearly hear her words. The shock was numbing. In the three torturous days of witch trials, he'd never head anything that sounded one-tenth as guilty as the words coming from Abigail West's mouth. And her behavior with the cat. She was cuddling him as if he were a human baby. The sight made his blood run cold.

"How about some goat's milk?" Abigail asked the cat.

"Meow." Familiar's purr echoed in the still night.

"That's your reward for guarding me." Abigail turned back toward her open door.

Samuel held his breath, hoping she would return inside without seeing him. He watched as she stepped under the branches of the tree. Suddenly the cat stiffened.

"What?" Abigail asked.

Before she could tighten her hold, the cat jumped from her arms and ran straight for the tree—and Samuel.

"Meow!" Familiar's greeting was distinct.

Abigail followed the cat, stopping when she saw the outline of a tall man beside the tree trunk. "Who are you?"

Samuel admired the fact that her voice lacked fear. He stepped out. "Samuel Truesdale, Mistress West."

"You've come to borrow a cup of sugar, no doubt?"

Abigail's strange talk confused him, but it was easy to read the sarcasm in her voice. "No, I came to visit you."

"Visit or spy?"

He hesitated. "Both." Once again he was struck by a terrible desire to reach across the night and touch her cheek, perhaps the corner of her mouth, which was held in such an angry frown.

"Explain yourself." Abigail mustered her anger around her. The handsome man standing in her yard was unsettling. There was a calmness about him, touched with sadness. He was not like the other men of the community, the ones who stared after her with ugly interest and a greedy desire.

"I came to spy on you because I was worried about you. But I wanted to visit. I was watching, hoping for a glimpse of you." He realized how that sounded and hurried on. "A glimpse to make certain that you were safe. That no one was trying to injure you."

"And do you anticipate that someone will try to harm me?" Fear made her breath short but she fought against showing it. Deep in her bones she also felt that sense of impending doom. The black cat's arrival had been an omen, but she'd felt tragedy headed her way even before then.

"Yes," he answered softly. "Your conduct begs examination."

"Because I'm not a stupid fool who's afraid of every shadow and cat. Because I manage my property with competency. Because I am a woman who chooses to live alone."

"All of those things, and because you are so very beautiful."

His statement startled her, defusing the head of anger she had begun to build at the unfairness of the villagers.

"You must be more careful." He pressed his advantage. "I heard you talking—to the cat." He couldn't help the shudder of apprehension that touched him at the memory. "You speak to it as if it can understand you. That alone is enough to make you hang."

Abigail knew true fear at that moment. She recalled perfectly what she'd said. "Yes, if the court hears of my behavior, they'll certainly charge me with witchcraft. Someone is already spying on me."

Samuel nodded. "I came to warn you."

"Why?" Abigail let the question slip.

Samuel considered his answer. "I don't know. You... don't belong here. You're in danger because of that. Watch yourself." He turned abruptly and walked away, leaving Abigail and the cat alone beneath the tree.

"He's a strange one, isn't he?" Abigail spoke to the cat despite Samuel's warning.

"Meow."

She felt the prickle of a hundred eyes watching her from the darkness. Unfriendly eyes. "Let's get inside, fast." The cat at her heels, she hurried back to the safety of her house.

Once inside, Abigail prepared the bowl of goat's milk, which Familiar approached with some trepidation. Abigail took her place on a stool and picked up the yarn that was wound in a basket at her feet. The idea of making something was amusingly quaint. But then she dropped the yarn, got up, and went to examine a small stack of books she'd seen in the drawing room.

Worn, but still in good shape, was a Bible. Beside it was a copy of *Pilgrim's Progress* and a slender volume of stories. "*Beowulf,* every graduate student's nightmare." At the sound of her own voice her skin prickled. What had she said? What did the words mean? How did she know the story contained in the book—she'd never seen that book before, to her knowledge. And what was a graduate student?

Easing the book onto the table, she stepped back, moving clumsily to the kitchen where the light of the fire gave her some sense of comfort. Just as she passed the door there was a loud, rapid knock. Her heart leapt into her throat, and she had to grab the wall for support.

"Abigail, will you open the door for us? Please."

The woman's voice was frightened.

Responding to the need she heard, Abigail pulled the door open. The woman who stood in front of her was covered from head to toe in a dark cloak. Beside her was a little girl, an elfin creature with curls and dark, questioning eyes. The woman looked down and pulled the child against her leg. "Abigail?" She spoke with uncertainty. "What's wrong? Won't you allow us to enter?"

Abigail felt her senses reel. She knew this woman, and yet it was not possible.

"Abby, are you ill?" The woman stepped forward into the house and gently brushed Abigail's cheek with her cool hand. "Don't you know me?"

"Hester, what are you doing here?" Abigail cast a look out into the night to make certain no one was still watching her, then closed and braced the door.

"I've come to...I'm leaving Massachusetts Colony. Pearl and I wanted to say goodbye. We can no longer stay here."

Abigail motioned them into the kitchen where she grabbed the back of a chair for support. Her knees were weak, her head spinning. The woman who stood in front of her was Hester Prynne. There was no doubt about it. And she was a friend.

Almost defiantly Hester removed her cloak and draped it over a chair. When she turned back to face Abigail, the light from the fire caught the gleaming red threads of the scarlet *A* she wore emblazoned on her chest.

"Where will you go?"

Hester tossed her head, shaking her hair free of the white cap. "It doesn't matter. I've been such a fool, taking all of the blame and letting that spineless Arthur Dimmsdale escape. You know, I always thought he'd step forward and say that he was as much to blame as I was." She slumped into the chair. "But he won't. The man has no character. He's perfectly willing to let everyone believe that he was an innocent." She covered her eyes with one hand. "I was such a fool."

Abigail moved to stand behind her, her arms slipping around Hester for a hug. "You believed in him. You cared for him. Now you see him for what he is."

"A fake. An impostor." Hester looked up. "A coward."

"That and more," Abigail agreed. "Just think how lucky you are he didn't want to marry you. You'd spend the rest of your life trying to shore him up."

Hester's smile transformed her face.

"And look." Abigail pointed to the child who was sitting in front of the fireplace and playing with the cat. "You have Pearl. You have the best of anything he could have given you."

"And it is for Pearl's sake that we are leaving. I don't want her to grow up and be ashamed of me, and the people of Boston will make certain that she is if we stay there."

Abigail put a kettle of water on to heat and then slipped into a chair at her table. "It's a wise move, Hester. I'm happy for you." She looked at the woman again, still a little unnerved. Hester Prynne. She was a real woman. Sitting right at her table.

"I came to ask if you want to come with me, Abigail. The witch trials are only going to get worse. I'm afraid for you here. It's one thing to be branded an adulteress. It's another to be convicted as a witch." Hester reached across the table and took Abigail's hand. "They'll hang you."

Abigail tried to find a laugh deep inside, but it wasn't there. Hester would have been able to see through her false joviality, anyway.

"I stopped at the inn in Salem Town. I heard two men talking." Hester's dark eyes widened as she bit her lip. "They say that there will be more hangings. Many more. They say that Satan has been seen walking the roads of Salem Village. I was almost too afraid to come here, since it was dark."

"Then you must stay the night. Tomorrow I'll walk you back to the town."

"I have to find a ship. I've heard exciting stories about the West Indie Islands. One reason I came to Salem Village was to talk to Tituba. She is still with the reverend, isn't she?"

"Tituba tells of many wondrous things in her homeland." Abigail said the black woman's name with some trepidation. "Of course, she's in prison now, soon to be tried for witchcraft herself."

"Tituba? I had not heard." Hester's face registered real concern. "She's only a slave with a talent for storytelling."

"You know that. I know that. But the magistrate is all too eager to believe otherwise."

Hester grabbed Abigail's hands and clutched them firmly. "You must get away from here yourself, Abby. And I should never have come here. I've put you in more jeopardy." She shrugged. "A woman who sins without asking for forgiveness is not the ideal guest."

Abigail smiled. "I cannot have the friends of my own choosing? I've been told today not to befriend an injured cat. Soon I will not be able to prepare the simple medicines

I use to treat the sick. Little by little, my life is being taken from me."

"So you'll come with me and Pearl?" Hester was hopeful.

The idea was tempting. Abigail looked around the room that was so familiar and yet kindled not a single actual memory. She could walk away from Salem Village without a backward glance. Old man Elika Adams would take her sheep and cows and care for them as best he could. The property could be sold.

Abigail got up, still without answering her friend, and went to the window to look out into the darkness that was her front yard. It would be so easy to leave. Why wouldn't she?

"You will not leave, will you?" Hester turned in her chair but didn't rise.

"I can't."

"Why not? You have no family here. No one to care about and no one to care about you. We could start over together, Abigail. We could go somewhere and find a new life. Maybe one with some love in it."

The pull of Hester's words was almost more than Abigail could bear. Oh, she wanted to go, to leave the coldness and harshness of the coming winter, to frolic on some white, sandy beach where the water was the color of a precious gem. But she couldn't.

"It's hard to explain, but I feel that I have to stay here."

"Because you're afraid to try someplace new." Hester dared her friend to look at her.

Still facing the window, Abigail smiled. "No, I relish someplace new. But I sense there is something here I must do before I leave."

"Get yourself hanged?"

Abigail laughed this time, turning to see the anger on her friend's face. "I hope not. But it is something to do with the trials. They're wrong, Hester. Very wrong. This whole foolishness has to be stopped."

"And what can you, a woman, do to stop it?" Hester threw up her hands. "Why don't you hang yourself now? At least I'll be here to see that you're properly buried."

Abigail went to her friend and circled her with her arms. "No, I don't want to die. I want to stop others from dying."

Hester finally calmed. "How? How will you do this?"

"I don't know," Abigail admitted. "I only know that I can't leave without trying."

"Even if it costs your life?" Hester grasped her friend's shoulders. "Think of the danger, Abby. Think long and hard on it before you commit yourself to a path that leads only to the grave."

Chapter Three

The pounding on the door woke Abigail from a sound sleep. As she started to rise from the bed a large black paw caught her shoulder and held her. She was eye to golden eye with the black cat who'd obviously been sleeping on the pillow beside her. His black fur was bristled in anger, or fear.

"Okay, I'll be careful." She got out from under the covers and found her cloak to wrap around her dressing gown. At the door she paused, her heart hammering. "Who is it?"

"Open the door," a gruff male voice ordered.

"Who is it?" Abigail repeated.

"On the order of the magistrate, open the door."

Paralysis gripped Abigail. When she could finally move, she looked up to see Hester and Pearl cowering on the steep ladder that led to the loft. Motioning them to come down, she took a deep breath. "A moment for me to dress."

"Open the door. The magistrate has ordered a search of this house."

"When I'm dressed, you're welcome to search."

Motioning frantically, Abigail pulled Hester and Pearl to her side. She went to the fireplace and her fingers searched the stones on the left side. In a moment a narrow section of the wall opened and she pushed Pearl inside, hustling Familiar in with the child. She knelt down to speak to the little girl.

"Pearl, they'll kill the cat if they find him. You must stay in here, in the dark, and keep him quiet. His life depends on it. And possibly mine."

"Yes, Abby." The little girl was solemn, but she smiled. "I can do this. The cat likes me."

Choking back panic, Abigail closed the panel and then looked at Hester. "Get dressed quickly. I'll hold them as long as possible. And for God's sake, cover up that *A*."

Hester took a bit of courage from that. "Let them search. You've nothing to hide."

Abigail had no choice. There was the sound of something battering into the door. "Wait!" she cried, and went to lift the heavy wooden bar that was used as a lock.

Standing on the steps was Silas Grayson. Behind him were two more men, and at the edge of the property stood a solemn Samuel Truesdale. Abigail had expected Silas and the others, but the sight of Samuel made her suddenly more afraid. He'd heard her talking to the cat. He knew Familiar was in the house. Had he told?

"What right have you to search my home?" She blocked the doorway, though she was no match for the strength of the men who demanded entry.

"By right of the magistrate. It's been reported that you have a strange creature in your home. A familiar."

Abigail summoned up the courage to laugh. "Indeed, and is this a small green man who hops and dances in the road?"

"'Tis no laughing matter, Mistress West. The charges are serious." Silas eyed her long and hard. "The penalty is death."

It was the look of pleasure in his eyes more than his words that truly frightened Abigail. She opened the door as soon as she saw Hester coming down the steps. "Search as much as you like. I have nothing to hide."

Silas brushed past her, moving into the house with the two other men. One man stood outside the door, as if to prevent her escape. Samuel stepped forward to the doorway.

"I did not expect to see you on this type of errand." She met his gaze directly, daring him to tell all that he knew of her.

Samuel felt the corners of his mouth twitch. Strange that he should want to smile at such a time. When he'd heard Silas rouse out of bed in the middle of the night and tell Sarah that he'd been ordered to search Abigail West's home, Samuel had insisted on accompanying the search party. To Silas's great displeasure.

Taking a step away from the guard at the door, Samuel signaled Abigail outside. Although she was stiff and angry, he managed to get her to follow him safely out of hearing of anyone in the house. "I was not invited to attend." He did allow the briefest of smiles. "Silas is unhappy with my presence here, but I wanted to be sure that if he found something, it was not something he brought with him."

Abigail's eyes widened. "He would do such a thing?"

"I have no proof, but I have begun to suspect that not all of the evidence brought before the magistrate is real."

"We have to stop..." She swirled quickly and started to run back into the cottage.

Samuel's strong fingers circled her upper arm, holding her. He'd meant only to detain her, to keep her from rushing back into the cottage. But the touch of her firm flesh, even through the layers of clothes, ignited a sudden, powerful desire.

At the feel of his fingers on her arm, Abigail instantly stopped. A man did not touch a woman other than his wife. It was not done. She glanced back to the doorway to see if the guard had noticed. Luckily the man was looking into the open doorway of the house. Abigail shook her arm free.

"Let them search," he cautioned her. "Pretend you do not care."

Abigail clamped her mouth shut. She did not want her house searched. She did not want her space violated. As an

American citizen, she had rights against such behavior. The
Constitution guaranteed those rights....

She felt her legs weaken. She turned to Samuel, her head
swimming with a million conflicting thoughts. Constitution? Rights? What were those things and where had she
heard of them? Citizen? What was that? She was in the
Massachusetts Bay Colony, and women had no rights.

"Mistress West?" Samuel saw her eyelids flutter.

"Help...me." Abigail managed to croak out the words
before the tide of black washed over her. Her legs buckled
and she felt herself falling.

Samuel was near enough to catch her before she hit the
ground. She was a tall woman, and as his arms encircled her,
he could feel the lush curve of her waist and hips. One hand
brushed her full breasts as he tried to maneuver her into his
arms. The desire he felt for her was so sudden, and so apparent, that he was glad the folds of her cloak fell across
him.

"Hey, you!" he called to the guard. "Help me."

The man rushed forward and with his assistance Samuel
was able to shift the unconscious Abigail into his arms. As
soon as he had her safely nestled against him, he ordered the
man away. Without further ado, he carried her into the
house and made for the ground-floor bedroom, which he
assumed to be hers.

"What is it? What's happened?" A strange woman with
her hair disheveled but pushed beneath a white cap rushed
at him.

"She fainted, I think." Samuel wasn't exactly certain
what had happened to Abigail. All he knew was that something serious had happened to him. The feel of her in his
arms, her gentle breathing against the side of his neck, all
acted as the most potent of aphrodisiacs. With great reluctance he lowered her onto her bed.

"Out of my way," the woman ordered, pushing against him to make room for her to step forward. She waved a tiny vial under Abigail's nose.

"It's th-the law," Abigail sputtered, her eyes rolling and blinking rapidly as she came to her senses. She pushed up on the corn-shuck mattress covered in clean linen sheets. She looked beyond Samuel to the gaunt man who stood lurking in the bedroom doorway. "Get out of my house. You have no right here."

Silas Grayson stepped into the room. "I have every right, Mistress West." From his side he lifted his hand. In it was a small figure, a doll made from a corn cob and the husks. The golden silks had been arranged into two glistening braids. "Has Tituba been teaching you the art of voo-doo?"

"You foolish man." Hester snatched the figure from his hand. "It's my..." She caught herself. "It's a doll. For a child to play with."

"I see no children in this house." Silas's smile was one of victory. "I see only two women, one of them known to be an adulteress, Madame Prynne."

Although Hester was flustered by the fact that he recognized her, she held her composure. "I brought the doll from Boston. I wanted Abigail to help me make them so I could sell them." Hester stood her ground. "I need money to support myself and my daughter."

"Your daughter?" Silas arched one bristling eyebrow.

"My daughter, Pearl. Since you know so much of my private affairs, I'm sure you know of her."

"Where is the child?"

"Since you are not the father, that is none of your concern."

Thunder darkened Silas Grayson's brow. "You will speak to me with the respect I deserve, or you will pay the consequences."

Samuel stepped between the two and moved directly into Silas's face. "Mistress West has taken ill. If you've finished your search we should leave her home. We have no quarrel with her guest."

"George, have you searched the upstairs?" Silas called.

"Yes. There's no one up there. And no black creature."

"You've searched thoroughly?" Silas stared at Abigail. His gaze shifted over her form on the bed, lingering on her breasts as he continued to talk. "A witness saw her with the black creature, talking and kissing it."

Samuel saw the look, and his hands at his side clenched into fists.

Abigail, too, saw what was passing between the men. She sat up, swung her feet to the floor and stood. The sensation of weakness was gone, but her questions were not. She knew something, something about the future. She didn't know how, or why, but she felt a sense of purpose that had not been there an hour before.

"Get out of my house, Silas Grayson. Take yourself home and to your own bed. You shall not share mine."

At the look of fury on his face, she knew she'd scored a direct hit, but she also knew she would pay for that remark.

"You cannot tempt me, witch." Silas spoke the last word with relish.

"I have no wish to tempt you. I want none of you. But, be warned. I am not an ignorant woman, not someone you can intimidate and bully. Get out of my house before I make you truly sorry."

Before Samuel could do a thing, George grabbed Silas by the arm. "She speaks so strangely." He gave her a terrified look. "She is strong. Hurry!" He tugged at Silas.

"You have done your search here, Silas, and found nothing but a child's dolly. Leave," Samuel said, his tone far more gentle than it had been before. He dared not look at

Abigail. She was standing at the bed, her mismatched eyes blazing fury, daring Silas Grayson to do his worst.

Samuel could not look at Abigail, for he knew she had signed her own death warrant. Hester knew it, too. He could read it in her eyes and the paleness of her skin.

"I will go." Silas smiled. "But I will be back. With a warrant for your arrest." He left the room, joined by his men as they exited the house. They did not bother to close the door as they left, and Silas's voice carried clearly back to Abigail, Samuel and Hester.

"She will hang before the week is out," Silas said, and there was great satisfaction in his voice.

For a moment no one in the house spoke, then Hester started forward. She slammed the door and barred it again, then hurried to the fireplace. "Pearl!"

Abigail hurried after her, leaving a very concerned Samuel to follow. When he arrived in the kitchen, Abigail was swinging the secret panel open to reveal a young girl and the big black cat.

"My daughter," Hester explained.

"And my cat, Familiar." Abigail looked up at him, her face defiant.

"I see." It was all Samuel could manage. His emotions were in terrible turmoil. Kneeling at the hearth, her hand stroking the cat, Samuel knew Abigail was the most beautiful woman he'd ever seen. And the most doomed. She had humiliated Silas Grayson in a manner he would never forgive. And Silas would not rest until he made certain the charge of witchcraft had been brought against her.

"Abigail." It was Hester who spoke, her voice breaking with the tension. "Pack a few things. We'll leave immediately. We stand a better chance in the forest with the Indians than we do staying here. As soon as it is daybreak, that man will have a warrant for your arrest. Once you're in prison, you'll never escape. We have to leave now." As she spoke she started pacing the kitchen. Her fingers found first one object, then another, as she picked them up and looked at them, then discarded them as unnecessary. "Just clothes, and some bread and cheese, if you have any. What money you might have stored away. We can manage with that." She didn't look at anyone as she paced.

"Mother, are we going to the islands?" Pearl spoke up with some confusion. "Tonight? I thought we were to visit here for a time."

"We're going nowhere." Abigail's voice was firm.

"You're still woozy from the faint." Hester confronted her directly. "Do you deliberately fail to understand? That man is going to have you hanged."

"But I'm not a witch."

Hester rolled her eyes and looked to Samuel for help.

"It doesn't matter, Mistress West. I don't believe Goodwife Bishop was a witch. She is dead nonetheless. Sarah Good, Elizabeth How, Susannah Martin, Rebecca Nurse, Sarah Wilds—they are not witches, but they will hang because they have been accused." Samuel felt a twist in his heart. "You must listen to your friend and leave here at once. You will be safer with the Indians." As he spoke he felt the wrenching loss of her. She was a woman he'd spoken with for the first time only the day before, but already he knew he would miss her for the rest of his life. She had indeed bewitched him.

Abigail looked at Samuel, then Hester, and finally at the black cat who was staring solemnly at her from the hearth. Even little Pearl was waiting for her response.

"I'm not going anywhere." Her thoughts were still confused, but things were becoming more and more clear to her. She pressed the flat of her palm against her chest and her fingers automatically found the elongated crystal that always hung between her breasts.

"I have some coffee." She smiled as she said it, knowing that Hester and Samuel would find her behavior insane. "There are some things I need to tell you both. Things you are going to find hard to believe because I don't believe them myself." She was uncertain exactly what to tell them. So much of what she felt was intuitive, and she had not the first scrap of proof, other than the pendant.

And the cat.

She looked at Familiar and saw the intelligence in his eyes. Yes, it was the cat, too. And Samuel. And Hester. They were somehow all bound in this together. An involuntary shudder took her. She disguised it by filling the kettle from a bucket of water and lighting a small fire in the hearth.

"Coffee, then we'll talk." She spoke more to calm herself than anything else. She pointed to chairs around the table as she lit more candles until the kitchen gave off a soft glow.

"If they're watching you, they'll claim you're holding some type of ceremony," Samuel warned her, noting the excess of lighted candles.

"Let them burn in hell." Abigail grinned at the impact of her words. "You see, Samuel..." She dropped all formal manner of address. "Where I come from, relegating people to hell is a common practice. It may not be very polite, but it certainly isn't an offense punishable by death."

"Abigail!" Hester rose, half in shock. "Where did you learn to talk in such a manner?"

"Somewhere in the future, Hester. Out of books, from movies, from my parents and friends." As she spoke, the sense of truth rushed through her with elation. "Yes, from the future. From a time where people finally understand that there are no such things as witches or warlocks."

"God save you," Samuel said, his face a mask of complete dejection and horror. "God save you, Abigail West, because if you behave in this fashion you are surely doomed to hang."

I'M AN EXTREMELY intelligent creature with a lifetime of incredible experiences behind me, and I'm having a hard time grasping what's going on here. So I don't expect Pilgrim Man and Hester, who was a fictional character from a book, to be able to grasp the premise of traveling here from the future. As difficult as it is to believe, there's no other explanation for what's happened to me.

Last I remember I saw this knockout dame hoofing it across Pennsylvania Avenue. She didn't see the car coming, and I knocked her out of the way. Then the car struck me. Whammo! Bammo!

I wake up in this strange place, drift in and out of a coma for several days, then keel over by that stone fence. Next thing I know, I open my peepers and there she is, the woman I knocked out of the street. Only she's dressed in the ugliest fashion I've ever seen, and she's talking all stiff and funny— like everyone else around her. You'd think they had a broom…never mind, that may not be a good word to use— what with all this witch hysteria I'm hearing about.

The best I can deduce, though I may be a little iffy from being stuffed into the side of the fireplace, is that we're somewhere back in time. Late 1600s, I'd say. We're near Boston. And we're in major, big-time, serious, cat-killing trouble.

The question is, why? Why are we here? How did we get here? More important, how are we going to get back?

At least Abigail is beginning to catch on to the fact that we're visitors from another time. Once she accepts it, then I'll have an ally in getting out of here and back to the future.

Samuel, I'm not so sure about. He seems vaguely familiar, no pun intended at this point, but I can't be certain.

And, Hester! Whew! Right out of Nathaniel Hawthorne's novel, bearing the sign of her sin, no less.

Well, Abigail is trying to tell them about the future. She's pacing the room, talking about cars and movies, and now she's getting down to the Revolutionary War and Indepen-

dence and the constitution and, yes, indeedy, the Bill of Rights.

Samuel thinks she's flipped over the edge. Hester wants only to pack and run.

And me? What do I want? That's what's troubling me. Why are we here in Salem Village at a time when innocent women and men are being killed as witches? It's the worst possible place and time for a black cat.

And the most challenging.

What if Madame Mysterious and I could actually do something to stop the witch trials? What if we could figure out who's really behind all of these accusations?

I feel the need for some action, and I've got to get out of this house and do a little exploring. My very extraordinary kitty sense tells me that something is rotten in Salem Village, to bastardize my old friend, Will.

Yes, I do believe Madame Mysterious and I are going to make an impressive team—and change the course of history, to boot. If these heathens don't hang the both of us before we get a chance to act.

"ABBY." Hester got up from her seat at the table and went over to her friend. She knelt beside her, her hand going to Abby's forehead to feel for a sign of fever. "Listen to me, and listen carefully. If one person in this village hears you talk of such things, they will hang you. They will not doubt that you are a witch. They will not care that you are ill." She shook her head, freeing the tears that had been trapped in her eyelashes. "Men riding in machines that go a hundred miles in a single hour. Big machines flying in the sky. Pictures of people in a box that tell stories."

"It's blasphemy," Samuel said softly.

Abigail looked from one to the other, aware that she had frightened them far worse than she'd intended. In describing the wonders of the world she was remembering more clearly with each passing moment, she'd terrified Hester and

Samuel. Hester, a name from a classic novel, and Samuel, a man who somehow seemed . . . part of her future. At the looks on their faces, she had a blistering jolt of self-doubt. What if she was crazy?

"Meow." Familiar got up from beside Pearl. He leapt onto the table and walked directly to Abigail. His black paw went gently to her chest, and he pressed the pendant into the tender flesh. "Meow."

Abigail looked at Samuel and Hester. Very slowly she caught the necklace that was hidden beneath her dressing gown and cloak. Inch by inch she pulled the pendant up until it was free of the clothing. Slipping it from her neck, she dangled it in front of the candle. The multifaceted cut of the stone captured the golden candlelight and shattered it into a rainbow that fell across the table.

"What is it?" Hester asked.

"I don't know," Abigail admitted. "I've always worn it, that's all I know. And it has some power."

Familiar swatted it toward the light. Swinging wildly, the crystal sent the rainbow hues dancing across the table.

"If Silas Grayson had found that trinket around your neck . . ." Samuel didn't finish. He saw no harm in pretty adornments, but to the stern pilgrims of Salem Village, such foolishness was against all of their religious creeds. Abigail was courting destruction on so many fronts he didn't know where to begin to try to save her.

"Now that you've told us your wild story, are you ready to leave?" Hester hadn't given up on making a run for it.

"I'm not going anywhere," Abigail answered. There was no room for argument in her voice.

"Please, Abigail, consider what will happen. As sure as dawn comes, Silas will be back. And he will arrest you."

Abigail looked at Samuel. "And you will defend me, correct?"

The impact of her words was like a blow to his chest. "I will try, but I've not been able to do much to save the other women, and their charges were so much milder than yours."

"But you will try?"

The taste of doom was so thick in his throat that Samuel could not answer, only nod.

"I believe I have been sent here for a purpose." Abigail went to the cat and pulled him into her arms. "Familiar and I are here because we have to stop these trials and the death of innocent people."

"You will accomplish nothing from a dungeon cell, Abigail." Hester's voice was cold. "Remember, I've been imprisoned. You are helpless there."

Abigail looked at them. "It is my destiny."

Chapter Four

Dawn was almost at hand. The fire had burned into dull red embers, yet Samuel lingered. Hester and Pearl were asleep in the loft bedroom, and Abigail had finally worn herself down. She took the last sip of precious coffee from her cup and replaced it on the table. Her voice was tired. "I know it sounds like I'm lying," she said finally.

"It's a strange story." Samuel also drained his cup and put the thick mug beside hers. It was time for him to go—before they both suffered for it. Besides, he had a lot of sorting out to do. The wild and strange story Abigail had spun throughout the long hours of the night had aroused a host of different emotions in him. Some things he did not understand, but one thing that he was clear about troubled him greatly. He was drawn to Abigail West in a strange and compelling manner. Part of it was physical—just to look at her made him desire to touch her. But there was something else, too, something more elusive yet much deeper. Was it possible she'd actually cast a spell on him? He didn't believe in witches or witchcraft, but the woman had a powerful effect on him. Enough to make him edgy.

"Do you believe me?" Abigail asked. Once she had begun to comprehend what had happened to her, she'd been eager to pour out the details of her trip from the future. But looking at Samuel's face, she had to take into account the fact that he was a stranger to her. Spilling her guts to him might have been a miscalculation. One with deadly consequences. As she'd watched the firelight flicker over the strong planes of his face, she'd forgotten that Samuel's accusations could send her to the hanging tree as quickly as those made by Silas Grayson or the young girls of the village. She felt a terrible constriction near her heart as she watched concern and anxiety play across his face. What if he thought her mad? Or a witch?

"I need some time to think all of this over. It's hard to grasp. You're a challenging woman, Abigail." His gaze held hers briefly, then fell to stare at her hands.

"I don't know what else to say." Abigail stroked the black cat who'd fallen asleep in her lap. "I had to tell all of this to someone, Samuel. I've had this terrible feeling for the past three days that I was caught up in something much bigger than me." She tugged the cap off her hair, freeing the unruly curls. "I don't know how I came to be here, or why, but I know I'm not *from* here." She looked around the house. "These are not my things. This isn't my home."

Samuel wanted to reach out and touch her hair, but he didn't. For more than four hours he'd sat at her table and listened to the fantastic and damning words spill from her lips. And now all he could think was that her hair was too beautiful to be true. He was indeed bewitched.

Sighing, he spoke again. "You should get out of here with your friend. Make an escape while the getting's good."

As he talked with Abigail, he was finding it easier and easier to fall into the same diction that she used. Even more troubling was the fact that her own stories had brought up matching images in his own mind. If Abigail had the same effect on others in Salem Village, she would definitely hang.

She would hang by her own words and deeds. And the black cat she persisted in defending would hang beside her.

"I can't leave...."

"I can go into Salem Town at daybreak and find a... clipper." He fought to keep his language uncluttered with her unusual words. Whether she had captured him in her spell or whether it was simple mimicry, he couldn't begin to say. But if he started talking and acting like her—he'd hang just as quickly.

"Flight is your only salvation," he said with determination.

"I'm not leaving."

Her gaze was direct, level. Nothing at all like the gaze of a proper woman. "You have to leave, Abigail. They'll hang you as sure as you're sitting here."

She leaned forward, her mismatched eyes begging him to listen. "Don't you see? If I've come from the future, as I believe, then I'm here for a purpose."

Samuel saw the single candle that still burned reflected in her intense eyes. "You think you came back in time over three hundred years to die at the end of a rope?" Before she could answer, Samuel continued. All of the concern and anger he'd bottled up inside demanded release. "You speak, with all sincerity, about a future that sounds like something Satan made in one of the pits of hell. Your eyes shine as you describe it. You fairly beg to be called a witch. You've not seen the prisons. The suffering of those accused is not imaginable to you. They stand in cells not big enough to allow them to lie down. They stand! And they starve, with the rats at their feet." He turned away. The horrors he'd seen in the past three days were almost too much.

Abigail's hand went to her chest, her fingers finding the pendant beneath the multiple layers of her clothing. His words frightened her. She wasn't foolish, or a martyr. "What you say only makes me believe more strongly that I've been sent here to stop all of this."

"And how do you intend to stop it?" He stood, then turned back to face her. "Once you're in that hellhole of a prison, exactly what do you intend to do, provoke the occupants there to riot? Or do you think you can somehow unlock their chains and deliver them to safety?" Shocked at his own words, he sat down.

Abigail's gaze on him was like a touch, and when he looked up at her he was surprised by the gleam of amusement in her eyes. "What puts that expression in your eyes?" he demanded.

"And all this time I thought you were so cool and in control. It's nice to see you spit fire." She leaned forward. "Where were you born, Samuel?"

The innocent question made him pause. He'd known her only a single night, but he understood that Abigail was not a woman who wasted her time with idle conversation. "London."

"Oh, really. Strange that you don't have a British accent." Her smile widened.

"I've been in the States since I finished my schooling."

Abigail's grin was wolfish. "Oh, and where exactly might 'the States' be?"

Samuel opened his mouth, then shut it. He knew. The United States of America. But he also knew there was no such place. Had she somehow put that phrase in his mind, given him a picture of a vast map cut into different-colored shapes called "states"?

"You're from the future, aren't you?" Abigail leaned across the table and took his hand. "I've suspected as much for the past hour." She turned his hand palm up, concentrating on the lines in the dim candlelight.

Part of him wanted to withdraw his hand, to hide it in his pocket—until he realized his pants had no pockets. With that he gave in to the pleasure of her soft fingers tracing the lines of his hand. Pleasure spiced with a sense of intense longing, and a thimbleful of dread. What manner of craft was she practicing now? Was she a mortal woman, to elicit such hungers in him?

"You have the mark of the traveler," she said, bending closer to study his palm. "Right there." She pressed into the pad at the base of his index finger. "Your entire life is a journey." She traced a line down his palm. "Tell me about your sister."

"I have no sister," he answered without thinking. But then the memory of a tall, slender girl with dark gray eyes came to him. She was reaching up to touch a flower in the lapel of his suit, a smile on her solemn face as she stood on tiptoe to whisper something in his ear. Something scandalous—and funny. Karen. That was her name.

"Ah, but you do. She lives in the future." Abigail closed his hand into a fist and yet she still held it, her fingers stroking the skin on the back of his hand and wrist.

"God had better be on your side, Abigail." Her touch was so potent that it was almost painful. He wanted to pull his hand back, as he would from a fire. But he could not. Just as he could not break the gaze they shared as the candle flickered between them.

"It'll be light soon." Abigail lowered his hand to the table, her fingers dancing lightly across it as she released him.

"Please, go with your friend. If it's the trials you hope to stop, I promise you that I'll do everything in my power to protect the accused."

"You could give your life and not save a single one of them." Abigail put her fingers to her temples as if struck by a sudden, intense pain.

"Abigail, are you injured?" He got up and went to her, putting his hands over hers on her temples. "What ails you?"

"There's something I have to remember. I can almost catch it, sometimes. Something just there, and it's very important." She squeezed her eyes shut more tightly, in concentration. "But I can't remember." Her eyes were closed and she was bent forward over her knees. Very slowly she straightened, shaking her head. "It slips away from me whenever I try to catch it."

The pink gold of a summer morning had begun to climb the windows of Abigail's house. Samuel slowly rose, reluctant to leave the woman beside him. "My presence here is another danger to you. They'll be more than glad to add a charge of fornication to one of witchcraft."

"Then I can wear a bright red *F* on my dress when they hang me." Abigail hadn't meant the words to sound so bitter or so fatalistic. But she saw the results of her retort in Samuel's gray eyes.

"I'm sorry," she said, rising, also. "You're right. For your own safety, you should leave."

Nodding, Samuel made his way to the door. With a quick movement he lifted the wooden bar and opened it wide. "Silas will be back. If not today, then tomorrow. What will you do?"

"I don't know." She felt once again the tiny bud of knowledge that she needed to capture. Once again, it eluded her. "I have to think. Before he gets here. I have to have a plan."

"You can count on me to help in any way that I can."

She stood motionless. "Can I?" She'd revealed so much that she hoped she could.

He nodded.

"Good. Meet me tonight, down by the stream. I want to know what happens at Goodwife Nurse's trial today. I doubt I'd be welcome in the meetinghouse, and I don't think it's wise for you to come here again."

"What about Hester and Pearl?"

"I hope to see them on a ship tomorrow. The West Indies may be just the place for them. There are people here, in this village, who would accuse Hester for no reason."

He started to urge her to go, also, but he knew she wouldn't leave. Was she a witch? She'd captured him with her stories and visions. Yet he could detect no single trace of malice or evil in her. "Tonight at nine o'clock." He ducked his head, stepped through the door and strode across the yard to the gray sand of the path that had begun to glow faintly pink in the dawn.

ABIGAIL SIGNED her name to the document with a flourish, then scattered sand across the signature.

"I believe you act in haste." Hester Prynne held both of her hands behind her back.

"If you aren't going to the islands, the least you can do is take this to the governor of Massachusetts. The man has a right to know that citizens under his charge are being brutalized and murdered."

Hester took the paper and rolled it into a tight scroll without reading it. "The governor will not put much credence in a document delivered by a woman who wears the scarlet *A* on her chest."

"Well, for heaven's sake, Hester, wear a cloak."

"Abby! The letter is my punishment."

"And what letter does Dimmsdale wear? *C* for coward?" Abigail grabbed hold of her temper. "Sorry. It's just that you've served your sentence. If you didn't wear the *A*, people would forget."

"Which is the point, I believe." Hester's mouth twisted into a wry line. "Perhaps the governor will appreciate a hint of scandal in his life. In this time that you come from, do men in authority abide a woman interfering in the business of justice or government?"

Abigail turned to her. "Fiddle dee dee, Hester." She smiled at her own imitation of Scarlett O'Hara. "You're a resourceful woman. I'm sure you can get the message to him whether he 'abides' the idea or not." Abigail's thoughts had already moved on. "Now, I have to determine what to do in the meantime."

"The sound of that is ominous." Hester's brow furrowed. "Where is my Pearl?"

"She went to the stream."

Hester nodded. She'd given up her plans to go to the West Indies. Her friend's life was in jeopardy—even if Abigail was too hardheaded to believe it. Instead she'd agreed to try to deliver a message to the governor of Massachusetts Colony. A desperate letter urging the governor to intercede in the judicial proceedings that were passing as trials in Salem Village. Hester didn't believe it would do any good, but it was part of Abigail's new personality that women had a right to have a voice in how things were run. That kind of talk was blasphemy, if not sorcery.

"Promise me that you'll be careful, Hester. You've had enough sorrow in your life. You and little Pearl."

As if by magic Pearl's footsteps could be heard running along the hard-packed path to the front door. Three seconds later the door burst open and Pearl stood, ribs heaving.

"Abigail, hurry!"

For only a second Abigail froze. "What is it?"

"The cat." Pearl swallowed and gasped for air. "He saved my life! But she saw him, and now she's gone to get that horrible old man who was here last night."

While Hester put her hands on Pearl's shoulders to calm her, Abigail knelt beside her. "What happened?"

"I was sitting by the stream, and this stick came floating by. Or at least, I thought it was a stick. When I reached for it, it struck at me."

"A snake!" Hester's hands tightened.

"It was," Pearl agreed. "But Familiar jumped into the shallow water and slapped the snake away from me."

"And then?" Abigail prompted.

"I saw the girl hiding in the bushes, watching. She said that the cat was a playmate of the devil's, and that I was an evil child and that she was going to get that mean man and have us all taken to the dungeon." Pearl started to cry. "She said we'd hang as witches, all of us."

Abigail wiped the tears away. "Where is the cat?" she asked gently.

"He was hissing at her." Pearl struggled to regain her composure. "He was so brave. He saved me, and that girl wants to have him killed."

Abigail looked up into Hester's eyes. "There's no time to waste. You must take Pearl and get out of here. And the cat."

Hester pulled her child into her arms and held her tightly. After a few seconds she released her, pushing her toward the ladder to the loft. "Get our things. And be quick. Abigail is right, we have to get out of here."

Abigail went to the kitchen area and wrapped a hunk of cheese, bread and salted meat in a cloth, then put it all in a coarse cloth sack. "It isn't much, but it will do until you can find other provisions." She went to a small jar and poured half of the coins into her palm, then gave them to Hester.

"I can't take your savings."

"For the cat," Abigail said. "Take care of him for me."

Hester nodded, then hurried to tie Pearl's cape and bonnet. Her fingers shook but she finished the task. Standing, she grabbed Abigail's hands. "How can we leave you here in this godforsaken place?"

Abigail's smile was tinged with determination. "You aren't leaving me. I've chosen to stay. And as soon as I come up with a plan, you'll see that I made the right choice." Even as she spoke she tried to quell her own self-doubts. Could she make a difference to the villagers accused of witchcraft? Or would she die beside them? Her fingers strayed to the pendant that hung between her breasts. She had to believe—in herself and in her mission.

She turned to the door and went in search of the cat. Familiar was a fine companion, and she would miss him. For his own safety, he had to go with Hester and Pearl. Her friends would take good care of him, of that she had no doubt. But after ten minutes of frantic search, she had to give up the idea of sending the feline to safety.

"Go." There was no time left to discuss the merits of leaving the cat. "Go now, and Godspeed." She kissed Hester's cheek.

"I'll deliver your letter." Hester's words were a vow. "And I'll be back to help you."

Abigail shook her head. "Stay away from Salem Village. For Pearl's sake." She gave them a slight nudge out the door and then closed the heavy wood behind them before she could change her mind and run after them.

SO, THE CAT IS OUT of the bag, so to speak. I've been seen by one of those sneaky little urchins. Mary Wadsworth? Was that her name? And to add insult to injury, Madame Mysterious was going to send me away with Hester and Pearl. She was going to trust my fate to fictional characters. Or, at least, I'd always thought they were fictional. And I'm proud to see that Hester has not allowed that sniveling Dimmsdale to ruin her life. But enough about them. What I'm concerned about now is me. Whoever thought that saving a nine-year-old child from snakebite could result in accusations of being a witch's familiar? This is grossly unfair.

Whining aside, I've come to some basic conclusions. First, Abigail West is no ordinary woman. Excluding her beauty and her brains, she's still cut from a different bolt of cloth. There's something... extraordinary about her. How do I know this? you ask. Oh, from minor observations. Just little things, like being in her proximity has resulted in a leap back in time of more than three hundred years. That was my first clue!

I've been giving this serious thought, and the last thing I remember from my 1995 life was a fierce pain in my head as I made cranial contact with the bumper of a really striking little BMW. I had just pushed a dame—one that looked ex-

actly like Mistress West—to safety. The next thing I know, I'm here.

It seems to reason that Abigail and I came here together. And she thinks Pilgrim Man might be from the future, too. While I feigned sleep last night, I listened to him. He talks like an alien when he's around Abigail, but it could be that he's easily influenced. Fellow traveler or not, he seems to be the only one in Salem Village interested in stopping these horrible trials.

Okay, there go Hester and Pearl. Now that Abigail can't send me away, I can mosey on home and help her think up a plan. Even though I was sitting beside the old babbling brook, my mind was in high gear. Why are these young girls allowed to bring charges against others? These are children. Unreliable at best. Why are they suddenly being believed?

And isn't it strange that most of the accused are women? Single women. Women who have property. Oh, there is a man or two accused, but these are men who have challenged the credibility of the children.

Knowing what I know about humans, I find that greed and jealousy are always prime motives in any crime. This isn't always the case, but it often is. Fear is another motivating factor. Is it possible these girls honestly fear these women?

If the motive isn't greed or fear, what else could it be? Is it possible that these little girls are simply mean? Now that is a scary thought. I know that humans are capable of such meanness. I've seen it in action. But it is still hard to accept, especially from young girls.

I'd rather believe that perhaps they've become caught up in the center of a great drama. Never underestimate the human ego, not even in the rug-rat-size humanoid. I can see a likely scenario where the girls made an accusation and the response to what they said was far greater than anything they'd expected. Suddenly they're stars, the center of attention. The entire town is focusing on everything they do and say. That would be very appealing for young girls who see nothing but a life of toil in front of them. Yes, I can clearly see how this might have happened.

And once the first accusation was made, the girls couldn't stop. Fear of being caught in the lie would make them continue, as well as a need for the attention. Now they are accusing everyone. But surely if this is the case they would recant when they saw that people were being hanged. Surely. Then again, maybe not. Humans seem to have a positive lust for the limelight. And if these children have gotten caught up in a lie, how can they stop now? Innocent people have already suffered greatly.

Here comes Abigail, and I can see by the look in her eyes that she's angry with me. I know she wanted to send me to a place of safety, but that was out of the question. If she's here on some kind of mission, then I must be, too. Should I step out and surrender myself to her? Or maybe I should wait until she hunts long enough to become worried. Then she'll be glad to see me. Cats have learned to value the delayed response. It's one little tool we have to keep humans on their toes.

"DAGNABBIT! Familiar, where are you?" Abigail hurried around the corner of the house. The cat was watching her. She could almost feel his wily gaze on her, calculating the best time to show himself. Perhaps he didn't realize his elegant black hide was in danger. She wanted to put him in the safety nook of the fireplace before the young girl and Silas Grayson made an appearance to cast yet another accusation at her feet.

"Familiar!" She stopped at the road, noticing the small band of black-clad people who were moving her way. She recognized Silas Grayson's tall form, and that of a young girl. Fear tripped in her chest but she didn't move. Now it was too late to find the cat and put him in a place of safety.

Familiar would just have to look out for himself, because she had the feeling that she was going to have her hands full protecting herself.

"Mistress West." Silas Grayson bowed, but not before he smiled. "We have it on good authority that you have been consorting with one of Satan's familiars. A black cat."

"I saw him strike a snake in the head!" The young girl stepped forward, her blond curls spilling out from beneath the cap she wore. If it had not been for the expression on her face, she would have been a lovely child. Her plump cheeks were dimpled, her skin flawless. But it was the set of her mouth and the anger in her eyes that told of her true nature.

"You saw a cat and a snake?" Abigail asked the question gently. "Are you sure?"

"I am sure." The child stepped forward. "I accuse you of witchcraft." She pointed her finger at Abigail.

"I have no black cat." Abigail still spoke softly, but she didn't flinch as others who had been accused had done.

"I saw him. He was at the creek with that young girl. The snake floated down, and the girl was going to pick it up but the cat saved her."

"A young girl. A snake. A cat that saves children. Where are all of these magnificent things that you've seen?"

Silas Grayson shifted uncomfortably. The smile that had been on his face was gone. The other two men with him murmured together.

"I think this young lady sees what she wants to see." Abigail's tone was no longer soft. "There is no child in my house. There is no cat. Search if you will, but you'll find nothing because there is nothing there. I am no witch, but this girl is a liar."

Before Abigail could say another word the girl pitched forward into the road and began to scream and writhe. "She's pinching me! She's pinching me!" She screamed. "Make her stop! Make her stop!"

Chapter Five

Agile as a cat, Abigail eluded the grasp of the three men as they lunged at her. In a moment she had Mary Wadsworth by the forearm and had tugged her to her feet. She pulled back and slapped the girl across the face with a resounding crack.

For several seconds there was only silence.

Disbelief, shock, then fear marched across the blond teenager's face as she stared at Abigail in openmouthed wonder.

"I don't know who you think was pinching you, but if you don't stand up and behave yourself, I'm going to take a switch and beat the hide off your legs." Abigail was startled at her own words. She hadn't heard such talk since her grandmother had switched her for throwing red mud balls at a neighbor's newly painted white house. It had effectively curbed Abigail's wayward desires for vandalism and trouble-making.

"Who are you?" Mary Wadsworth was still in awe.

"I am not a witch, that's for certain, and you'd better watch yourself, young lady, or you'll find yourself in hot..." She stopped herself. She didn't think a threat of hot water would be understood—or appreciated—by her current audience. She dropped Mary's arm. "Now quit making a spectacle of yourself in the middle of the road."

"Mary?" Silas Grayson's face was a thundercloud. "Is she a witch or not?"

Abigail looked at a bridal wreath bush that grew beside her house. The long, slender branches would make excellent switches.

Mary followed Abigail's gaze. "I don't think so," she said. She backed a few steps away from Abigail.

"What about the cat? What about the snake? What did you see?" Silas pressed.

Abigail put her hands on her hips and arched her eyebrows. "What did you see, Mistress Mary?"

"I don't remember," the girl answered. She backed away several more steps. "I couldn't see clearly. Maybe it wasn't a snake."

"As I said before, I don't have any children in the house, and I don't have any pet . . . cats. You're welcome to search if you wish, but you'll waste your time and find nothing." Abigail started toward the house. "My time is valuable. I have sheep to tend and cows to milk. Excuse me." Without looking behind her, she walked around the house to the barn.

Once out of sight she collapsed against the rough wood of her barn. To her conscious mind she could not remember ever feeding sheep or milking cows—until she'd woken up in Salem Village. But she'd done it for the past three days, and she was becoming quite efficient at it. The animals had taken to her. And they were also a comfort. Right at this particular moment, she was due for some comfort.

Samuel's face came unbidden to her mind, and she allowed herself a few seconds to mentally go over the strong jaw, the clear gray eyes and the intelligence she saw so clearly there. Was he really from the future? Would he eventually come to realize that, or would he turn away from it, and her?

A growing seed of doubt that had begun to loom larger and larger in Abigail's mind sprouted into full blossom. What if she never figured out how to get home?

She thought back over the most recent incident. Silas Grayson was definitely out to get her. She'd sidestepped this particular effort, but how much longer could she outmaneuver him? Not for long. And just because she was from the future didn't mean she couldn't die in Salem Village.

That chilling thought made her close her eyes and seek comfort in the memory of Samuel's face. Aside from Hester, he was her only real friend. If he didn't become too frightened of her. With that thought she took a deep breath, opened her eyes and started forward again.

Entering the barn she threw hay to the cows and then got the bucket and sat on the stool to milk. At the zinging sound of the milk in the can she leaned her forehead against the cow's side, inhaling the clean smell of the animal. Ole Sally, the cow, munched hay and mooed a soft bit of sympathy at her.

"What am I going to do?" Abigail asked the cow.

"Meow!" From the darkened corner of the barn Familiar stepped forward. "Meow."

"Right. You're part of the reason I'm in hot water." She was feeling less than happy with the cat.

"Meow!" Familiar was indignant.

"No, I didn't expect you to let the snake bite Pearl. But what were you doing down there with her?"

At the sound of the cat's strange meow, Abigail looked up. A tall man was standing in the doorway of the barn. With the intense light from the setting sun at his back and in her face, Abigail couldn't get a good look at him, and she felt terror sink hard claws into her before she finally managed to find her voice. "Who is it?"

Samuel stepped into the barn. "They found Rebecca Nurse guilty." He sounded slightly dazed, as if he didn't believe the verdict.

Abigail let go of Sally's udder and stood, looking at him over the cow's back. "Was she sentenced?"

"To hang. Two days hence."

Abigail sat back down and started milking once again. The rhythm was soothing, the sound of the milk in the pail the only noise in the barn. "Is there nothing you can do?" she finally asked.

"Nothing. I tried everything I knew."

"And was it the testimony of Mary Wadsworth and her friends?"

"Indeed, it was. They put on a performance that would have frightened Boris Karloff."

Abigail's smile was weary. "And who is Boris Karloff, Samuel?"

The tall man took a step back. "I don't know," he answered. "I honestly don't know why I said that."

"It's the future slipping into your brain." Finished with Sally, Abigail moved the milk pail and her stool as she stood. "I only wonder why you fight it so hard. Familiar and I have accepted the fact that we're from the future."

"Let's not linger on this topic." Samuel stepped toward her again. In the rich golden light filtering through the barn door, Abigail looked like something from a painting. The golden tones of light painted her skin a soft peach, and a few tendrils of her russet hair had escaped her white cap to catch the light in fiery ringlets.

"You don't want to talk about the future, and I don't want to talk about the present." She sighed. "At least Hester and Pearl got out of here. They're taking a letter to the governor. I hope he'll come to Salem Village and see for himself what a travesty these witch trials are."

Samuel didn't hold much hope that the governor would intervene in any fashion, much less a timely one. But he saw no reason to destroy Abigail's only hope. "I hope Hester has a safe journey. By the way, Silas Grayson left the proceedings today after he was certain Rebecca would be hanged. Did you see him?'' At the fleeting expression of concern that Abigail worked hard to hide, Samuel felt genuine fear. ''He was here, wasn't he?''

''Yes. But he's gone. And that lying little heathen is gone with him.''

''Mary?''

''Aye, Mary.'' Abigail used the archaic speech deliberately. '' 'Tis a fetching liar she is, but a liar nonetheless.''

Samuel shook his head. ''Did she accuse you?''

''No. Grayson wanted her to, but she wouldn't. She was a little afraid to accuse me of anything after I slapped her.''

Samuel stepped around the cow and caught Abigail's arm. ''You what?''

''I slapped her.'' She felt a twinge of guilt. ''Not all that hard, but enough to make her stop thrashing around in the dirt and pretending that I was having some invisible demon pinch her.''

''She went into a fit?'' Samuel was aghast.

''She did. But when I jerked her up and slapped her, just like my granny used to do to me when I pitched a temper fit, she stopped.''

''And she failed to accuse you of witchcraft?''

''I told her I'd switch the hide off her legs.'' Abigail looked down at the milk in the pail. ''I probably shouldn't have done it, but she made me mad. Surely any fool can see that those girls are putting on a show. You see it. I see it. Why don't the others?''

Samuel kept a grip on Abigail's arm and led her to the stack of hay that was in plentiful supply against the south wall of the barn. He took the milk bucket from her hand and put it down, then sat back in the hay, pulling her down with him.

''I wonder your head is still connected to your body without a rope between the two.''

''Huh! Once I called her bluff, she wasn't going to accuse me.''

"Not while you could reach across and punish her again. But she'll be back, Abigail." Samuel lifted a hand to touch her face, turning her so that their gazes met and held. "What am I to do with you?"

Abigail looked into his eyes. Ever since waking up in Salem Village, she'd felt so terribly alone. She'd hidden that feeling, from everyone including herself, but now she knew she needed Samuel. Whatever he was capable of giving.

"Kiss me," she said softly. The words shocked her as much as Samuel.

Samuel felt desire wash away his initial surprise. He lowered his lips to hers and kissed gently, adjusting to the feel of her soft lips beneath his.

Abigail raised her hand to his hair, fingers curling in the thick, dark waves. She turned so she could put her other hand in his hair.

Samuel slipped an arm around Abigail, pulling her against him as he parted her lips and began to explore her mouth. He could feel the surge of blood that seemed to sing in his ears, feel the heat beginning to drum. Abigail's response was wanton. She pressed into him, bringing the fullness of her breasts against his chest. He could feel the rapid movement of her breathing, and it heightened his desire for her. His hand moved along her rib cage.

"Meow!"

Somewhere in the distance he heard the cry of the cat, but he ignored him. With one strong pull, he dragged Abigail against his lap, into a more comfortable position in the hay.

"Meow!" Familiar's unsheathed claws made contact just at the back of Samuel's thigh.

"Hey!" He broke the embrace and sat up, looking for the cat.

"Meow." Familiar's voice had calmed but he stood in the open doorway.

"I think he wants us to look out," Abigail explained. She could hear a strange noise, a rumble of low sounds that also had some high-pitched tones.

She got to her feet and offered her hand to Samuel, who remained in the hay. When he didn't take her hand, she turned to look at him more closely. He was staring at her with something akin to awe. "What?" she asked, letting her hand fall to her side.

"I wanted to make love to you. I would have if the cat had not interrupted us. Right here in this barn. Without another thought of the future." He spoke as if he were amazed.

"I don't know whether to strangle that cat or thank him." She felt the blush touch her cheeks. "I feel as if I've known you for a long time, Samuel. I wanted to make love with you, too."

"That's what concerns me."

Abigail's shy pleasure turned to shock. She took one look at Samuel and could plainly see that he was troubled. "What is it, Samuel? What's wrong?"

"It's sin we're discussing, Abigail. And you act as if it were no more than sharing a cup of tea."

"A sin?" She felt as if all the air had been knocked from her lungs. The sound in the distance was growing louder, but she knelt beside Samuel. "Is it a sin to care for someone?"

"Behavior of this sort is punished here." He slowly got to his feet, leaving her kneeling.

"Putting aside what's punished and what isn't punished, do you think what we did was wrong?" Abigail remained as she was. She and Samuel had to settle this issue once and for all. If his seventeenth-century sensibilities were going to cause trouble for them, she wanted to face it now. Things between them had moved fast—faster than she'd ever expected. But she felt no guilt for her feelings for Samuel. Nor any remorse. If he did, then he needed to say so.

He walked to the doorway, seemingly absorbed in the scene outside, but he saw nothing, not even the beginning of the procession that was coming down the road. He went back to Abigail and held out his hand to her, pulling her to her feet. He'd hurt her with his reaction. She'd given herself with such passion, and he'd acted as if she'd done something wrong. But there was something he had to ask. One question. "Just tell me once and for all, Abby, have you bewitched me?"

She wanted to smile at the question, but he was sincere. Not afraid, and not wary. Simply sincere. "What do you think, Samuel?" she asked gently.

"That's not an answer."

"It's the best answer. What do you think? Do you believe I've bewitched you?"

"If this is a spell, I want no part of it. I want to come to love a woman because of who she is, not because she's tricked me into seeing her as something else."

"And you think I've tricked you somehow?"

He hesitated. "It's hard for me to believe your beauty, or the way I've come to feel about you in such a short time."

"So it must be witchcraft?" She couldn't resist the smile.

"You're mocking me," he said, but there was no reprimand in it, only relief.

"No, not mocking. What you say gives me a great deal of pleasure. And it also makes me smile because you are so sincere, so without the pretenses of... modern man."

"But you still haven't answered my question."

Her smile widened. "I can't give you that answer. You see, you have to decide for yourself, Samuel. No matter what I say, it all comes back to what you believe."

He nodded, a faint smile lifting the right corner of his mouth. "Then I don't know whether to ask for more of the magic you've used on me or whether to run as fast as I can. I don't remember a lot of my earlier life, before coming here to Salem Village, but I know I've certainly never felt this way about a woman before.''

Abigail lifted her hand to his cheek, then stood on tiptoe to kiss him lightly on the lips. "That's good."

The sound outside the barn was too loud for them to ignore any longer. Abigail walked to the door, then pushed Samuel back as he started to follow.

"Stay back," she warned him. "It's Silas Grayson. It won't do your health any good to be seen in my barn."

"Are they coming here?"

Abigail looked out the door. She watched the crowd of men and women led by Silas Grayson. It was a motley assortment of folks, including two of the teenage girls who'd been making the charges of witchcraft against the other members of the community. But the procession didn't appear to be headed to her house. Silas had already passed the path that led to her door, and he hadn't yet spied her in the barn.

"No. They're going toward town, I believe." She looked closer, scanning the tense faces of the crowd. In the middle was a young woman who looked terrified. Her hands were clutched in front of her chest, and it took Abigail a moment to realize they were tied, and that she was tethered to a rope held by Silas Grayson. Several of the crowd around her were poking her with sticks and jeering at her as she was being led down the road. No one made a single effort to defend her.

"They've arrested another woman." Abigail started to walk out of the barn as she spoke. "That crazy old fool has accused another innocent woman."

She was startled to feel herself being pulled back into the barn. Struggling to free herself, she argued, "We have to stop this now, before she's actually charged. We have to…"

"We have to do nothing." Samuel pulled her back into the shadows where he held her tight against his body.

"Let me go." Abigail struggled against his firm hold. "We have to help her."

"If you go out there and try to defend her, you'll only make it worse for her and get yourself arrested. I've seen that happen." He gave her a small shake to stop her struggling. "If anyone comes to the defense of a person accused of witchcraft, then the defender is automatically accused of witchcraft, also. The logic is that the defender has been put under the spell and therefore must die, too."

"Someone has to help her!" Abigail struggled, but Samuel held her firm.

"Look, Abby," he whispered in her ear, finally calming her furious struggles.

A tall, thin woman had come up the road in the opposite direction. At the spectacle of the woman being dragged along the road, she stopped, hands on hips, and raised a challenge.

"Silas Grayson, what manner of action is this that a defenseless woman is so persecuted?" Her strong, clear voice ran out over the crowd. "This woman has done no wrong. Release her."

Abigail instantly recognized Georgianna March, and so did Samuel. The woman had both property and respect in Salem Village.

"She is charged with witchcraft," Silas answered, his tone less surly than Abigail had ever heard it. "She must be tried."

"'Tis a mockery you make of trial," Georgianna said, her fury and frustration plain even at a distance.

"Be off with you, woman, before you find yourself marching beside her." With that, Silas jerked the rope that was tied to the woman's wrists, and the procession continued down the road. Georgianna March was left standing alone in the road, shaking her head.

"Who is the woman who is charged?"

Samuel came to stand beside her, his breath leaving in a sigh of dismay and disgust. "Elizabeth Adams. She's taken in several Indian children who had smallpox. She's kind-hearted and completely unafraid."

Abigail wanted to turn away but she forced herself to watch. "She's afraid now. And she should be. Where will they take her?" She realized she had no idea what Salem Village looked like. Once she saw it, she'd know everything she needed to get around—she was certain of that. Just as she knew where everything in her house was, and how to milk and care for livestock. But there was no picture in her mind that she could pull up and study.

Samuel gave her a look, then answered. "The dungeon is beneath the magistrate's hall. It's crowded to overflowing, but they still manage to cram newly accused victims in."

Abigail couldn't suppress the shudder. She could suddenly picture the evil place. Did that mean that she had been there before? Or that she was headed there soon?

Samuel's arm went around her and pulled her against him. "It isn't a place you'd care for, Abigail, and I intend to do everything I can to keep you out of there. There's very little protection I can offer you here. Even though I'm involved with the trials in an official capacity, I have no real power here. Please, consider leaving." He spoke from his heart, his words strong and forceful.

Abigail shook her head. "No. I'm here for a purpose. And so are you. I know we've been sent back in time to stop these horrible trials. The only problem is, I have no idea how to go about it. These people won't listen to reason." She began to pace the barn. "If I tried to prove anything scientifically, they'd hang me on the spot. Besides, chemistry was never my strong suit."

Samuel paced beside her. "There's nothing I can do legally to help the accused. No matter what angle I bring up, I am disputed. If it isn't Silas Grayson, then it's Caleb Hawthorne, the prosecutor, or those girls. Every time I think I'm about to make a point on behalf of one of the accused, one of those girls begins writhing and screaming and the place erupts in panic."

"Do you believe the magistrate is actually afraid of witches?"

Samuel pondered the question. "I think he's afraid of displeasing the people, and many of them are afraid of the influences of the Dark One." Even before he could finish talking, he saw the spark of sudden excitement in Abigail's eyes. "What? What are you thinking?" He was instantly concerned.

"The Dark One, huh? Do you remember the old saying, if you can't beat 'em, join 'em?"

Samuel nodded. It was very familiar to him. He had an image of the dark-haired girl that Abigail had assured him was his sister saying those exact words as she prepared to do something mischievous. "I don't like the way this sounds."

"Oh, you're going to love it," Abigail assured him. "We need a black coat, some phosphorous, a little sulfur, some coal and some gunpowder."

"Phosphorous? Sulfur?" With each syllable, Samuel was more uncomfortable. "What are you going to do?"

"Samuel, my tall, dark stranger, I'm going to give this crowd exactly what they want. They think Satan is in their midst, well, he's going to make an appearance." She laughed out loud with excitement. "Yes, indeed, the Dark One is going to ride tonight."

"I don't like the sound of this." Did she actually plan to conjure up the devil? Was it within her power to do so? Was he falling in league with Satan by allowing himself to become involved with this woman's schemes?

"This is going to be fun," Abigail insisted, too busy planning to notice Samuel's face. "And it's going to put a scare into Silas Grayson that he'll never forget. If we work our cards right, we'll have the good Mister Grayson accused of consorting with the devil by the very girls he uses to accuse others."

"Abigail!" Samuel grasped her shoulders, but the wicked smile on her face was enough to tell him that he'd never change her mind. The least he could do was try to protect her, from herself and whatever unknown force she would tempt with her actions.

"You don't have to become involved." Abigail saw his hesitation.

"No, I'll help," he said. He could not abandon her, no matter what.

"Before you even know what I'm going to do?" Abigail was amazed. Samuel was rapidly shedding the shackles of his seventeenth-century ways.

"I don't feel I have a choice. You'll do it with or without me."

Abigail smiled, the eyebrow over her gray eye arching. "Are you a fast runner?"

Samuel shook his head. "I already regret this decision. The answer is, yes, fairly fast."

"Good. Where I come from, people jog. It's a bit difficult to do in these awful clothes that women here wear, but I'm fit and I know the two of us can outrun Silas."

Samuel's concern tripled. "This isn't a game, Abby. I don't think we should be making sport of Silas, no matter how fast we can run."

"This isn't a game, not by a long shot." Even though she was serious, there was still a glint in her eye. "Satan is going to pay Silas Grayson a little visit later tonight. I believe that if he's busy defending his own self against charges of witchcraft, he won't have time to persecute the likes of Elizabeth and me."

Samuel knew instantly that Abigail's plan was sound. Dangerous, but sound. An accusation against Silas would throw a monkey wrench into the works. Samuel turned to Abigail. "What's a monkey wrench?"

Chapter Six

The hard wood of the door skinned Abigail's fingers as she pounded on it and then ran for her life. She'd barely gained the protection of the woods around Mary Wadsworth's home when the door was flung open and a big, burly man stood in the light of several candles.

"Who comes to my door and then hides?" he called. Behind him was Mary's voice asking what was happening.

In a moment the man bent to pick up the note that Abigail had so carefully written.

"What's this? A letter left by a cringing messenger?" The man ripped the sealing wax free and opened the note. He read silently once, then turned toward the lighted room. "Mary, what manner of tryst is this? Who is this Joseph who leaves you a message to meet him at Courtney's Hollow? Explain yourself, girl, or I'll box your ears until your head rings like beggar's bells."

"I don't know, Father." There was worry in Mary's voice, and fear. "I know no Joseph."

"Oh, it sounds as if you know the lad. He says he wants to 'gaze upon your beauty by the light of the moon.'" There was rage in the father's voice.

For a brief moment Abigail was afraid maybe she'd gone too far with the wording of the note. She wanted only to make sure that Mary and her father would be walking down the Mill Pond road in half an hour. She hadn't intended to get the girl in trouble with her father, but it was so difficult to gauge the way people were going to react in 1692. By 1995 standards, the note had been formal, very proper. But Mary's father was acting as if she'd been accused of something horrible.

"I don't know him, Father. I swear it. Besides, what boy would write me a note? What boy would dare?" She was angry. "They're all afraid of me. They fear I'll point my finger at them."

Abigail's fingers dug into her knees as she crouched in the bushes and eavesdropped. Damn! The girl was smart and extremely manipulative. She was wiggling out of her tight jam.

"Then what does this note mean, and how did it come to rest upon our doorstep?" Wadsworth demanded.

"Could it be that someone is trying to trick me into going to that place?"

Abigail felt her stomach twist with sudden anxiety. If Mary and her father failed to go along with the plan, Samuel would be endangering himself for no reason.

"Aye, a trick. Then we certainly shan't disappoint this young man," Wadsworth said, his voice gravelly. "If he wanted a meeting with a pure young girl who can sense the evil in another, then that's exactly what he shall get. Get your cape and bonnet, and don't bother to try to hide from me. We'll make the rendezvous and see what this young rapscallion is up to. When I get my hands on him he'll find himself down in the dungeon with all of the other troublemakers in Salem Village!"

"Father!" Mary protested loudly. "I don't want to go to Courtney's Hollow. I hate the dark!" Her voice rose. "The Dark One is out and about tonight. I feel him."

"Ye've made your bed, Mary, girl. I can see you've encouraged this Joseph. He thinks he can write you notes such as this and escape without punishment. Well, you're my daughter, and I must protect your good name if I'm ever to marry you off. This beggar will pay a high price for his moon-mad antics. Hey! Don't try to scuttle backward now. Get your cape and let's be off. There's a gentleman waiting to gaze upon your beauty.''

Wadsworth's harsh laughter was still ringing in Abigail's ears as she crept through the bushes and back to the road where she began to run toward Silas Grayson's house and the scenario that Samuel had already begun to put into effect. If circumstances had been different, she might have felt pity for Mary Wadsworth and her domineering father, she thought as she hurried through the dark woods. But Mary and her cohorts had already sent at least two innocent people to hang. Abigail didn't waste her tender feelings on the girl's domestic plight.

She arrived just in time to see Samuel toss the gunpowder into the small bonfire he'd built in the middle of the road. In the sudden flare of the firelight his soot-blackened face was truly frightening and the black cloak she'd supplied him disguised his muscular frame. Clutching a crooked staff that he'd found in the woods, he gave more than a passable imitation of the Dark One.

''Silas Grayson, come out and meet with your friend,'' Samuel called loudly.

Behind her, Abigail heard the sound of someone hurrying down the road. She ducked into the small clearing in the trees where she'd tied her only two horses, already saddled and bridled. Peeking through the dense foliage, she calmed the horses with a few murmured words and watched the scene develop. Silas Grayson came out the front door of his house just as Mary Wadsworth and her father rounded the curve in the road.

With the timing of a master showman, Samuel tossed a handful of gunpowder and sulfur into the fire. The flames leapt high with a roar and a sizzle, and the yellow smoke that followed carried the distinctive odor of brimstone.

"Silas, your master calls!" he bellowed. "You dare to keep me waiting!" He tossed another handful of gunpowder into the fire.

At the sight of Samuel's angry, soot-blackened features and his lanky frame lit by the flare of the bonfire, Mary screamed and almost fainted, stumbling back into her father. He lost his footing and the two of them fell into the dirt and began thrashing to separate and get away.

In the doorway Silas let out a shriek of fear and jumped back into the house, slamming the door. With everyone in confusion, Samuel ducked behind the bonfire and cut through the woods to the place where Abigail waited with the horses.

As soon as he parted the bushes and entered the clearing, Abigail threw him the reins of her bay gelding and she climbed into the saddle on the smaller chestnut mare.

"Ride," she whispered, barely able to contain her mirth.

"I fear we've frightened them badly," Samuel answered as he turned the gelding toward the thicker woods. His voice was tinged with laughter.

"It's exactly what they deserve," Abigail answered as she urged her mare into a trot and led the way to the old hunting trail that would eventually take them home without risking the use of the main road.

Ignoring the small branches that tugged at their clothes, they rode for the next fifteen minutes without talking. As soon as they were in the barn they unsaddled the horses and put them in stalls for the night. Finally, when all the work was done, Abigail turned to Samuel.

"You make a fine Satan," she said, laughter bubbling beneath her words.

"I'm not sure that's a compliment." He brushed a twig from her hair, his fingers lingering to trace her cheek. He'd never tell her, but he was more than a little relieved that her "magic" had not actually conjured up a hoofed man with a pitchfork tail.

"Believe me, it is."

"I'd better wash my face and hurry to the Graysons' home. I wonder what story Silas will have for me about his visitor?"

Abigail detected the worry in his voice. "How will you explain where you've been?" It was a matter she'd failed to think through. The idea that she might have put Samuel in danger made her heart beat faster.

"I'll think of something, but I have to get this charcoal off my face. It's more than a little incriminating."

Abigail got the bucket of water she'd left in the barn and the soap and cloth. She lit a small lantern and then sat on her milking stool as Samuel removed the cloak and his shirt and bent to wash his face.

The lamplight played across the muscles of his back as he leaned over the water. The night had gone better than even she had expected, but her mind was not on Silas Grayson and the effects of his unexpected visit from the Dark One. Instead she found herself remembering the way Samuel's lips had felt on hers. His kiss had been sensual, tender yet hungry. She was tempted to go over and help him wash away the evidence of his adventure, but she knew that he had to leave immediately. Once she touched him, she wouldn't want him to go.

He dried his face on the towel she handed him and brushed the damp hair from his forehead. "You're very quiet. Do you regret our actions?"

"No." She stood. "I regret that we're here, in a place where we don't belong. I can't help but wonder what we would be doing if we were back in Washington in 1995."

Samuel held the towel bunched in front of him. He wanted to reach for her, to pull her into his arms and kiss her lips, which were slightly parted with the desire he saw so clearly in her eyes. Was she a witch? At the moment he didn't care.

Abigail broke the tension by handing him his shirt. "You need to go," she whispered, her voice husky. "You'd be shocked by my thoughts."

He took the shirt, his fingers catching hers and holding them. "I find I like to be shocked by you."

Abigail wanted nothing more than to feel his arms around her, to surrender to his kiss, but there was no time. "Then hurry to the Graysons' so we can both remain free to shock each other another day." She held herself away from him by sheer will. They had played the scene successfully so far. It was dangerous to tempt fate by making any mistakes.

In a moment Samuel had his shirt and coat on. Abigail blew out the lantern and together they crossed the moonlit stretch of yard to her house.

"Tomorrow? There's a secluded area about a half mile along the eastern bank of the Mill Pond."

"At four," Abigail said. "You really can't be seen here, Samuel. It could mean your life if Silas persists in accusing me."

"At four." He turned and walked away, his long stride taking him into the darkness in only a moment.

Opening her door, Abigail slipped inside and lowered the heavy wooden bar. Now that the evening was over, now that Samuel was gone, she felt her knees weaken with fear as she sat down in a chair beside the cold fireplace. Although she'd hidden her deepest fears from Samuel, she was no fool. She had just played her hand at a game where the stakes were high. Very high. If her luck held, she'd bought herself a reprieve from Silas Grayson's unexplained wrath. If she'd failed, the next morning could bring a summons to the magistrate and a charge of witchcraft against her.

THE MORNING HOURS dragged by with a slowness that made Abigail want to scream. She was afraid to go into the village proper to see what the news was. No one had come walking down the road whom she could ask for news. She tended her sheep and horses, milked Sally, and waited for four o'clock.

Unable to eat, she cooked lobster for Familiar and then sat with him on her lap and waited for the afternoon to pass. The black cat seemed restless, too, and though he asked repeatedly to go outside, she refused to open the door.

"They'll string you up, foolish cat," she cautioned him. He didn't argue, but he sat by the door, waiting.

The road outside was bare of all traffic. Neither human nor animal came along to catch Abigail's eager eye. It was as if everyone had gone into town—and intended to stay.

At last the sun began to shift down the western sky, and Abigail picked up the picnic basket she'd packed with such care. She had to hear what Samuel had learned, but almost as important, she had to see Samuel. The only pleasant moments of the day had been while she'd cut the bread and cheese and prepared the small delicacies that she'd found in her kitchen. There were jam and cookies, and an intriguingly dusty bottle that contained some type of homemade wine. She'd buried that in the bottom of the basket knowing that such liquor would be in the top "sin" category of the Puritan village. Well, she intended to drink the wine, and indulge in a few tempestuous kisses with Samuel. To hell with the 1692 values of a bunch of drab men and women.

"Familiar, you stay put," she ordered the cat. It wasn't that she didn't want his company, but she was afraid that he'd stray out in public and someone would see him. As smart as he was, he wouldn't stand a chance with an entire village chasing him, intent on killing him.

She slipped quickly through the door, taking care not to let him out. She hesitated, wondering if she should put him in the safe hiding place behind the chimney. Surely he would stay out of the windows. He'd displayed incredible good sense so far.

Eager to meet Samuel, she hurried around the house and to the old trail they'd ridden the night before. The longer she stayed off the main road, the less her chance of running into Silas Grayson or one of his finger-pointing minions.

The Mill Pond and Courtney's Hollow were some three miles from her house. It would be a good forty-five-minute walk in Reeboks and gym shorts. In tight underclothes, layers of petticoats and a heavy flannel dress, Abigail found that she had to stop and rest every half mile. By the time she got there she would be a hot, sweaty mess. She had the impulse to rip off her clothes. The underwear—any one particular layer of it—was heavy enough to hide her body, but if she were caught traveling down the road in her chemise, they'd lynch her without a trial. She tried to find the humor in the situation and keep moving.

At the end of the road was Samuel. That was what she had to keep in mind. Samuel *and* news about what effect their prank had had on the witch trials.

At last the trail fed back into the main road and Abigail forced herself to ignore the sweat trickling down her back and walked faster. It was almost July, and the days would get hotter and hotter. She could only wish that if she were going to be forced to wear such clothes that she could have visited 1692 in the winter months instead of summer. But she hadn't been given a choice.

She passed the time by trying to remember who she was in 1995. What did she do for a living? An artist, perhaps? A teacher? Maybe a mother? She felt a tickle of certainty that she was not a mother. Surely if she had children of her own, even at a distance of three hundred years, she'd be able to remember. Maybe a jeweler? She remembered the crystal pendant and the fine craftsmanship that had gone into it. Yes, she was a jeweler. Too bad the women of Salem had no use for gewgaws and trinkets.

She saw the pond up ahead and increased her lagging footsteps. She was still half an hour early to meet Samuel.

Although she'd never been to the pond before, she found the secluded place he'd mentioned.

She spread out the linen cloth and the food items. There was still time to kill, and Abigail cast a longing look at the cool water. She had no swimsuit, but even if she did, it would still be thought indecent. At the idea of herself in a bikini in a crowd of Salem Villagers, she chuckled out loud.

Even as she tried to mentally talk herself out of it, her fingers worked the coarse buttons of her dress. She stepped out of it, then the heavy cotton slip, then another, until there was only the plain cloth of her last layer of underclothing. Stepping out of the poorly fitting clogs she'd found to wear, she stepped into the water.

It was an initial shock, but in six strides she was shoulder deep and feeling as if she'd been set free. The water was cold, but not unbearable. She bobbed down into the water, executing an underwater flip and then surfacing to shoot a stream of water into the air. She hadn't felt so carefree or childlike since she'd awakened to find herself in the middle of the witch trials.

For the first time since her arrival she could see the beauty of the area. The land was harsh and unforgiving in some regards, but it was also starkly beautiful. She could only imagine the fall when the leaves would turn into glorious reds and yellows.

She did several breaststrokes away from the shore and then struck out in a crawl. The exercise in the bracing water made every cell of her body tingle with life. But she knew her time was short. She had to get out and get dressed before Samuel arrived.

Any other man might relish the idea of finding her swimming in her underwear, but not Samuel. He'd be scandalized—and tempted. She burst to the surface of the lake, laughing.

"I know for certain you're a witch. Witches can't be drowned."

At the sound of Samuel's serious voice she looked up at the shore. He was sitting on the picnic cloth and watching her, her clothing in his hands.

She swam forward enough to put her feet on solid ground but to keep her body beneath the shield of water. "I meant to be out and dressed before you got here."

"You swim like one of the sea animals. I've never seen a woman with such grace."

Abigail felt a glow of pleasure at his words, but since she'd stopped swimming, the water was becoming chillier and chillier. "In 1995 almost everyone knows how to swim."

"Do you have leeches in 1995?"

"Leeches?" Even the sound of the word was ugly. "Those bloodsucking parasites that look like snails?"

"Those are the ones." His smile was slow. "The waters of the Mill Pond are famous for them. We capture them and sell them to the apothecaries all over the New World. Summer is the best time to catch them."

Abigail didn't bother to scream. She ran out of the lake heedless of the fact that her underwear, long and cotton though it was, clung to every curve.

Samuel stood, still holding her clothes. "Maybe I should check you for leeches," he said, walking toward her.

"Oh, God, make sure those terrible things aren't on me." Abigail was searching her arms and legs, but she couldn't see her neck or back.

"Take it easy." Samuel lifted her sodden hair and looked at her back and shoulders. He turned her around, his eyes lingering on her breasts, which showed clearly under the wet cloth. "I think I need a closer look." He leaned down and kissed her neck, his hands moving down her ribs to her waist. With sudden desire, he pulled her against him.

Abigail forgot the leeches and the cold wetness of her clothes. She forgot everything except the hot desire that Samuel Truesdale stoked in her. If she had thought she would scandalize him, she'd been mistaken. His reluctance to participate in sinful behavior had flown right out the window.

With his fingers at the laces of her clothes she knew a rush of need so strong she felt her knees weaken. Samuel took that as a signal to lead her over to the linen cloth that had been intended to serve as a table. It would serve as well for a bed.

"What about the leeches?" she asked. Once his lips were off hers, the concern returned.

"I was teasing," he said.

"There are no leeches in the pond?"

"Well, there might be, but I haven't seen any."

"You lied." Abigail was astonished.

"I fibbed," he said, pulling her down onto the cloth beside him. "I thought it was the modern thing to do."

"For what purpose did you fib?"

"I wanted you to come out of the water. I wanted to see what you looked like, but I didn't want to tell you."

Abigail saw the smile on his lips. He was hungry for her, but he was also amused, and a little sad. "But you're telling me now."

"I know. But now I'm positive you've bewitched me so it doesn't matter if I confess my carnal desires to you. I'm already yours, to command to do your slightest wish. The way I figure it, I'm only doing what you have required me to do."

She placed her hand on his chest where she could feel his heart beating. "Do you really believe I've bewitched you?" She didn't want him to believe that. Was that the sadness in his eyes?

Samuel kissed her lips lightly. "No, I don't believe that. Not really. But it makes it easier for me to touch you, like this, without regard for the consequences. If anyone saw us, Abigail if they suspected..." He kissed her again. "Are these not considerations in the world of 1995? Perhaps it would be best for us to go there, because I think I want to spend a great deal of time doing these things with you."

Abigail laughed. "You are an unusual man, Samuel. Sometimes I'm positive you're from the future, and then I think maybe I'm mistaken. I don't want to..." She searched for the right word. "Corrupt you with modern ways and thoughts if you really belong here."

"Corrupt me," he commanded. "Now."

He brought his lips to hers and his hands began again the exploration of her laces.

Abigail was only too willing to oblige. The buttons of his coat and shirt were thick and hard to work, but her fingers were determined. Samuel gave a soft sigh of pleasure as she finally managed to unbutton his shirt and free it from his pants. The release of her laces sent a rush of anticipation through her.

Her hand brushed along the flat planes of his stomach, giving him a hint of what was to come. Locked together in a kiss, she could feel his involuntary shudder of pleasure.

Abigail was completely unprepared for the shriek of pure terror that came not a hundred yards away. She sat up, her undergarments falling around her shoulders, as Samuel almost leapt to his feet, his shirttail flapping behind him.

"Please! Not the pond! Please! I cannot swim!"

The woman's voice was pitiful, and Abigail reached for her laces and then her petticoats. She had no doubt what was happening. The poor woman, Elizabeth Adams, was about to be put to the water test for witchcraft.

"Samuel!" She looked up at him, afraid for Elizabeth, not for herself. "What can we do?"

He was already dressed and bending to gather up the picnic supplies. "I don't know what we can do," he answered, unable to meet her gaze.

"We can't let them tie her to the dunking stool. You know as well as I that she'll drown."

"And be proven innocent," Samuel said bitterly. He turned away from her abruptly as he tried to regain his temper. "It is unjust. And I don't know how to stop it."

From thirty feet in the woods came the sound of an enraged animal. Abigail, her arms caught in her dress, jumped to her feet.

With a quick jerk, Samuel pulled her dress down and freed her hands and head. "Let's get out of here." It was clear from his tone of voice that he knew exactly what was happening.

"What was that noise?" Abigail demanded.

"It sounded a great deal like an angry bear. A very angry bear. And it's coming this way." His prediction was punctuated by the sound of an animal crashing through the brush.

"Samuel." Abigail held her ground and pointed just as a young bear cub came streaking out of the woods. Instead of anger, the three-hundred-pound cub was squalling with terror. Caught up in its own fears, it ran by Abigail and Samuel without giving them a look. Five seconds later a large black cat leapt out of the bushes and swatted the cub on the rump, sending it shooting forward with another fearsome cry of horror.

"It's your cat!" Samuel was amazed. "He's chasing the bear cub."

From the woods came the sound of a much bigger, more furious roar. "Sweet Moses," Abigail said. "It's the mother bear! She's coming after her baby." She grabbed the picnic basket and began hunting for something the mother bear might eat.

"I wouldn't worry about feeding her," Samuel said. "It's the cub she wants. And Familiar's hide, I'd say."

Abigail turned back to glance in the direction where Elizabeth was about to meet her fate. It was exactly the same direction Familiar had been herding the cub. Was it possible? "Samuel, the cat is herding the cub over to disrupt the dunking."

"But the mother bear will follow! And Elizabeth's a prisoner!" Samuel took her hand and they darted into the cool shade of the woods as they made their way around the edge of the pond, careful to stay out of sight of the witch-hunters and out of sight of the mama bear.

They arrived just as Familiar drove the cub straight out of the woods. The young grizzly squalled in outrage and fear—and was immediately answered by the mama bear, who had gained ground. She came out of the woods, charging forward until she was within twenty yards of the terrified humans. Her eyes red with anger, she stood on her hind legs, a good three feet taller than the men, and swat-ted her deadly claws in the air in front of her.

The crowd that had gathered around the accused witch seemed partially paralyzed. They stood frozen, then slowly began to back away, never taking their gazes from the tow-ering bear who roared her fury. Only Elizabeth, who was tied to the dunking stool, was unable to move.

Abigail scanned the crowd for Silas Grayson, but he was noticeably absent. It appeared that Ezekiel Lecter had taken over as lead persecutor of the witches, followed by several other men, among them, Mary Wadsworth's father.

"Run!" Ezekiel cried, pushing aside one of the older women as he made for safety in the woods. Pandemonium broke loose and the persecutors ran for their lives, pushing and trampling each other in the process.

Abigail started forward, but Samuel held her back. "Wait," he whispered. "Don't let them see you."

"But the bear!" Abigail tried to pull free of him.

"Wait!" He held her, pinning her struggling arms.

"The bear! It's going to get her!"

Even as she spoke, the cub was making directly for the terrified woman who was tied to the stool. She struggled to get away, but her bonds were too tight.

As soon as the last of the witch-hunters had fled for their lives into the woods, Samuel released Abigail. Ten seconds later he was halfway to Elizabeth. With a quick scoop of his arm, he picked up the hefty bear cub, spun around and put the angry baby down—running in the direction of its infuriated mother.

Just at the edge of the clearing, cub and mama were reunited in a loud roar. Together they went lumbering back into the woods at a quick shuffle.

Samuel bent over Elizabeth's hands and quickly freed them, then her feet.

"Can you manage in the woods?" he asked her. "It isn't safe for you to go home. If you can make it through tonight, tomorrow I will find someone to take you to Boston."

Abigail had rushed out to join them, making sure the frightened woman was not physically injured. As she turned to look for Familiar, she saw something that made her catch her breath. Standing at the edge of the woods, cat in his arms, was an Indian.

"Samuel!" Abigail practically hissed the word. "I think the bear was only the first wave of attack."

With a cry of delight, Elizabeth darted past Samuel and ran toward the Indian. She slid quickly into his arms, her relief and happiness evident on her face.

Samuel took Abigail's arm and they walked toward the Indian, who had dropped Familiar lightly to the ground in order to hold Elizabeth.

"Thank you," the Indian said. "You saved my wife."

Without showing a trace of surprise, Samuel nodded. "Take her with you, Sanshu. She isn't safe here any longer."

Sanshu looked at Abigail, then the cat. "He is your creature? I would like him to live with me. He has a great spirit."

Familiar moved against Abigail's leg, then turned to put his claws into her dress, begging to be lifted. She obliged.

"Yes, he's mine. And we have work to do together, although there are times I'd dearly love to give him away."

Sanshu looked at her long and hard as his hand stroked Elizabeth's shoulder. "Yes. I think you have much work that requires the cat." He turned to face Samuel. "We have taken the children who were in Elizabeth's care. They are safe with us now, thanks to her medicine. Now it is time for us to go. She has proven herself and will be welcome with my people." He didn't flinch, but a flicker of sadness touched his features. "We will not be back to this village in peace, Truesdale. Tell the people of the village that when we return, it will be as enemies."

"I will tell them." Samuel held out his hand and the two men shook. Sanshu, his arm still around Elizabeth, turned back into the woods.

"But…" Abigail started to speak, but Samuel grasped her arm and turned her away.

"No buts, Abigail. This is the way it has to be. We have enough troubles to settle with the witch trials. I don't think we can stop the Indian wars, too."

"But they will die in a slaughter." Abigail tried to turn back, to warn the man and woman who had already disappeared into the dense woods. "They don't have guns. They don't have anything. It'll be a bloody slaughter that will end in the death of their entire tribe."

Samuel refused to let her turn around, but he did stop. She looked up into his face and felt as if she'd been struck. She knew instantly what had occurred. "You know, don't you?"

He took a breath. "Yes, I know. And I wish to God I didn't."

Chapter Seven

Abigail and Samuel, with Familiar meandering behind them, stopped at the edge of the woods beside her house. "Are you sure you're going to be okay?" She didn't like the drawn look on his face. The reality of the past three hundred years had hit him like a ton of bricks.

"This is the past. It's already happened." His gray eyes were tormented as he looked at her. "We *can't* change the past, Abigail. Think of the consequences. If we do one little thing that actually changes the course of history, everything could be drastically changed. It's mind-boggling."

What he said was true, but Abigail knew she'd been sent back in time for the specific purpose of changing the witch trials. She couldn't say how she knew, but she knew. And the black cat did, too.

"We're tired. Let's think about this later." She was bone weary with the weight of what was happening around her. "At least Elizabeth is safe. And the Indian children. She'll be able to ease their suffering with the medicine she knows." She turned suddenly. "You never told me what happened with Silas. We got a little sidetracked."

At the hint of her smile, Samuel couldn't suppress his own. "Yes, we did, didn't we? Something we need to discuss further."

The look in his eyes was suddenly hungry. "Silas," she reminded him.

Samuel forced his thoughts back to Silas Grayson. "He was a no-show at the trial. It's odd, but neither Mary nor her father made a single accusation." Samuel frowned. "The entire procedure was diverted by the accusations against Elizabeth. Everyone in town knew she was helping those sick Indian children, and no one thought anything about it until little Emily Waters said she'd seen Satan sitting in a chair by the fire rocking those babies."

Abigail shook her head. "It's ridiculous what these people believe."

"What they want to believe," Samuel said. He reached out to pick up a strand of her russet hair, letting the silky texture slide through his fingers.

"Do you think that Elizabeth was a diversion, to draw attention away from Silas Grayson and his little adventure last night?" Abigail mentally tried to push the facts into a neat line. Why was Elizabeth suddenly a victim? Why Rebecca Nurse?

"I've thought of that. If we could only get to the root of all this. If I remember my history correctly, almost everything is motivated by economic gain. At the bottom of all wars, all great religious conflict, it's always basic human greed."

"Exactly." She liked the feel of his fingers tugging at her hair and was tempted to remove the stupid white cap that was de rigueur for women of 1692. But the sexual desire they felt for each other was so near the surface that if she offered the least encouragement, Samuel would follow her into the house—and that could cost both of them their lives. She already knew the witch-hunters were after her. Samuel had been a thorn in their flesh as he tried to keep the trials from completely dissolving into hysterical mass hangings. The Silas Graysons of Salem Village would be only too glad to use any excuse to get rid of both of them. And if little girls were seeing Satan rocking babies in Elizabeth's home, there's no telling what they would see if they could catch her and Samuel together under the same roof.

"Who is gaining by these accusations?" Samuel asked. He continued with his train of thought. "Of the women executed, they generally have no relatives that I've been able to find. If they do, no one comes forward to claim their property."

"What has happened to the property?"

Samuel thought a moment, his fingers absently reaching up to pull more hair from beneath her cap. "Nothing yet. It will be sold at auction, I suppose, if no family member claims it. Of course the village itself will take some fees from the sale."

"Fees?"

Samuel shook his head in disbelief. "Yes, those who have been executed owe fees. For their incarceration, for the trial, for their execution. It's incredible, really. The prisoners are charged for their food, Abby. As the dungeon fills, more and more are starving because they can't pay for food. They have land, but no ready cash."

"What can we do?" She thought of the people locked in the dank cells beneath the magistrate's courtroom.

"I've been taking food down to them, hidden in my cloak. Just some bread and things. Hardly nutritious, but it's the best I can manage."

"Perhaps I could smuggle some food down there. There ought to be some purpose to these horrid dresses and petticoats. I could sew food in the petticoats!" She was inspired by the idea.

Samuel gently touched the corners of her eyes. "You would, too, wouldn't you? But if you dare to show yourself, they'll never let you out again. To provide succor to a witch is a sign that you've been bewitched. Or in your case, I think they'd make a case that you were feeding your minions."

"Right!" Her enthusiasm turned to disgust as she realized Samuel was correct. "So what do we do?"

"Right now, I have to get to the Graysons'. Silas was suspicious of me last night when I returned so late. Of course he didn't say anything because his own butt was in a pickle, but he won't remain passive for long. I don't want to be his next target if I can avoid it."

Abigail kissed his cheek. "Go now. We'll meet tomorrow."

"At four. In the loft of your barn. The woods are too dangerous for you."

"I—"

He cut her off. "They are, Abigail. Sanshu taught me a lesson today. That could just as well have been Indians angry about the diseases and treatment they've been given at the hands of the settlers. Not to mention the bear!"

"Familiar stirred that hornet's nest." She looked behind her to find the black cat grooming a paw. He completely ignored them, though she knew he was listening to every word. If the Salem witch-hunters ever suspected the cat's intellect, they'd really believe in witches.

"Perhaps, but the bear was there for him to stir. This isn't Yellowstone. These animals aren't used to seeing humans."

"Go." Dusk was falling hard and fast.

"Promise me you'll stay on your property and mind your own business tomorrow."

"Oh, Samuel. I thought you'd accepted the fact that you were from 1995. You sound like one of these men ordering their women around." She was exasperated.

His grin was quick. "Now that's one part of this system I like."

She lifted an eyebrow. "Be off with ye, Samuel Truesdale, or I'll turn ye into a toad."

With a wave of his hand he stepped back into the woods. His laughter lingered a moment longer, and then he was gone.

WELL, WELL, so Pilgrim Man has finally come to his senses and realized he's from the future. I was beginning to wonder if I was going to have to knock him on the head or something. I've been making some of my usual astute observations about humanoids. Now, they're inferior creatures to us felines, no doubt about that. But it's mortifying to me, a male feline, to discover that the male gender of Homo sapiens is even dumber than the female of the species. Not dumb as in taught knowledge, but as in common sense and just plain paying attention to details.

Pilgrim Man is smart. But he isn't aware. If I had to place odds on which of the two would survive this extremely hostile world we've been sent back to, I'd take Madame Mysterious any day. But then I begin to think that Abigail has a little edge on both of us males. There's something about her that's positively... witchy.

Well, I'd better catch up to her before she goes in the house. She's forgotten that she thought she left me locked inside. Wait until she discovers that Silas Gruesome paid her a little visit—and tossed her house in the process.

Lucky for me I'm a sly and devious fellow. I eased right out the door and he never even saw me. All I can add is that I'm glad Abigail washes my dishes every time I eat. Otherwise, I think it would have been hard to explain a saucer of lobster and a bowl of milk on the floor. That would look suspicious to a blind man.

Uh-oh. She beat me to the house. I do believe I hear the sweet chimes of her voice tinkling out some very 1995 language. I'd better go plug the geyser before someone walks by and hears her.

ABIGAIL PUT the last towel back on the shelf and went to sit by the fire she'd built. Familiar hopped into her lap and she began to stroke him. "At least you escaped without being caught. I tell you, Familiar, when I get my hands on that low-life, sneaky, ratso, I'm going to make him squeal."

Familiar reached up to put a paw on her lips. His green gaze held her own.

She removed his paw. "Listen, you sassy cat, Samuel is trying to tell me what to do. The villagers are trying to hang me for doing nothing. I'm not going to be bossed by a black cat."

Familiar's gaze was unrelenting.

"Okay, I'll watch my language." She stroked his head. There was something peculiar about the cat. He *understood* what she said. She knew he did. And he had saved her life back in 1995. She remembered how she was walking across the street to go to an appointment at Cassandra's Tea Room. It was a small tea shop around the corner that offered a wide variety of herbal and spiced teas. And she often met friends there. But she couldn't remember specifically who she was meeting. In fact, there were a lot of things about her personal life in 1995 that she couldn't remember.

When she sat down and really thought about it, it was troubling. What role had Samuel played in her life before they'd found themselves dumped backward in time to 1692? Was he her lover? She didn't think so. Then why him? Why was he the man sent back in time? And Familiar? She looked at the cat who watched her so intently. "Where do you fit in my life, Familiar?"

His only answer was a louder purr.

Abigail looked out the window. Darkness had fallen over Salem Village and the night was still warm. She put the cat on the floor and set about making something to eat for both of them. As she took in the stock provisions, she sighed. "Why do I get the feeling that I was a vegetarian?" She thought of Sally the cow and shuddered at the idea of eating her. But there was only the joint of smoked pork, the milk she had to get from Sally, some bread and cheese and some eggs from her chickens. "This is a cholesterol nightmare. I think I'd better find the garden if I'm going to stay here."

Motioning for Familiar to follow, she went to the barn and finished taking care of Sally and the sheep. With the bucket of warm milk in her hand she stopped at the barn door. It was a beautiful night. The stars overhead were bright beyond words. For all the lack of modern conveniences—such as a vegetable steamer and a grocery store—the natural beauty of the land was impossible to ignore. Could she stay in this time, if there was no way back?

"Oh, my, Familiar, what are we going to do?" She fought back a sudden wave of homesickness. "This is stupid. I can't even remember what my home was like. How can I miss it?"

"Meow." He rubbed against her legs in a statement of sympathy.

"You have a family and I know they're looking for you. What must they think?" Since there was no answer that would help the situation, Abigail started toward the house. From the barnyard the house looked inviting and warm. The cook fire burned in the hearth and the candles were lit on the table. It was a cozy house, well built and apparently loved by the prior owner. And where had she gone? What had happened to the 1692 Abigail? These were all questions to which Abby had no answers.

In the distance she could see the sudden flicker of light. At first Abigail thought she'd imagined it. Standing in the dark with the warm milk and the cat, she searched the dense blackness where her pasture ended and the woods began. Tiny pinpricks of light glimmered momentarily in another gust, then disappeared. "Torches?" she asked out loud. The thick trees of the forest hid them, except when the wind pushed the thickly leaved tree limbs around. "Torches?" she asked the cat.

He put both paws on her dress. Still holding the milk, she bent over and lifted him so that he could see the dancing lights. They seemed to be coming from deep in the woods.

"Probably a band of Indians planning a takeover. Or maybe a coven of witches," Abigail said, then immediately regretted her words at the march of goose bumps that rushed over her. "Of course, there's no such thing as witches," she reminded herself and the cat.

Sudden inspiration struck. "But it wouldn't hurt to check it out, would it?"

"Meow!" Familiar jumped to the ground and started back to the house.

"Oh, don't be an old pantywaist. We won't get into trouble. We'll be very quiet."

"Me-ow, yow!" Familiar stood his ground.

Abigail was certain he'd said something about her promise to Samuel to stay home and safe.

"I never actually gave my word," she argued. "Stay here if you want, I'm going to see what's happening. It takes a foolhardy group of folks to meet in the woods when everyone is being accused of witchcraft. Maybe we should find out who these people are."

She started walking, and she knew without looking that Familiar was following. He might not like her decision, but he wasn't going to leave her alone in the woods with lions and witches and bears.

Abigail's brash confidence began to wane as she drew closer and closer to the flickering lights. There was a strange sound in the forest. She was certain it wasn't being made by animals, but it didn't sound human, either. It was a low drone, almost a language, but not quite.

As the sound got louder, she slowed her pace. Putting one foot forward and slowly testing the ground for the snap of a stick before she lowered her full weight, she inched her way ever deeper into the woods. Behind her, Familiar didn't make a sound. The only time she knew he was there was when a stray flicker of light lit his golden eyes. She could only hope she was as well concealed in her dark clothes.

The sound was human, that much she could determine as she got closer. It was a chant of some kind. She felt a thrill of fear. Of course she didn't believe in witches! What was wrong with her?

She stepped out from behind a large fir tree and finally saw the lights. There was a small fire surrounded by what must have been a dozen torches. The flares flickered in the gentle summer breeze. But it wasn't the fire or the torches that caught her attention and held her transfixed. Three dark figures moved around the fire in a strange, choreographed dance. They all wore black cloaks with hoods that were pulled low over their faces.

At first Abigail couldn't make out the details, so she crept closer. Her heart pounded and she thought she'd faint from the fear and excitement, but she wasn't about to leave without getting a closer look. The people who ringed the fire were chanting and moving slowly around it in a circle. Their faces were turned up to the sky—to the full moon.

Abigail crept closer. She could feel Familiar tugging at the hem of her dress, but she ignored the cat.

The rhythm of the chanting became faster. It was a monotone, but as Abigail moved closer still, she thought she could detect Latin words mixed in. The sound was mesmerizing. Not soothing, but compelling. Behind her, Familiar hissed, but she kept inching closer.

The full skirt of her dress hung on a limb, and there was the loud crack of the branch snapping. To Abigail it sounded like a gunshot, but the people around the fire ignored it. They were moving faster around the circle, as if they'd begun a slow dance to the chanting. Visually, it was hypnotizing, the dark figures passing in front of the bright fire. A force stronger than her own will seemed to pull her toward the flames.

The pain in her left hand was intense, and she looked down, astounded, to find Familiar's claws sunk deep into her skin. As soon as he had her attention, he retracted his claws, then moved to block her way to the fire.

"You have a point," she whispered. She'd been about to step out into the clearing. At the thought, she felt a shudder of fear. Who were those people? And what were they doing?

She snuggled down behind a dense bush with Familiar in her arms. She didn't want to be stupid, but neither did she want to leave without finding out who the chanters were. Their behavior—and more important, the effect it had had on her—was sinister.

The movement and the darkness worked against her, but she concentrated all her energy on seeing. Suddenly one of the dancers dipped low and turned to the fire. Abigail caught the scream in her throat just before she released it.

The figure had the face of a goat!

Abigail fell over backward and released her grip on Familiar. The cat took off through the dense undergrowth and Abigail followed, on her hands and knees, crawling as fast as she could away from the frightening scene.

When she was a short distance away, she turned back. The dance had increased in speed and the chanting was louder. She knew now what it was. A ritual of some kind. In the flickering firelight the dancers moved with a sensuous energy that brought their faces low to the fire. Each had the face of an animal.

Abigail forced herself to watch, to memorize each detail of the grotesque scene playing out in front of her. She knew what the people were. Worshipers of evil. But the dancers and chanters around the woodland fire were not witches. Not by a long shot. They were something far more dangerous.... No wonder the witch hysteria had taken over Salem Village.

"Let's go," Abigail whispered to the cat. She crawled backward, her gaze constantly on the fire. If the people ever caught her spying on them, they'd kill her in a split second.

When she could no longer make out the dancing figures or distinguish the chanting from a low whisper of evil in the woods, she got up and ran, the black cat leading the way home.

Once inside her house Abigail barred the door and then leaned against it. Without regard, she ripped her dress open, stepped out of it and began shedding her petticoats. She was exhausted from running and the tight confines of her undergarments were suffocating her. She'd had enough of the conventions of 1692. And more than enough of the stupidity.

While the town was busy hanging poor elderly women whose only sin was to mind their own business and prosper, a band of truly evil people were cavorting in the woods.

It was more than a sane woman could bear.

Abigail paced. What was she to do? She knew about as much about Satanism as she did about the history of the witch trials. Which was next to nothing. How could she fight something she didn't fully understand?

And Samuel would not be much help. She wasn't certain what he'd been in the future, but she had the keen feeling he wasn't a historian or an anthropologist. Nope, they'd have to depend solely on their own wits. No future knowledge was available to help them.

Who had been dancing in the woods? Now that she was safe behind her own door, she tried to bring forth the visual details. She realized there had only been three people, a small number, but Salem Village was a small community. They had been average-size people, as best as she could tell by the cloaks. At least none had been extra-large members. Men or women? The cloaks had hidden such detail, and she couldn't make a determination by their movements. Certainly the animal masks had protected their identities.

The masks themselves were interesting. They had been crafted with some skill. Another shudder took her as she thought of the expertise that had gone into making the masks. She'd seen public television shows on African tribes that still used masks made from the skulls of dead animals. No doubt that was the medium this craftsman had employed. Plastic hadn't been invented yet.

She paced more while Familiar watched her with a wary eye.

"Let's go find Samuel," she said. It had been fifteen minutes since she'd arrived home. Sleep was impossible.

"Meow!" Familiar went and stood to block the door.

"Oh, don't be such an old fraidycat. He said he was sleeping in the loft. We can throw rocks against the window. He'll wake up and we can tell him. Maybe, if he'll go with us, we can return and identify the people." She was still sore with herself for not having gotten more and better information. Reviewing all she'd seen, she realized she'd discovered nothing that would lead to the identities of the dancers. If she and Samuel went back, they could at least follow two of them home and learn that much.

Familiar growled as he blocked the door.

"I'm going, cat," she warned him. "Stay, or come along, but I'm going." She picked up the broom and brandished it at him. When he held his ground, she brushed him aside, then opened the door. Suddenly she realized she had to put her dress back on. "Damn it all to hell and back!" She picked up the petticoat, then threw it down in a fit of rebellion. She'd found some trousers and a worn cotton shirt, along with suspenders. She'd wear that and be comfortable while she crawled around in the woods at night.

"After all, if they catch me spying, it won't matter whether I have on a dress or pants." She looked away from the scowl Familiar gave her and put on the boy's clothes.

In two shakes of a lamb's tail, she was out the door, Familiar shadowing her, his displeasure apparent in the way he carried himself.

She took the back path to the Grayson house. Though she searched the night for the sound of the chanting and the flicker of the fire, she couldn't see it. She had to get a little deeper into the woods, but first she had to get Samuel.

The closer she got to the Grayson house, the slower she walked, until she found herself standing beneath a giant elm tree. Something was nagging at her, but she wasn't certain what.

Once she stopped, she heard it. The sound of footsteps was coming from behind her. They'd been almost perfectly matched to hers. Familiar had heard them long before, and tried to warn her, but she'd ignored him. She was going to have to learn to listen to that darn cat.

She ducked behind the tree, Familiar beside her. The steps were louder. Was it someone from the ritual in the woods? For the first time in her life she knew what it meant to say her blood ran cold. She pressed against the tree so hard the bark cut into her palms, but she needed the tree to steady herself.

The figure appeared on the road as if by magic. At first he wasn't there, then he was, striding out of the light of the moon.

He was a tall man, well-built, and he carried a cloak under his arm. He walked with a confident, self-assured stride, a man in a hurry to get home.

Abigail held herself still until he passed. He was too far away to identify, but she felt he must have come from the ritual in the woods. Why else the cloak on a June evening? When he was safely past, she fell into step behind him.

She didn't have far to go. The tall man went directly to the Silas Grayson house where a lamp still burned inside. The man passed in front of the window, silhouetting himself in the lamplight.

"It's Silas! He's behind the Satan cult, and that's why he's persecuting the witches, to draw attention away from his own evil." She understood at once. It was a devious, but brilliant, camouflage maneuver.

Just as she was ready to look for a rock to throw at Samuel's window, the returning figure opened the door. For a second he stood in the doorway, then entered.

It wasn't long, but it was long enough for Abigail to be certain that it was not Silas Grayson returning home.

It was Samuel.

Chapter Eight

The long hours of the day finally passed. At three-thirty, Abigail took the note she'd written at least twenty times, thrown away and rewritten again. Her head pounded from trying to make rational sense of a situation that was irrational, and her eyes burned from the sleepless night she'd had.

She went to the loft of the barn and pinned the note to the top step of the ladder. She'd finally decided on something nonspecific, nonaccusatory. Her first drafts had been outraged accusations against Samuel. She'd seen him, cloak in hand, returning from the woods. She knew what he was about. She wanted to bludgeon him with the facts.

But common sense—and Familiar—had intervened. So she'd opted for a note that simply stated she was unable to make their rendezvous. Something had come up.

No way in 1692—or 1995 for that matter—was she going to be caught alone with a man who could prance around a campfire with an animal skull over his face.

Not when she suspected where those rituals were leading. Damn, but she should have spent more time listening to Maury, Montel and Sally Jessy. They were always having something about Satan worshipers on their talk shows, but she'd never had time to pay it much attention. And who said daytime television was a void? Well, let those critics wake up in 1692 and figure out which things from the future were useful and which weren't.

She knew she was expending her mental energy on foolishness, but she had to think about anything to keep her mind off the pain that came with every thought of Samuel. It was the betrayal that hurt the worst. She'd trusted him. Believed in him. And she'd needed to believe in someone so badly.

Her only saving grace was that each jolt of pain was followed by an equally burning fork of anger. In all her long hours of worrying about the situation, she'd still not been able to come up with a reason for Samuel's conduct. Why would he befriend her? Like everything else surrounding the witch trials, there wasn't a sensible answer.

Back in the house Abigail picked up the heavy basket she'd loaded with food. While Samuel was poking around the barn looking for her, she intended to get the food down to the dungeons. She didn't know how she was going to do it, but she was. As a preparation—and to pass the hours of the lonely night—she'd sewn pockets into the lining of her petticoat. It wasn't a good method, but it might work. If she could get the guards to allow her into the prison in the first place.

That was the problem.

Well, she'd cross that bridge when she came to it.

She looked at Familiar, who was sitting innocently on a chair, preparing for a nap. It wasn't like the cat to mind his own business. He was up to something, too. Well, he'd just have to follow his own plans, like her.

She carried the heavy basket of cheese and pork, bread and jam, out the door. It was awkward, but she could manage. She secured her door. Of course, Silas, or Samuel, could break in anytime they wanted, so it was pointless to lock it.

Lugging the heavy basket, she set off to make her first trip into the village. Her inclination was to keep walking all the way to Salem Town and book passage on the first ship out, no matter where it was going. If she didn't have this driving sense of purpose, she would do it, too.

Although she had no actual memory of ever having walked the road to the village, Abigail knew each landmark along the way. It was eerie, but she was growing accustomed to her sense of knowing. As she came over the crest of the hill she saw the cluster of buildings that made up the village. Salem Town, hugging the natural harbor, was not visible, but she knew it wasn't far. She stood a moment, calculating her odds. As a precaution, she hid the food and decided to explore the building where the prison was located.

She had the peculiar feeling that someone was following her, but each time she turned around, the path was clear. Familiar had been left in the house. The last thing she needed if she was to succeed in this errand of mercy was to have a black cat accompanying her.

She straightened her cap and collar and started down to the village. She kept her eyes downcast in a modest fashion, more to avoid eye contact and questions than in acquiescence to the "rules" of conduct for women. The village and its wares were as drab as the clothes everyone wore. Still, it was interesting to see the men and women going about their daily lives.

She came to the stone building that now served as a jail. The legal proceedings—they certainly weren't trials by any standards she knew—were over for the day, but there were still people standing around discussing the day's testimony. The tall figure of her neighbor, Georgianna March, caught her eye. Georgianna's face was pulled into a frown and she hurried down the steps with a confidence that few women dared show in Salem. It was the one ray of hope in Abigail's observations. Georgianna disappeared, but two other women caught Abigail's attention.

Edging closer, she eavesdropped without any guilt.

"Aye, 'tis a hard one to swallow, even when little Mary pointed her finger and fell onto the floor. Had I not seen the bite marks with my own eyes, I would not have believed it possible."

The woman who was talking was middle-aged, her full face worn by a hard life and unhappy emotions. She spoke with another woman, one who also showed shock and dismay.

"I've known Ann all of my life. I saw the bite marks on Mary Wadsworth myself, but I'll not believe Ann made them."

"Then, who?"

"Answer that riddle and ye'll answer the entire web of this foolishness." The first woman's face had grown red with anger, but she looked warily over her shoulder to be sure she wasn't being overheard. She cast a hard look at Abigail, who bent as if to remove a rock from her shoe. The two women drew closer together and lowered their voices as they spoke.

"Then you believe all of these accusations against witches to be false?" The second woman was alarmed.

"I do." The first woman lowered her voice. "My son has been forced to clean the prisons. He rightly pointed out to me that if the accused were indeed witches, why wouldn't they fly out of those horrible cells and escape? If they had these powers, why would they not use them?"

The second woman's mouth opened. "Why, he's found the bone of truth in the stew. The boy has made a point."

"Except no one listens. And he's been told that he, too, is displaying signs of being under a spell. I told him to clean the cells and keep mum."

"Good advice," the second woman said. She looked around. "Any of us could be accused, at any moment."

"Just like Ann." The first had a more defiant look in her eye as she scanned the vicinity. They were the only two spectators from the trial left. Abigail had hidden behind a large sycamore tree.

"What can we do?" the second woman asked.

"Obey our husbands. That will give them no reason to complain."

"Aye." The woman spoke with some bitterness.

"And I am going to present the magistrate with two of my fattest sheep."

"No! Your family needs those sheep. Winter will be here."

"More than sheep, my family needs their mother, and their father."

"You'll try to bribe the justice?"

The first woman made a derisive noise. "I will do whatever it takes to keep the label of witch from my name."

"Lucinda, that is dangerous talk."

"These are dangerous times. There is evil afoot, but it does not come from witches." The woman named Lucinda cast a furtive glance around to make sure she was not being overheard. Then she straightened her posture and composed her face. "Now, the cows need milking and the sheep must be fed. I'll not be back tomorrow, or ever again. These people are innocent, and I cannot watch while they are tortured and sentenced to die."

"Nor I. Mind you, keep your thoughts to yourself."

Exchanging knowing glances, they hurried off in different directions.

So, there were sensible people in Salem Village, but they were afraid to speak out. From the little Samuel had told her, Abigail understood why. Every person who had made an attempt to defend someone accused of witchcraft had been singled out for prosecution themselves.

But she had learned something interesting. Lucinda's son worked in the prison, and he was sympathetic to the accused. Sticking close to the sides of the building, Abigail walked around it, casing it to determine how she would enter with the food.

A stocky, dour man stood at the front door. He wasn't an official guard, but it was apparent he was guarding the entrance. The windows were not accessible. Abigail found the back entrance, but it was locked, with the added measure of a wooden bar on the outside.

She was about to give in to her frustration when a harsh hand clamped over her face.

"Mistress Abigail, hush!"

She allowed herself to be dragged into the recess by the back door.

"Don't scream. It's me, Walter."

She nodded that she understood and was rewarded by being released. She turned around to confront a big boy, almost a man, who was more than a little worried.

"What are ye doing in this godforsaken place? Your name has been linked with the witches. 'Tis only a matter of time before you will be accused, and yet you are here, begging for their attention." He brushed his hands over his long, fair hair in frustration.

"Easy, Walter." She knew him. He was a big, kind boy who went out of his way to help others. She couldn't remember a specific event, but she knew this. This was Lucinda's son, Walter Edgarton.

"'Tis your life that hangs in the balance. And if ye could see the poor lost souls down below us." He almost wrung his hands.

"That's exactly what I've come to do. See the prisoners." Abigail had found her entrance to the jail. "I have some food up on the hill. I know they're hungry, and I was trying to find a way to get it in to them."

"No!" Walter was horrified. "No, Mistress Abigail. They will hang us both if they find out. To feed those accused of witchcraft if they have no money to pay for the food is punishable by being named a witch."

Abigail put her hand on his arm, steadying him. He was literally stiff as a board with fright. "Okay, Walter. Okay." She felt the tension in his arm lessen. "How many are there in jail?"

"Every day there's more and more. At least fifty now. The magistrate cannot hear the charges fast enough."

"Do you have a key to this door?"

His eyes widened.

"Walter, I won't involve you. If anything happens, I'll take the rap. I'll say I bewitched you and lifted the key. But nothing's going to happen, so I'll return the key in an hour. I'll leave it here. I promise I won't get you in trouble."

He inched back from her. "Ye talk so strange."

Abigail shut her mouth. She'd forgotten the fact that she was three hundred years ahead in slang. "'Tis something new I'm studying." She did her best to fumble through the awkward phrasing.

"I cannot give ye the key." He shook his head for emphasis. "They would hang me and my family, too."

"Leave it here," she said. She had to trust his kind heart. She had to. "I'm going up to…yon grassy knoll to fetch my basket of goodies." She felt like an idiot. "Leave the key, and I'll replace it. You have to do it, Walter. Those people are starving to death." Before he could argue with her, she hurried back up the hill to the place she'd hidden the basket of food.

The basket was tucked in a copse of beech trees. Panting slightly from her uncomfortable clothes and the climb up the hill, Abigail ducked into the trees and made straight for the basket. She'd hidden it behind a rock, which required her to lean down a slight incline. So intent on her task was she that she didn't hear the soft footsteps behind her.

She grabbed the handle of the basket and stood up. Brushing her dress back down, she hefted the heavy wicker and turned around. She gave a slight shriek and stumbled backward.

Samuel's hand grabbed her wrist and caught her before she fell. "Too busy to meet with me?" He lifted an eyebrow. "Too busy doing what?"

"How did you..." She didn't finish when she saw Familiar sitting not ten feet away, a self-satisfied kitty expression lighting his eyes. "You traitor!"

"Food for the prisoners." Samuel took one look at the basket and knew its contents. "You'd risk your life to feed the hungry." Samuel was angry and he reached out as if to take the basket from her.

Abigail shifted it to her left hand. "Stay away from me."

Samuel stopped, his hand in midair. She wasn't angry at his interference, she was afraid of him. He saw it in her beautiful mismatched eyes. "What's going on here?"

"Stay away from me." Her voice lowered but took on a deadly intent. She'd intended to be calm, to stay clear of him in the future. Never to reveal the fact that she knew his secret—until she could make the charge stick. But her sense of betrayal, the pain of it, was too much to keep bottled up inside.

"Abigail..."

"I saw you last night, coming out of the woods. I know what you do in there. Deny it if you will, but I saw you with my own eyes!"

Samuel stared at her face. "So you saw?"

Abigail's heart plummeted. She'd expected him to deny it, at least. To make some explanation. To try to make her believe it wasn't true.

"I saw." She spoke more boldly than she felt.

"And who else did you see?"

Real fear began to gnaw at her. He was so cool, so collected. She had evidence that would get him hung indeed. Yet he acted as if he were discussing a football score.

"I'll tell the magistrate when I'm ready to."

Samuel reached suddenly and took the basket of food. "He won't bother to listen if you're already in jail accused of aiding those charged with witchcraft."

Abigail snatched the basket back. "That's my worry. You're not involved in any of my decisions any longer. Now leave me alone, or you'll regret it." She felt as if something inside her was being torn so badly it would never heal. But it had to be this way. She'd made the mistake of caring about someone she didn't know, and this was the price for such carelessness.

Samuel stepped back, allowing her to walk past him.

"If you saw me, then surely you saw someone else?"

She didn't want to stop, but she did. There was something in his voice. "What are you saying?"

"Think, Abigail. I saw no one there that I could identify."

She swung around to look at him. "Speak plainly."

"They wore masks. I never saw their faces, though I hid in the woods for a long time and waited. You could not have seen my face since I was hidden in the woods away from the light. I was merely wondering how you'd managed to see me in a place I was not."

The relief was sweet enough to counter the bitter shame of her accusation. "You were hiding, watching them?"

"I can't believe you thought I was part of that...cult."

"Oh, Samuel..." She took three steps toward him, then stopped. He wouldn't want her to touch him. Not now. Not after she'd accused him of something so terrible. "I saw you going back to the Graysons' with the cloak. You were coming from that direction. I assumed you were part of it."

"You honestly believed I would be part of such a thing?" He compressed his lips in a bitter line. "It seems we don't know each other nearly as well as I thought we did."

"Be fair. What would you think? Everything here is crazy. I'm from 1995. There are psychos out walking the streets. People lie about everything."

His smile was sad. "Not me. I don't lie."

Abigail felt a twist at her heart, which was almost as painful as her sense of betrayal had been the night before. Except now she was the cause of it. She'd tried and convicted Samuel in her heart, without even asking him the truth.

"I'm sorry." She put the basket down and waited. "I jumped to a conclusion that was wrong. Instead of seeking more evidence, I assumed. But I couldn't come out and ask you, Samuel. I couldn't. To ask would have put me in danger if it were true."

He nodded, the hurt in his eyes lessening somewhat. "I can see that. It did look guilty."

Abigail ventured a step closer, hoping Samuel would close the remaining distance. "How did you discover the fires?"

Samuel gave a small grin. "I heard Silas leaving the house. I was curious as to why he was leaving just after we'd eaten and all. I assumed he was going to spy on someone else, and I thought I could follow him, figure out who the next victim of the accusations will be. So I did follow him, but he was too far ahead of me in the woods for me to actually keep up."

Abigail felt her excitement halt. "You lost him?"

"I did." Samuel shook his head. "I was tailing him by listening to him. Then there were others around me." He went to Abigail, lifting her hand and holding it between both of his own. "I had to duck under a fallen log, and just in the nick of time. Two of them stepped right over me."

"Did you see?"

He shook his head. "Too dark. And then I couldn't be certain whether Silas had joined the others or if he'd gone on somewhere by himself."

"But you think he was there?"

"I *think* so. But that doesn't make it true."

Abigail's smile was contrite. "I see your point." The touch of his hands felt so good, wonderfully good. Especially since she'd thought he'd never touch her again. But there were hungry people in cells without food. And Walter had left the key for an hour. She pulled her hand back. "I have to go."

"No." He recaptured it, holding tightly. "No."

"I am, Samuel. I must. There's nothing you can do to stop me." She took her free hand and touched his face. "Nothing you would want to do."

"Then I'll go with you."

She shook her head. "No. We've already discussed the fact that if I'm accused, I won't drag you down with me. You'll be my only hope to freedom."

"Abigail, this is crazy."

"I said I wasn't a witch. I didn't say I wasn't crazy."

"If they catch you doing this..."

"I have to make certain they won't catch me."

Chapter Nine

The key weighed at least eight ounces, and the lock was ancient. Abigail had seen such things only in movies, but she managed to open the door. Before she could stop him, Familiar made a dash inside and darted down a dark, stone hallway. She sighed, giving up on trying to keep the little rat fink safe. As soon as she'd left with the basket of food, Familiar had hotfooted it straight to get Samuel. Even as she thought it, she smiled. He was one heck of a cat.

She let her mind dwell on Familiar and his antics as she followed the corridor, one hand on the wall to keep her balance in the dark. If she let her mind stray to her surroundings, or the danger she was in, she'd be imagining all sorts of Frankenstein terrors.

Ahead of her came the rustle of something alive.

She lifted the basket higher, took a breath and forced herself on. If it was a rat, Familiar would take care of it.

A low moan drifted down the hallway to her. It was a sound as old as human suffering, and as filled with anguish and hopelessness. Abigail steeled herself for what was to come. Samuel had told her the conditions were dreadful. But she'd never been face-to-face with people who'd been tortured. Could she bear it?

The rustling came again, like dry bones in the wind. She wanted to speak out, to let the prisoners know that she had come to help, but Walter hadn't told her if the place was guarded by someone other than himself. She couldn't risk giving herself away because she was spooked. But where in the world had Familiar gone?

She kept her right hand on the harsh stones of the wall. When suddenly she reached into emptiness, she stumbled and almost fell. It was as if her hand had pushed through a hole in the stone. Gasping, she struggled to regain her balance. She was almost steady when something clamped onto her hand.

It was dry bones, cold from the grave, clutching on to her. Abigail tried to pull free, but the hands held her, pulling her frantically closer to the wall. She stumbled again, lost her balance, and fell into the stones. As she twisted her body, her face was pressed against cold bars, and the smell of captivity rose up in a stench.

"Help me," the voice whispered from the other side of the bars.

Abigail thought she'd faint from fear, but she didn't. "I've come to help," she said. "I have food, but you have to let me go."

Her hand was instantly released, and Abigail reached into the basket and brought out cheese and bread.

"Thank you, thank you." The hands grasped it eagerly.

The cell was completely dark and Abigail stood outside it, heart pounding madly. "Who are you?" she asked.

"Goodwife Jenkins. I've been in here three weeks without more than a crust of bread. They would starve me into confessing, but I won't. They will never make me swear to such dreadful lies. I'm wrongly accused."

"Eat slowly," Abigail cautioned. She could hear the poor woman tearing into the bread and swallowing. "I have more."

"No more. This will sustain me. There are some who have been held here longer than me. They, too, have not been charged." The voice grew edgy with panic. "We will all die here before we are even tried."

"How many?" Abigail asked.

"I don't know. More each day. There are three and four crowded together in the larger cells. The space I have is so small, I have room only to stand. My bones beg to lie down. I can't even kneel to say my prayers."

Abigail swallowed back the despair she felt. "Is there a light down here?"

"For those who can afford candles." The woman's laugh was bitter. "They think they're better off than we are, but they'll keep them here longer, running up the cost of candles and food and the few niceties of life. Once their money is gone, they'll hang just like the rest of us."

"Perhaps you won't hang." Abigail wanted to be able to give her some reassurances, but she had nothing solid to give.

"If you're caught here, with us condemned, you'll hang beside us." The woman came up to the bars, reaching out and catching Abigail's shoulder. "Who are you, Mistress?"

"'Tis better I remain a stranger to you."

The bitterness increased in the laughter. "Better *and* safer." The woman withdrew her arm. "Take care, my unknown angel. Watch for the guard. He returns in half an hour."

"How can you tell time?" Abigail asked. The area was pitch black.

"There is routine even in this hellhole. He'll be back at half past eight, and he carries a lantern."

"Thank you," Abigail said.

"Thank you. And God bless you."

Abigail walked on. In the few cells where there was lighting, the conditions were so appalling that she did not want to look. It took her less than ten minutes to distribute the food she'd brought, and there was not nearly enough to go around.

"I'll be back," she promised the prisoners. "And know that we are working to set you free."

Instead of derision and laughter, she was met with silence.

"How can you help us?" a woman asked. "There is no defense against these charges. We're doomed."

"I don't know," Abigail said. "But I got here, with food for you. No one thought I could do that. I'll think of something."

"Hurry out of here, Mistress. And God bless ye," one of the older women called to her.

Abigail's basket was empty, and there was no sense tempting fate. She could do nothing to help the accused. The locks were ancient, but it was beyond her skills to open them. It would take a stick of dynamite to unlock the iron hinges.

"I won't abandon you," she called over her shoulder as she and Familiar hurried back the way they'd come, climbing the stairs to the incredible relief of a warm summer night.

As she sucked in the sweet air, she felt more than a little guilty. Conditions were deplorable; the plight of many of the people there was beyond desperate. Where was Amnesty International or the ACLU when you really needed them? Where was George Washington, or Thomas Paine, or Ben Franklin, those fathers of liberty?

"We're even a good seventy-five years ahead of the father of our country," she mumbled to Familiar as she locked the door and slid the key back beneath the ivy where Walter had left it for her.

Darkness had fallen completely as Abigail tucked Familiar into her basket and started toward home. Sally would be raising sand with a full udder and a hungry stomach.

Samuel materialized out of the night, a tall, dark shadow on the road. She recognized him so he didn't frighten her.

"You're still alive," he said with a mixture of relief and disbelief.

"So far. I think we should spring those people out of that hellhole."

"With what? I haven't exactly seen an arms arsenal around here anywhere. A few automatic weapons and some tear gas and we might stand a chance against muzzle loaders and rocks."

"Don't be so sarcastic." But she couldn't help but smile at the mental image his words created.

"I've been thinking about our ritualists." He paused as they continued hurrying toward her home.

"Well, spill it," she said.

Samuel stopped in the center of the road. "Did you hear something?" he asked.

"You're trying to dodge my question." Abigail had heard nothing. And Familiar, with his head popped out of the basket and his keen kitty ears twitching forward and back, had not heard anything, either.

"I swear, I thought I heard an owl or something. Probably Indians."

"Samuel..." Abigail tried to think of a good threat. He'd come up with a plan and suddenly decided not to share it with her. Probably because it was dangerous. "What were you thinking?"

He looked down the road, then down at his shoes, and finally at Familiar, who blinked twice. "I was thinking that since Old Brimstone had made such a dramatic appearance in front of Silas Grayson's house, wouldn't it be interesting if he actually showed up for a chat with those who think they worship him."

Abigail's grin was as wide as her face. "Brilliant!" She hefted the basket to her hip and reached up with her free hand to encircle his neck. "You are brilliant," she said, kissing him. "Brilliant and very, very sexy."

Familiar's harsh hiss broke them apart, and just in time. Another tall man came walking out of the darkness toward them.

"Good grief," Abigail said under her breath as she recognized Silas himself. "It's old Sulfur Britches."

Samuel wanted to laugh, but he knew better. He took the basket from Abigail and held it himself as they both started walking toward Silas.

"Truesdale," Silas Grayson addressed Samuel, pointedly ignoring Abigail. "What are ye doing out in the night with the likes of her?"

"Mistress Abigail had taken eggs and butter to the market to sell," he said, indicating the basket and lifting it as if it were empty. "I found her walking home alone and decided it was my duty to see her to her door."

"'Tis you who should beware. Her master protects her." Silas's words were clear—and deadly.

"I have no master," Abigail said loudly. "Isn't that what troubles you, Silas Grayson? That I answer to no man and continue to make a better profit on my farm than you do on yours? If you would stay home and tend your stock and your family instead of poking your long nose in—" She stopped with a grunt at the painful wrench Samuel gave her arm.

"Satan speaks with your tongue, woman. Beware, you will be found out and named. That is my promise to ye. The name of witch will be twined with thy own, and ye shall burn in hellfire forever."

Silas whipped past them, his long legs churning.

"That wasn't very smart," Samuel said, his fingers holding her arm in a grip so firm that it actually hurt.

"I didn't mean to be smart. He's a jerk. A chauvinistic jerk. I'd like to get him back to my century for thirty minutes. I'd like to..."

"Swing from a rope?" Samuel propelled her forward as he started to walk on. "I didn't realize you were suicidal."

Now that her burning anger was cooling, she felt the chill of concern. Her actions had been foolhardy. But the man was unbearable. And she was from a place and time where a woman didn't have to put up with such treatment. Unfortunately, she didn't know how to get back to that place and time.

She glanced at Samuel, and in the moonlight saw that a thundercloud was sitting on his brow. He was angry with her, and for just cause. She'd endangered herself for the pleasure of irritating a man too stupid to waste energy on.

"I'm sorry," she said. "I shouldn't have done that. It was foolish."

Samuel sighed, but his grip on her arm loosened and he gently rubbed the spot he'd held. "He could see to it that you're killed, Abigail. We know him for what he is, but he has great power among the people here. He and his wife, Sarah, have only to point their fingers."

"Or to persuade those young girls to do their dirty work."

"That's true." Samuel pointed to her house, which had just appeared on the horizon. "I'll bet he was searching your home again."

Abigail didn't even bother to show her anger. She had to accept the realities of 1692. She was a woman and she had no rights. Until she figured out a way to change things!

At her door Samuel put down her basket and allowed Familiar to jump out. Then he took Abigail in his arms.

"I'd give anything to stay here with you tonight."

They kissed with a passion that made both of them feel breathless and light-headed, but Abigail ended the exchange.

"Silas will be counting the seconds until you return."

"No doubt." Samuel hid his growing concern.

"I'm going to prepare some more food for those people." Abigail felt her frustration grow. Feeding condemned people wasn't exactly her idea of solving the problem.

"When do you think we can expect to see our chanting friends again?" Samuel asked. "They must meet on a regular basis."

"The new moon." Abigail answered without thinking. It wasn't until she felt Samuel's intense gaze on her that she even thought of what she'd said.

"Well, I think the phases of the moon have something to do with the rituals." She shrugged. "I must have read about it in some magazine or something. I don't know how I know."

Samuel lowered his more-than-curious gaze. "Abigail, think about leaving here." He looked up and put his finger gently against her lips to stop her protest. "I listen to you and every word that falls from your lips condemns you. Tonight, when you confronted Silas, you sealed your fate."

"No..." she broke in. "I was foolish to do that, but he hasn't accused me yet."

"Not yet. But when he does, no one can help you. Go to Boston. Plead with the governor in person. You're a passionate woman, and I believe you can sway him if you go there yourself." Samuel put everything into his own impassioned plea. He knew with dead certainty that Abigail would soon be named. Once Silas and the witch-hunters had her firmly in their grip, they would torture her with pleasure, and then execute her with a sense of holy purpose.

Abigail felt herself listening. What Samuel said made sense. Her letter had been impassioned, but she had always been better at arguing her ideas in person. Maybe her role was to go to the governor. She absolutely didn't want to be imprisoned. Her stomach roiled at the mere thought. And she would be of no help to anyone if she was locked away.

"I don't want to leave you here," she said. "Is it that I'm being selfish to stay?"

Relief was like a cool hand on Samuel's forehead. "Go to Boston. Bring the governor back here, to Salem Village."

"And you? What about you? What if they accuse you in my absence?" The idea of such a thing made her heart hurt.

Samuel's smile was wry. "I have no property, and I am an appointee of the governor. That's no shield, but it does make Silas and the others think twice before they point the finger at me."

Abigail still hesitated, but his argument made sense. That much she had to acknowledge. "I'll think more about it," she promised.

Samuel swept her into his arms and kissed her with a deep hunger. "We have to put an end to these trials so we can turn our attention to figuring a way to get home. I seem to remember such things as hot showers—for two, beds big enough—for two, and charming little romantic restaurants with excellent wine—for two."

"Hold me, Samuel," she whispered, pressing her body against the solid strength of his. "Hold me tight. I'm afraid we'll never get home."

AT FIRST LIGHT Abigail rose from her short, corn-shuck mattress and stretched. Her body ached from tension and the terrible bed. Samuel had left her the night before with promises that they would find the key to return to the future. The words were nice, but it had been his touch, his kisses, that had finally calmed her fears. He was the only thing, except the peculiar black cat, that she liked about 1692.

During the long hours of the night, she'd decided she would pay a visit to the governor. But she'd also decided that she had to have some hard facts to take with her. It wasn't enough to go and beg for his intervention. He'd think she was a fool. What she needed was hard evidence that someone was deliberately manipulating the witch trials for personal gain. Somehow, she intended to get that information.

She hurriedly dressed and completed her chores, then searched her limited wardrobe for a disguise. She settled once again on the boy's clothing she'd worn before. With a proper hat and some tight-fitting undergarments to compress her breasts, she'd pass as a boy. She was tall for a woman, but slender enough. And with a little carefully applied dust to hide her soft complexion, she'd be able to attend one of the trials. She had to have specific detail to make the governor believe her.

As she walked to the village she tried to make her body mimic the walk and demeanor of a teenage boy. If it were 1995, she'd need a swagger, a boom box and some three-hundred-dollar athletic shoes. In Salem Village, it was a completely different story. As she neared the village, she observed the stiff, formal manner in which even the young people moved. She did her best to assume the role and fell into the milling crowd that awaited the opening of the stone building where the trial of another witch was to be held.

Though she searched the crowd for Lucinda Edgarton, Abigail could not find her. Feeling more alone than ever, Abigail pulled her hat firmly down on her head and prayed that she wouldn't have to remove it in the hearing room. What were the rules for hats in 1692?

She fell in behind four women who looked as stern and unpleasant as the dour men who made up the group. Salem Village was not a place where a smile greeted the day.

When the spectators were finally allowed to enter the building, Abigail did her best to blend with the crowd. She made it past the man who stood at the door, examining all who entered as if he could find the mark of Satan upon them by simply looking.

As she entered the doorway, she felt a slight release of tension. Once in the room that served as a court, she shifted to the back and took a place among several young people.

A few curious glances were thrown her way, and she realized she'd miscalculated. Everyone in the village more than likely knew each other. Especially the young people. How would she explain herself?

"Are ye a stranger to Salem Village?" a boy of about seventeen asked her, his glance openly curious.

Abigail considered pretending to be mute, but was afraid it would get her accused of witchcraft. The horrid thing about wild accusations was that anyone with any type of infirmity could be accused on "physical evidence."

"From Boston." She lowered her voice and mumbled.

The boy's curiosity deepened. "Will you be living here in Salem?"

Abigail hesitated. "I'm in search of work." The others were looking at her with more than a few questions. She was saved as the members of the court, Samuel among them, entered the room. There was little preamble as Magistrate Jonathan Appleton brought the room to order. Abigail's concern about the boys fled as she turned her attention to the trial. Appleton was a porcine man who wore his excesses on his face.

In the grim pilgrim village of Salem, he'd foregone his powdered and curled hair, but Abigail could tell by the way he carried himself that he fancied the ways of the British barristers and judges. He did love his moment of drama.

The prosecutor, Caleb Hawthorne, was the extreme opposite. He was a lean man with a razor-blade nose and a sneer that showed his contempt for excesses of any kind— except punishment. Every line in his face spoke of a cruel nature. As he glanced around the packed room, Abigail felt his gaze brush hers. It was as chill as a touch from the grave. When she looked up and saw his eyes lingering on her, she thought her heart would stop completely.

Samuel, too, noticed the exchange of glances, and when he turned to see what Hawthorne was looking at, he blanched. He recognized Abigail instantly.

"What are the charges?" Appleton's voice was snappish, demanding the attention of the other players in the drama.

Hawthorne turned back to his business, and Abigail let her breath out until she heard the prosecutor's next words.

"We charge Elizabeth Adams, a known sinner, with consorting with the devil. It is commonly known that the accused has abandoned her own people to live in the company of red savages. She now consorts openly with the Dark One, using his powers to heal our enemies and to torment the children of Salem Village."

Abigail pressed herself into the wall as she heard the clanking of chains. The dark-haired Elizabeth Adams, her dress torn and her hair wild and disheveled, was dragged into the courtroom.

Once she was in front of the table where the magistrate and the other members of the court sat, Elizabeth shook off the men who had dragged her. She faced the court, her shoulders squared.

"I am innocent of these charges. In all my life I have done nothing but try to help other people. My own as well as the Indians. If you persecute me, you are persecuting an innocent woman, and I pray the wrath of God will fall upon you one and all."

"Silence!" Appleton thundered at her. "Prove yourself innocent, then, witch!"

Samuel stepped forward. "It is the duty of the court to prove her guilty."

"Not a difficult task," Hawthorne said, nodding to the murmurs of approval that broke out in the spectators. "I will prove her guilty and by the end of the day, she will hang beside the bones of the other witches."

"What are the Cl—p—ys?" Appleton's voice was shrill, demanding the attention of the other players in the

Hawthorne turned back to his business, and Abigail broke out until she heard the prosecutor's next words. "We charge this man, Thomas of Connecticut, with crimes. With the devil as a constant helper that the ac cused has influenced her own people in life in The communiy of respective the people most helped by the devil in a despite to gnaw us to destruction by setting the children of Salem Village.

Abigail wasn't sure if she was well or just talked out

Chapter Ten

Fear for Elizabeth Adams's life kept Abigail paralyzed and pressed against the wall as the proceedings continued.

The trial was a mockery, a sham. Hawthorne, his cold eyes assessing Elizabeth, took delight in reading the charges, which included eyewitness accounts from Mary Wadsworth and Emily Waters. With great detail, they told how they had seen the Dark One sitting beside the fire in Elizabeth's house. The girls said the devil had been rocking Indian infants in his arms, curing them of smallpox.

Elizabeth was also charged with fornicating with a savage—a charge to which no one could bear eyewitness evidence, but such details hardly mattered in Magistrate Appleton's courtroom.

There was a long list of lesser charges, which Hawthorne read. As he noticed that the interest of the audience was slipping, he called out for the two girls to be brought in.

Abigail was struck by the demure way in which the girls entered the room from a side door. Eyes cast down, hands clasped in front of them, they made the picture of perfectly well-behaved teenagers—for 1692.

As soon as they came near Elizabeth, though, the change was instant. They began screaming and crying, throwing up their hands as if they were being struck by terrible blows.

As they fell to the floor and began twisting and thrashing, they shouted, "Make her stop! Make her stop!"

Mary screamed in pain and cried, "She's biting me, please, make her stop!"

The crowd around Abigail surged forward, their emotions brought to a boil.

"Hang the witch!" someone cried. "Hang her now!"

"Filthy woman!" another yelled. "Hang her and burn her body as the savages do. If she wants to lie with them in life, let her lie with them in death!"

The young boys beside Abigail stirred but remained silent. Looking into their eyes, though, she saw the same fevered desire for blood. What had come over these people?

Emily and Mary had taken a breather from their antics. While the audience yelled and cried, they remained on the floor, pretending to be in a trance while they caught their breath.

"May I question the accusers?" Samuel's question was so softly put that Appleton tried to ignore it. But Samuel repeated it.

The audience, realizing that something was happening among the officials, quieted down. All strained to hear Samuel's soft-spoken question.

"Question the girls." Appleton waved a fat hand and adjusted the bow of his formal suit.

Samuel approached Mary. "Rise, Mistress Wadsworth, the court addresses you."

Mary started to thrash and moan, but before anyone could stop him, Samuel reached down and pulled her up by her arm. His voice was soft but steely; his gray eyes sparked with his fury. "Stand and restrain yourself," he said with a threat in his voice.

Stunned, Mary stiffened her wilting spine and stood erect and still.

"In making accusations against Elizabeth Adams, you claim that you saw Satan in a rocking chair before her fire, holding an Indian infant in his arms?"

"I saw it." Mary's gaze darted around. When she saw that the crowd was on her side, she visibly relaxed. "That's what I saw, and you can't make me tell a lie."

"I have no desire for you to lie." Samuel smiled at her, but it was not a pretty sight. "So, Mistress Mary, who was with you when you saw these things?"

"No one."

"You were alone?" Samuel rechecked the fact.

"Indeed."

"Is it often your father allows you to traipse the woods alone at night? Is he not concerned for your safety?"

"I demand that you halt these questions!" Caleb Hawthorne was red in the face and furious.

Samuel ignored the prosecutor and turned to face the audience. "Is it not a fact that the young women of Salem Village are well cared for? Is it not a fact that a loving father makes sure his daughter is safe within the confines of their home in the late hours of the evening? Is it not a fact that the young women here are guarded and not allowed to run wild in the night, especially when there are reports of Satan in the village?"

His questions had drawn frowns upon the faces of the spectators, but it had also brought complete silence. Mary Wadsworth cast about the room, looking for someone to help her out of the spot she was in.

"Where was your father, Mary?" Samuel asked.

"He was home...tending to the leaky roof." She nodded. "No one can fault his care of me. He looks out for me, he does."

"Then you escaped from your home without his permission? Surely a good father would not have given his consent for you to go out into the night alone? Which means that you are a disobedient child, a child who defies the authority of her father. Perhaps a child who might be said to draw the attention of..." He paused for dramatic effect. "Satan?"

Trapped again, Mary sought help, but none was forthcoming. Emily Waters had slowly sat up to watch with dread what was happening to her friend.

"Oh...oh, I don't feel well." Mary started to sink to her knees, her eyes rolling up in her head.

Samuel was too quick for her. He grabbed her arm and forced her back to her feet. "Stand up, Mary," he said, his voice a whip. "While you charge a woman with witchcraft, I bring the charge of liar against you."

Abigail saw what Samuel could not—the harsh emotion that passed across Caleb Hawthorne's face. He clenched his fist at his side but remained silent. Beside him, Magistrate Appleton had gone white.

So, it was worse than she feared. All of the court except Samuel were either completely corrupt or stupid. In this case, one was as bad as the other. Samuel was wasting his breath—and endangering his life.

Mary stood rigid under Samuel's glare. On the floor, Emily began to crawl away. Samuel stopped her with one angry command before he turned to address the quivering Appleton.

"These young women are not ill. They are not being tormented in any fashion, except by their own consciences." Samuel saw the futility of his plea as soon as he looked into the magistrate's eyes.

"The defense you bring on behalf of a woman known to cohabitate with a savage is interesting indeed," Appleton said, the fat around his jowls creased from the pressure of his disapproving frown. Once again, he adjusted his bow. "You give the appearance of a man caught in a spell of some sort."

A gasp went around the room, and the eager audience moved forward. The magistrate had all but accused Samuel of witchcraft!

Abigail started forward and caught herself. What could she do? If she showed so much as a shred of sympathy, it would go worse for Samuel. They'd hang him for sure.

The boy beside her leaned forward, also, and whispered, "'Tis a far better show than even I expected." His eyes were alight with pleasure. "Sure they'll hang them both before sunset."

"Her for sure," another boy answered. "Not him. They'll want to set him up for punishment for all to see."

Abigail focused her attention on Samuel. He was waiting for all the whispers to die down.

"If it be a spell which holds me, it is the sweet spell of reason," Samuel said. "I speak with common sense and a stout heart. *I* am not afraid of tales of evil, because I know my heart is pure. I believe it is those who make the accusations who have been placed under the thumb of evil. And those who listen to them because it suits their pocketbooks are even worse."

At that proclamation, another round of gasps and comments spread through the room.

"Is it your intention, Goodman Truesdale, to imply that—"

"My intentions are to prove Elizabeth Adams is innocent of all charges."

Appleton stood, his face actually quivering with emotion at Samuel's effrontery. "We shall halt these proceedings." He slammed his fist into the table and turned to leave the room.

Samuel gave a slight nod to Elizabeth before she was dragged away in chains. He had not proved her innocent, but he had gained a day for her. At what cost, though?

Abigail pressed back into the wall as the crowd got to its feet and began to hustle out the door. Many had taken time

way from their duties to attend the trial. Since the enter-
ainment was over, they were in a hurry to get back to their
arms.

Samuel had disappeared from sight, so Abigail fell in with
he crowd. She was getting ready to walk down the steps
vhen she felt a hand on her shoulder.

The fingers clamped into her collarbone in a bruising grip.

"You, boy. Some business awaits you in the dungeon."
The man who spoke was missing several of his front teeth.

Abigail tried to shake him off, but he held tight to her
shoulder, gripping with fingers that seemed to dig through
to the bone. She was afraid to cry out for fear she'd give her
gender away—and die for it.

"Who would want such a scrawny lad?" His grin was
mean, and his fingers gripped even harder. "I'm a desperate man to take on such riffraff as yourself. I have orders
from the magistrate to bring you around to his office, and
that's where I'm taking you." He leaned forward into her
face, his piglike eyes amused at her fear. "'Tis a cell that
may be waiting for you, lad. Cold stone and torture. That's
what's in the bottom of this old building. At night, when
they test the witches, their screams rise into this chamber.
The very walls quake with the suffering."

Abigail lurched forward in an attempt to break the man's
grip, but he wasn't easily dislodged. "Let me be," she
stormed.

"Or what? What would ye do to me?" He laughed,
dragging her backward through the exiting people.

Abigail cast a pleading look, but the men and women who
still remained stepped away from her as if she'd developed
a dreaded disease. With a sinking heart, she realized that
was exactly what had happened to her. She was infected with
the disease of suspicion. Who had turned her in? Would
Samuel be able to help her? She was swept away, through

the courtroom and into a small, private office. The door was open and she was unceremoniously flung inside.

To her surprise Samuel tossed a coin to the man. "Thank you. I have some chores for this boy to do for me."

"My own son is big, brawny," the man said.

"This lad will do." Samuel signaled for him to close the door, then turned to confront Abigail. "Well, well, I see you can't resist tempting fate." There was anger in his voice. "When I saw you in the courtroom today, I thought I would die of fear for you."

"I had to come. You were brilliant, Samuel. Brilliant!"

He ignored her compliment and began to pace. "Unless I can think of something to do tomorrow, Elizabeth will die. I'm not brilliant. What I am is desperate." He paced with his hands behind his back and his eyes lowered. "What can I do to save her? If she dies, Sanshu and the other warriors will come to the village. Women and children will die."

"They're dying now," Abigail observed. "Hanged by their own citizens. Perhaps the Indians will end these terrible trials."

Even as she spoke she could almost remember what event had actually stopped the witch trials. She could almost reach out and grasp it, but it slipped away. "Double damn!" she said, shaking her head. She refocused her frustration on him. "And by the way, how dare you have me dragged in here like a sack of garbage!"

"I had them bring you to me to help with my defense of Elizabeth."

Abigail was suddenly alert. "You had that oaf manhandle me and scare me half to death because you wanted my help?" She didn't know if she was mad or amused.

"I asked him to detain you."

"He implied I was going to the dungeon."

Samuel's smile was mocking. "You are. Since you seem so determined to spend your time in the dungeon, I've made arrangements for you to do so. As a janitor, of sorts."

"Janitor?" Abigail didn't like the sound of that at all. "You mean..."

"I mean, scrub the cells and floor, carry out waste materials, all the general work of a young *boy* employed to tend to prisoners."

"How kind you are." Abigail's tone dripped sarcasm.

Samuel shrugged. "You wanted to gain access to the prisoners. I thought you'd appreciate the work I did. But if you aren't interested in taking food to them any longer, then I don't suppose you care that they live in filth."

"You did this to keep an eye on me." Abigail suddenly saw his fine hand in the manipulations.

"I did. I thought it would serve your purpose as well as mine. You can feed the prisoners, and I'll know where you are."

Abigail stood and began to pace beside Samuel. She gave herself a few moments to digest the proposed plan. It was pretty good. She'd be able to come and go at will, and among her buckets and cleaning utensils, she could pack additional food for the hungry. In fact, it was a damn good plan. "You're right." She threw her arms around him. "It's an ingenious idea."

Abigail's dress was that of a boy, but her body was all female, and he felt the lush curves disguised beneath the coarse trousers and shirt. His desire for her was instantaneous. "My God, Abigail," he murmured, easing his hands down her ribs to the indentation of her waist. She was so feminine, so fiercely independent. "The things you do to me!" He lifted her to eye level, seeking her emotions in her beautiful eyes.

Abigail was bubbling with excitement. "I can speak with the accused. Perhaps they can tell me why they've been named. I mean, there has to be some rhyme or reason to these charges. Why Rebecca Nurse, an old woman? Why Elizabeth, who harms no one? Who is benefitting from these foolish charges?"

Samuel lowered her to the floor. "An excellent question. Perhaps those in the dungeon can answer it for you." He turned away and began to pace again.

"But what?" Abigail reached out to touch his arm. "It's a good question, but not good enough."

He shook his head. "Good but not quick enough. Not to save Elizabeth."

"What can we do?" Abigail asked.

"I can only hope that Sanshu has a plan," Samuel said. "And I can only pray that it doesn't involve the slaughter of innocent people."

ABIGAIL rose with the fresh milk and patted Sally's side. Making butter was a job that made her back sore and her arms burn. Cheese was even worse. What Salem Village needed was a local convenience store. And a good restaurant with a wine list. Some decent food and a glass of wine might put the entire village in a better mood.

As she hefted the heavy pail, Abigail resolved never, never, never to refer back to "the good old days" when she became a white-haired old woman. "Bah! Humbug to the good old days," she told Sally as she left the barn.

Outside, with the beauty of the night falling so softly on the landscape, her heart softened. "Why is it that with all of the bounty of this land, there is so much meanness afoot?" she asked the black cat who had stopped beside her.

She'd spent the remainder of the afternoon trying to figure out a way to save Elizabeth Adams from the hangman's noose. So far, she'd come up with nothing.

Samuel was meeting her at midnight in the hope of exploring the strange rituals going on in her woods. And also to discuss plans for the next day. He had vowed not to let Elizabeth hang, and Abigail felt a rush of fear at the thought that he would risk his own life to save the woman. There had to be another way, and she had to think about it.

She was almost to the house when she sensed another presence. She stepped to block Familiar, knowing that it was Silas Grayson come to spy on her. The man needed a wooden stake driven through his heart!

"Whoever you are, get off my property!" She held the pail at her side, determined to use it as a weapon if she had to.

"It was our land first." Out of the shadows of the tree, Sanshu emerged.

Abigail felt her heart trip-hammer, then level out. The Indian made her slightly uncomfortable, especially in view of his last words. He'd all but declared war.

"Where is my wife?" he asked in English that held only a trace of an awkward accent.

"She's been accused of witchcraft. She's in the dungeon." Abigail spoke with as much gentleness as she could. She knew Sanshu loved Elizabeth. Nothing could have been plainer.

"They will hang her." It wasn't a question.

"They want to, but Samuel and I are trying to stop them." Abigail felt the chill of death as she looked into Sanshu's eyes. If she and Samuel didn't come up with a plan, she knew Sanshu would do whatever it took to save Elizabeth—or at least avenge her. For a moment she considered the possibility that this was what she had come back three hundred years to facilitate. It would be one way to stop the witch trial madness. But in her heart she knew this was not true. There was malice among some of the participants of the trials. Malice and evil. But some were simple people who were honestly terrified. It was difficult for her to understand such terror, but in 1692, many aspects of life were tenuous and frightening.

She sighed and reached out to Sanshu. "We'll save her. You have my word on it. I don't know how, but we will."

Sanshu nodded. As quick and silent as a panther, he turned and disappeared into the woods.

He would give her and Samuel the first opportunity—and after that he would handle things in his own way.

Abigail went into the house, the milk pail dragging at her tired arm. If she had the power, would she simply wish herself back to the future?

"Auntie Em, Auntie Em, I want to go home," she whispered to hide her growing dismay.

MADAME MYSTERIOUS is at the breaking point, and I can see why. An Indian massacre isn't going to solve the problem here. In fact, if that happens, these frightened Puritans will find a reason to blame that on Satan and point the finger at God knows who!

Well, it's time for a little black cat action. I did a little re-connoitering of the dungeon. Jeez, that place is aptly named. There's the kid who left Abigail the key to the door, but he doesn't have the individual cell keys in his possession. Neither does old Silas Gruesome. So I'm wondering who has the key to the cells, and my best guess is Fattie Appleton or that prune-faced prosecutor, Hawthorne.

Samuel and Abigail are due to rendezvous tonight at the witching hour to check out the woods. While they're preoccupied and won't miss me, I'm going to do some checking of my very own. We have to act fast, but they didn't call me The Streak in my younger days for nothing.

Chapter Eleven

Abigail and Samuel slipped into her house and dropped their cloaks in disgust. They'd spent more than an hour crouched in the woods, waiting for something that never happened.

"You were right," he said. "It will be the new moon before they return."

"Or the half moon, or the second day after the rise of the sickle moon!" She slumped into a chair. "What are we going to do, Samuel? Time is running out. They're going to *kill* Elizabeth tomorrow. And whoever else they take a fancy to stringing up."

Samuel went to her and put his hands on her shoulders, pulling her against his chest. "I don't know what we're supposed to do."

She reached up and took his hands and held them. "We're both exhausted. We need sleep, but there's no time. Maybe we should go to the jail now and try to open the doors."

"You saw that dungeon. It isn't a matter of knocking a few wooden slats off the hinges. Those doors are embedded in stone. I can't say much for the comfort of the design, but the damn thing will stand for eternity."

"If we could get inside, do you think we could get Elizabeth out?" Abigail had pondered this while her legs cramped and finally went to sleep as she'd hid in the woods.

"It would be hard to leave the others." Samuel had also given it some thought. "But we would have to do that. Did Sanshu say how Elizabeth had come to be recaptured?"

Abigail shook her head. "No."

"Since I'm not allowed to consult with the accused," Samuel spoke with disgust, "I'm assuming that she went back for some medicine or something. She'd been gathering roots and things all spring and summer."

Abigail jumped up as if she'd been stung by a bee. "That's it! That's it!"

"What?" Samuel still held her shoulders and turned her around to face him.

"Elizabeth's herbs and roots. Surely there's something there that we could use as a sleeping potion. We could drug the guard and slip Elizabeth out with his keys."

Samuel's face fell. "The guards are not allowed keys to the cells. Appleton has already foreseen the situation where a guard might feel sympathy for a prisoner—or, as he puts it, 'Might come under the spell.'"

"Damn!" Abigail slapped the table. As she turned to the window, she drew in her breath and almost stumbled into Samuel's arms.

"Look!" She pointed, but the window was empty.

"What was it?"

"There were two large green eyes staring directly at us."

Samuel tensed, then started to laugh as Familiar jumped back up on the ledge and batted the window with his paw.

"It's only your Familiar," he said, going to open the door.

"I should have known he was being too well behaved to be in this house." Abigail put her hands on her hips. "He's impossible."

Before either of them could say anything else, Familiar darted into the room. He stopped at Abigail's feet and deposited a key ring with several iron keys.

"Familiar!" Samuel recognized them. "That's Appleton's keys to the dungeon." He picked them up with wonder. "How did you get them?"

Familiar gave the closest semblance of a Gaelic shrug that Samuel had ever seen, then licked his paw and applied it to his whiskers.

Samuel hefted the keys, looking first at Abigail and then at the cat. "Why do I get the feeling that you're no ordinary woman, and this is definitely not an ordinary cat."

Abigail swept Familiar into her arms. "Because it's true." She planted a kiss on Familiar's nose. "He's magic." She kissed him again.

"And so are you." Samuel swept cat and woman into his arms and kissed Abigail. Cozied up between them, Familiar gave a purr and then hopped down to the floor where he went to his bowl and attacked the lobster broiled in butter that Abigail had set out for him.

He cast a critical eye at the two of them, locked in an embrace that had grown hotter, more urgent, upon his departure. He blinked at them twice, then turned his attention back to his food.

The relief that came with the keys and a plan made Abigail dizzy, and Samuel's kiss was not helping her keep a level head. The passion they shared was like a warm wave that swept over her, engulfing everything except the moment, his hands and lips, the need for his touch that seemed to be something alive and independent of her will.

"It's late," Samuel whispered, his lips so close she could feel his breath on her cheek.

"Too late to sleep," she said. "We have to be at the dungeon early if we're going to make this work. And we have to stop by Elizabeth's place before dawn. No one can see us."

"I should go." But his embrace didn't loosen.

Abigail looked up at him. How had they come together in this place? What would their lives be like back in the Washington of 1995? Would there be anything there to bind

them together? Did it matter? It did, but not enough to halt
the headlong plunge her heart had already taken. "Stay with
me tonight," she said. "Everything we think and do is dangerous. At least give me one night of happiness."

Samuel tightened his hold on her. "Not one night, I
promise you that. Whatever else happens, we won't lose
each other."

The ache in Abigail's heart stopped the flow of her words.
She touched his cheek, feeling the day's growth of beard.
"If I ever had any powers as a witch, I would use them now.
To make you safe."

"To make us safe," he corrected her.

"No matter what happens, Samuel, we'll have this night
to remember." She kissed him with all the turmoil of emotions she felt. Taking his hand, Abigail led the way to her
bedroom.

The waning moon washed over the quilt that covered her
bed. Abigail's skin was silvery as she stood and let Samuel
undress her. With each lace, each button that was separated, she felt her excitement and desire grow.

When she was completely naked, her clothes pooled at her
feet, he cupped her face in his hands and then slowly lowered them down her body, caressing each curve. "You could
be from the past, from the future, or from the gods," he
whispered.

Abigail's heart sang as she caught his hands and molded
them to her breasts. "More likely the folks of Salem would
believe that I'm from somewhere worse," she said. She
lifted one of his hands to her left breast where a small beauty
mark was the only blemish on her skin. "Some would say
that this is a mark of the devil."

"They would." Samuel bent and gently kissed her breast.
"And some would say that I will burn in hell for the
thoughts I'm having of you now." His mouth became more
insistent. His hands pulled Abigail to him as they sup-
ported her back. Her body arched, and she gasped with

pleasure at what his lips accomplished. He lifted his head to meet her eyes. "But I am burning now." He shifted so that the bed was behind her. Very slowly, he lowered her.

Abigail reached up to pull him down beside her, but he caught her hand and held it while he gazed down on her. As she watched, he slowly removed his clothes.

Standing by the side of the bed, the moonlight playing across the muscles of his chest and abdomen, he was one of the most handsome men she'd ever seen. Classic, she thought. A figure that Michelangelo might have used as a model. Whoever would have thought that his Puritan garb could hide such a body? At the thought, she smiled.

"What amuses you?" He lightly moved his thumbnail from her breastbone slowly down between her breasts, inching down her torso to the flat of her stomach.

With each increment of progress, she felt her pulse intensify. She wanted to capture his hand, to halt its progress. And she wanted him to continue at a faster pace. "You amuse me," she answered. "You amuse me, and you frighten me."

His hand stopped instantly. "Frighten you?"

She moved beneath him, encouraging him to continue his exploration. "Not like that. You frighten me because I feel so much. And because the future is so uncertain."

"We have the here and now." His gray eyes held hers until he bent to follow with his mouth the trail his hands had already made. Before his lips touched her hot skin, he whispered, "And the here and now is all that anyone ever has, Abigail. No matter where they are."

NEITHER ABIGAIL nor Samuel had slept at all, but they were fully alert as Abigail slipped through the door of Elizabeth's unused cabin. They had come for the herbs, which Abigail thought she might be able to recognize.

She lit the candle that she had brought, afraid to risk the brighter light of a lantern. Using the stub of the candle, she went to Elizabeth's kitchen and began to go through the tins and boxes of dried leaves and roots and barks.

There was a vague familiarity to the names of some of the roots, but others Abigail had no knowledge of. She was acting completely on intuition, touching each tin and packet as she read the labels by the flickering light.

Her fingers brushed dried bark that was labeled Squaw Brush and she stopped. "This is it," she said.

"Are you certain?" Samuel had watched the whole procedure with a slightly eerie feeling. Abigail was acting as if she were calling upon some inner source that he did not understand.

"Yes. In some wine or..." She realized that alcohol was forbidden. "Or tea, I suppose. Wine would be better."

"Wine may be forbidden, but that doesn't mean it isn't used," Samuel said, as if reading her mind. "A goblet of wine left with some tempting morsel of food wouldn't be turned aside by the dungeon guard."

Abigail picked up the bark. "And you know exactly where to find some wine, don't you?"

"I do. Let's go," he said as he led the way to the village.

While Abigail waited in the dark, foreboding magistrate's hall, she heated the bark over a single candle that she was careful to hide from an outside view. By the time Samuel returned with the wine, she had a potent mixture ready. With great care she poured it into the wine and set out the pork and bread and cheese she'd brought along for the guard's treat.

"Stay here. I'll put it beside his chair." Samuel was nervous, but he finally convinced Abigail that even if he was caught, he could claim to have business in the dungeon. She, on the other hand, would not have a single excuse to be in that place.

Samuel was back in ten minutes, breathless but safe. As he'd expected, the guard had been asleep. He'd left the wine and food beside him, a gift from an unnamed benefactor.

Then Samuel had gone to the outside of the building and battered the door to make certain the guard would wake up.

"It shouldn't take longer than twenty minutes for the sedative to take effect." She looked at her wrist, aware that somewhere along the way of her time travels, she'd lost her watch.

"We'll still have time to get Elizabeth back to the woods under cover of darkness." Samuel began to pace. The night was slipping away from them. Daylight was their enemy in this attempt to free Elizabeth.

They waited until they could stand it no longer, then scurried behind the magistrate's private chambers where the entrance to the dungeon could be found. Abigail held Samuel's coattails as they descended the steep, narrow steps. She almost cried out as she and Samuel both stumbled over the prone body of the guard. He was sound asleep and breathing harshly as they stepped over him and made their way to the cells.

"Elizabeth. Elizabeth Adams," Samuel called into the darkness.

"Here." Her voice was terrified.

Abigail held the ring of keys and she went to the voice. "Where are you? Talk to us."

"Here. Who are you? What do you want of me?"

"Be quiet," Abigail warned her harshly.

"Who is it?" Other voices began to ask. Some had hope. Some, the fear of more torment. "What is going on out there?"

There was no time to explain. Abigail found the key and opened the cell where Elizabeth was contained alone. She was bent and stooped from the small confines, but she stepped out willingly and straightened. "Where are you—"

"Hush," Abigail warned her. "Just follow me."

"Wait!" One of the women sensed she was being left behind. "Take us. We're innocent. Please don't leave us here to die."

Abigail forced herself to be strong. "I won't abandon you," she promised. "Don't give up hope." She took Elizabeth's arm and pushed her forward toward freedom.

Halfway down the hallway Samuel held the lantern he'd taken from beside the guard, who was out cold.

"Samuel! Abigail!" Elizabeth turned to first one and then the other once they'd gained the top of the steps. "How can I thank you?"

"It's a little premature. You aren't safe yet, but we're going to take you to Sanshu. This time, Elizabeth, don't come back."

"I got a message that one of the Salem children was dying. They begged me to come back and save her." Elizabeth shuddered at the memory of her betrayal. "When I went to the place where the note said the child would be, Silas Grayson was waiting there for me. It was a trap."

"I never dreamed Silas could be so devious," Samuel said. He motioned them out into the night. "If I know Sanshu, he's been following Abigail and me this entire night. Let's start toward the west and hope he intercepts us."

"Jog," Abigail commanded even though she felt as if her legs would crumble from nerves and weariness.

"Jog?" Elizabeth's voice conveyed her amazement. "What is 'jog'?"

"A slow run," Samuel said, taking her elbow and assisting her into the questioned gait.

They were panting and huffing by the time they got to the top of the hill that overlooked the village, but they also felt somewhat safer. Samuel had noticed a slight movement in the woods to the west, and he was certain it was Sanshu. He wasn't startled when the Indian stepped from the trees.

With a cry, Elizabeth ran into his arms and pressed herself against him. Her tears were filled with joy and relief.

"Thank you again, Samuel," Sanshu said as he gathered Elizabeth against him. "We will not fall victim to another trick."

"Don't come back here, either of you," Samuel said. Dawn was just beginning to turn the eastern sky a dark gray. He found Abigail's hand and held it tightly.

"What will become of you?" Sanshu was in no hurry to abandon his friends.

"We'll be safe." Abigail spoke, though she wasn't certain she spoke the truth.

"Come with us. We will protect you." Sanshu stroked Elizabeth's hair.

She lifted a tear-stained face to Abigail. "Please don't stay in Salem. Down in the dungeon your name came up again and again. The last ten people who have been arrested have all been questioned about you, Abigail. The magistrate is determined to prosecute you."

"The magistrate?" Abigail wanted to be certain that Jonathan Appleton was behind the entire thing. He had been a suspect, but she'd never settled on any one person.

"The magistrate, or the prosecutor, or that horrid Silas Grayson!" Elizabeth's voice rose. "Who cares which man points the finger. The result is that you will hang."

"We care very much," Samuel said at the same time that he patted Elizabeth's shoulder. "We care because we intend to stop it. If you're certain Appleton is behind it, then we'll know better where to look."

Elizabeth brushed the tears from her face and steadied herself with Sanshu's arm. "I can't be certain. It is all gossip and talk in the dungeon. Everyone is terrified. We believe it is Appleton, because he is so cruel in the examinations." She cast a fearful look at Sanshu.

Samuel knew enough about the testing of witches to realize that Elizabeth wanted to keep this knowledge from Sanshu. If he knew that she had been stabbed with needles, pinched, poked, examined for witch's marks and a number of other humiliating actions, Sanshu would more than likely head straight to Jonathan Appleton's house and take his scalp and a few other relevant appendages.

"But you aren't certain?" Samuel asked.

The eastern sky had developed a silvery edge on the horizon. Time was dwindling. "No, I can't be certain," Elizabeth said with a sigh.

Sanshu put his hand on his knife. "If this man is so evil, I will kill him."

"No." Samuel put a restraining hand on the Indian's arm. "Killing him won't solve the problem, even if he is the main culprit. What we have to do is catch him, expose him and make him stand trial for all of his sins. Unless we can prove to the village that he is behind all of this foolishness, the witch trials will continue even if he is dead. These events have gone too far. The villagers are terrified. I hear that some children are accusing their own mothers."

"That is true," Elizabeth said. "There is a woman there, named by her teenage daughter, a friend of Emily Waters and Mary Wadsworth. The woman said she'd refused to allow her daughter to visit Mary's family."

"Oh, my," Abigail said. "These children don't fully understand the consequences of their actions. They couldn't possibly, or they wouldn't accuse innocent people."

Elizabeth looked at Abigail. "Find whoever is behind all of this and see that they are punished." She took Sanshu's hand. "We must go. And we must be quick about it. They will be down to test the newly accused in a very short while. My absence will be noticed, and the chase will begin."

"If you need me, you have only to leave a message in the black thorn tree beside the Mill Pond," Sanshu said. "Many thanks to you."

Holding Elizabeth's hand, they ran toward the woods just as the golden rim of the sun lifted on the horizon.

"We have to get home," Samuel said. He was exhausted, but satisfied that one innocent life had been saved. "I want to be in bed when Silas arises. And you must not be seen on the roads. Listen for the alarm. Search parties will be out, so make sure you've hidden those boy's clothes and

Familiar." He kissed her forehead, then turned her toward home. "Jog," he whispered as he took the opposite direction and began to run himself.

Abigail rushed into the door of her home to find Familiar stretched out on the rough wooden table. He gave her a yawn and a greeting.

"It's great for you to be so chipper. You haven't been organizing a jailbreak." She sank into a chair and ripped off her ugly, ill-fitting shoes. "I will never complain about Italian shoes again, if I ever get home and get a chance to wear a pair. I will never complain about panty hose again, just let me get home and find a store that sells them." She collapsed on her folded arms on the table.

Familiar stretched, walked over and nuzzled up against her hair. "Me-ow?" There was a definite question.

"I left the keys in the dungeon." Abigail had forgotten all about the darn keys until the cat asked. She looked up and met his concerned green gaze. "I forgot them."

Familiar hopped to the floor and then asked to go outside.

At first Abigail hesitated. The men would be around shortly in a house-by-house search for Elizabeth. She wanted to keep Familiar inside where he was safe. But the cat had uncommon good sense. She opened the door and let him out with a warning to stay hidden. If they did search the house, he was safer in the open.

Exhausted, she dragged herself to her bed and collapsed onto it, not even able to summon up enough energy to change clothes. The thought crossed her mind that she could not open the door for a search dressed in boys' garments, and she got up and changed into the floor-length cotton gown that was apparently the fashion of sleepwear in Salem Village. It was, at least, comfortable.

She had just begun to drift into a light sleep when there was a pounding at her door. "My goodness," she whispered, turning over and deciding to ignore it. Maybe they would go away.

The pounding grew louder. Then the deep voice of Silas Grayson penetrated her sleep.

"Open the door, Mistress West, or I shall be obliged to knock it down."

"Oh, jump up. . ." She sat and stopped the curse. If she was going to survive Salem, she was going to have to curb her favorite curses. "Hold your horses!" she cried as she got out of bed and found a robe.

The pounding came again, this time as if something big and wooden was being driven into her door.

"A battering ram, no doubt," she mumbled as she hurried across the floor. "Stop it! I'm opening the door."

"Open in the name of the magistrate of Salem Village."

She lifted the bar and opened the door. "What is it now, Silas? Have I been accused of sleeping too late?"

His stiff face hardened. "This is not a matter to make merry about. Elizabeth Adams has vanished from the jail."

"So?" She wanted to lean on the door, but she knew it would be construed as wanton and lascivious behavior so she stood erect. "What has that to do with me?"

"Are you hiding her in your home?"

"Look for yourself." She threw the door open, glad that Familiar had opted for an outdoor hideaway.

Instead of going inside, Silas remained where he was. "We do not anticipate taking her easily. She is very clever."

"A trait you don't share." Abigail wanted to bite her tongue, but she couldn't help herself. He was an arrogant, stupid, dangerous man. A bully.

"We will come back to search at a time of our choosing. Be aware, Mistress West, that in making good her escape, the witch has caused a death."

"A death?" Abigail was shocked and didn't bother to hide it.

"Yes." Silas grinned, delighted by her expression. "The guard was killed."

"That's impossible." Abigail distinctly remembered hearing the man's labored breathing.

"Why is it not possible?" Silas lifted his eyebrows. "Do you know something about this matter?"

"Nothing. But why would she kill the guard?"

"To prove her powers. Perhaps to warn us to stay away from her." Silas shrugged. "Perhaps because it is what her master ordered her to do."

"How was the guard killed?"

Silas leaned forward. "Poisoned." The word was almost a hiss.

Abigail quickly stepped back from him. "Poisoned?"

"Indeed. We found a goblet and food beside his corpse."

"And you believe that someone brought him poisoned food?"

Silas nodded. His smile was cold. "Someone in league with the devil. And when we bring the charge against her, it will be my personal pleasure to administer the severest of tests. Good day, Mistress West." He made a bow and stepped back from the doorway. He was smiling an evil smile.

Chapter Twelve

"I know I didn't kill him." Abigail sat at the table talking to herself. Not even Familiar was around to comfort her. But no matter how she thought about it, she couldn't forget Silas's words, or expression. The guard was *dead*. Not sleeping. Dead. And he had been poisoned. Was it possible that she'd taken the wrong herb from Elizabeth's cache? She'd been so certain she knew what she was doing. She had touched the squaw brush and knew instinctively that it was a sedative. How did she know this? Why hadn't she questioned her knowledge before she'd administered the drug to a man? She had put her faith in the fact that her knowledge came from her 1995 life.

She put her head down and moaned. In saving Elizabeth had she killed someone else?

She felt something brush her arms and sat up to discover Familiar. He leapt from the table to the large picnic basket and gave a cry.

Abigail stood abruptly. She had forgotten that she was to work in the dungeon. Even though she was greatly troubled by the news of the guard, she prepared the basket with food for the prisoners and found her boy's garb. With a determined warning to Familiar to stay out of sight, she left her house and began to walk to town.

Skirting the areas where people were already out and about their business, she made her way to the back door of the dungeon. Only a few short hours before, Walter Edgarson had reluctantly let her down into the dungeon, and the conditions she'd found had been horrid. Now she was doing something to help. She tucked cheese and meat and bread into the assorted pockets of her clothes and wherever she could find a safe place among her utensils. Heart hammering away, she pounded on the door and was allowed to enter. The man who warily eyed her was big, snaggle-toothed and unwashed.

"So, this is the lad Goodman Truesdale took on?" The guard eyed her critically. "You're hardly bigger than a mouse. My nephew has more heft and substance to him." He was clearly upset that his son had not been given the job. "Well, get busy and clean the cells of those who have the money to pay ye."

Abigail shuffled away from him, her pails clanging. He had seemed unperturbed by the death of his fellow guard. Surely he was the man who had found the body. The more Abigail thought about it, the eerier it became. And there had not been a word of gossip. Perhaps it was all a false story that someone had made up to give Silas Grayson a bad, bad evening. Or perhaps it was Silas, tweaking her nose, because of Elizabeth's escape.

It was a desperate hope, but it lifted her spirits nonetheless. As soon as she was clear of the guard's prying eyes, she began handing out the food she'd brought. Whenever anyone tried to thank her, she hushed them up. "Eat. Don't talk," she cautioned them. "I'll bring more tomorrow."

A woman's refined voice came out of the darkness of a larger cell to Abigail's left. "Don't eat it."

The voice was so strong, so clear, and so completely unexpected, that Abigail dropped a pail.

"What wicked things have ye done, my boy?" the guard called down the corridor.

"I dropped my bucket," Abigail called back, making her voice as low and hoarse as she possible could.

"Stay away from the prisoners who can't pay," the guard reminded her. "They steal the time of the court and ours, as well. Poor buggers, they have no one to pay for their food or upkeep. No one to care when they hang." He laughed. "Old Charlie used to say we should club them like rats, right in their cozy little cells. I say it was Satan who killed old Charlie. Smote him dead just as he sat upon his favorite chair, eating someone else's cold supper, no doubt."

Abigail grew suddenly very still, as did the prisoners. They all wanted to hear what had happened to Charlie Blackwell.

"Did ye hear that he was all black under the eyes, like he ate something a normal fellow wouldn't eat?" The guard laughed. "Probably cooked up one of the prisoners and ate him!"

The fear from the prisoners was palpable. They were completely at the mercy of the guards. "The guards eat our food," one of the prisoners murmured. "They eat and eat and when they are done they throw away the remains, knowing that we would eat even that."

Abigail gave the woman who spoke bread and cheese. As she'd suspected, she'd not brought nearly enough food. Everyone was starving.

"What happened to the guard?" Abigail whispered. The strain to make her voice deeper was beginning to wear at her throat. She'd be unable to speak at all if she had to keep it up.

From a cell to Abigail's right another female prisoner spoke up. "Stole someone's food and toppled over dead. Some say he was poisoned. If the truth is in that statement, then God has not abandoned us here. He was a cruel and evil man."

Before Abigail could respond, the educated voice came again. "Don't eat this food. I beg you."

It came from the cell to Abigail's left. At the imperial tone, Abigail felt a chill of fear, but she forced herself to go forward.

"The food is good. I ask nothing in return."

There was the flare of a lighter box and a short, stubby candle was lit. In the harsh glare, Abigail saw the features of a woman who had once been beautiful.

"You come with a good heart," the woman said, "but the consequences of your actions will be more suffering, worse than that of slow starvation." She held out one hand to show the ruined and mashed fingers where thumbscrews had been applied.

"The food will harm no one." Abigail tried to keep her language as formal as possible. She was risking her life. If any of the prisoners were tortured and could identify her, they might.

"The food is not the culprit. The lack of starvation will be the fact that calls attention to itself." The woman reached through the thick bars. "When these people stop starving, Magistrate Appleton will take it into his head that Satan is feeding us. What do you suppose will be the end result of that?"

The words were absolutely chilling. Abigail had not anticipated that her deed of kindness could result in more punishment for the people around her.

"But if they don't eat, they will die!" In her frustration she forgot to disguise her voice.

The hand pulled her forward to the bars. "So, you are a woman, not a boy. I thought as much. No boy would risk his life for a bunch of old crones and a few desperate men."

"Who are you?" Abigail was caught in the unflinching gaze of the woman.

"Brianna March."

"March?" The name was familiar.

"Georgianna March's twin sister."

Abigail remembered the tall woman who had confronted Silas Grayson on the road when he was dragging Elizabeth Adams to her fate. "Why are you here?"

"Like everyone else, I am a consort of the devil." She laughed, true amusement mixed with bitter anger. "I was one of the first accused, yet I have not seen the earth above ground in more than six weeks."

"What charges?" Abigail knew she needed to move along, to distribute the goods she'd brought and to get busy with her job before the guard came to check on her.

"Would that I knew. They change with each fancy of the prosecutor. Riding a broomstick with the Dark One, pinching and biting that curdle-brained dunce, Mary Wadsworth, and even dancing by the light of fires with familiars. But it wasn't me dancing in the night."

Abigail's heart dropped to her stomach. "You've seen someone dancing around a bondfire?"

"Aye. Someone or something. I stumbled upon them just the night before I was arrested." Her eyes were smart. "I believe I was charged because I saw something I wasn't supposed to see."

Abigail gripped the bars that separated them. "Figures in dark cloaks. They wore animal masks."

Brianna's eyes narrowed. "Either you've seen them prancing about the night—or you're one of them!"

"Not the latter." Abigail cast a glance down the hall. The guard was coming, and she'd done none of her work. "Did you recognize any of the people?"

"You believe they were witches?" Brianna was incredulous.

"Not really witches. Just part of a cult. There's a big difference. A very big difference, at least where I come from. But that doesn't matter. Did you see any of them?"

"I didn't get close enough to get a good look. Truth be told, I didn't want to get close. I was afraid of them and their hellish masks."

"I don't blame you." Abigail gathered her brooms and buckets. "I have to go. I'll be back tomorrow." She handed out the rest of her food, speaking soft words of comfort to those who wanted to listen. It was impossible to do any real cleaning in the dank, dark pit of a dungeon, so when she was through distributing food, she returned to the guard.

"Are ye done?" he asked.

"Aye."

"Then find Goodman Truesdale. His coin will warm your pockets." He laughed again. "No one else cares whether the dungeon is neat and tidy."

"Thanks, butthead," Abigail whispered under her breath as she hurried up the steep stairs to the fresh light of day. One thing her morning underground had reinforced—she didn't want to be confined there with the likes of the guard in charge of her fate.

Samuel was in the room where the trials were held, so Abigail found a corner in the back and huddled there to watch the remainder of the morning's activities. A man was being tried for making his neighbor's sheep sick.

Samuel argued in Brenton Holland's defense that a weed growing in the neighbor's pasture, which his sheep had eaten, had made them sicken and die. But Magistrate Appleton was having no logical excuses. Without a turn of a hair, he sentenced Brenton Holland to hang as a witch.

The attitude in the courtroom was one of vindicated pleasure, especially in the small pocket around Silas Grayson.

Abigail, her face dirty and her form disguised by the boy's clothes, couldn't help but shrink away from Grayson's eagle glare as he surveyed the courtroom looking for any whose expressions betrayed their horror at the verdict.

"Old toad," she murmured at him. "If I were a witch I'd turn you into a roach. Then I'd find the industrial-strength bug spray!"

She stopped mumbling to herself when she saw that one of the other young boys was giving her strange looks. She clamped her lips together and gave him a fierce stare. Then she turned away and walked back down the corridor that led to Samuel's office. Once the verdict had been rendered and the convicted man led away, Samuel had thrown his papers on the table in disgust and left the room.

"I'm sorry," Abigail whispered when she found him at his desk, his head held in his hands. "It wasn't your defense that was lacking. The judge had no intention of releasing him, no matter what evidence you produced." Samuel was a complex man with many moods. He had been the most passionate of lovers the night before, but now his passion was directed at the suffering of another. That was one of the reasons she loved him so.

"Not a single person accused has been found innocent." He looked up, his eyes tired and red, his hope almost doused by the verdict. "Brenton is an old farmer. He's ignorant, poor, superstitious. But he's no witch. And he isn't the kind of man who would injure another's animals."

Abigail went to him and put her hands on his cheeks. She stood behind him and started a slow massage of the muscles of his cheeks and temples, moving into his scalp.

With a sigh he relaxed against her. "What can I do? They'll hang him tomorrow." Her fingers were magic. How was it possible for her to be soothing and arousing at the same time? He responded to her on so many different levels.

Abigail continued her massage, not answering for a long while. "What happened to the guard, Samuel?" She swallowed even as she asked.

He read her pain and was instantly concerned for her. "*I* think it was a heart attack, but Caleb Hawthorne is determined to make it murder. He claims the guard was poisoned by Elizabeth Adams, or someone who broke her from prison."

"How far wrong are they?" Abigail's hands had stilled. "Did I poison that man by accident?"

Samuel reached up and captured her hands, pulling her around to face him. He could see the tears in her eyes. "My guess is a heart attack. Maybe he finally realized what a horrible thing he was doing and died of guilt."

"The guard today said the tissue beneath his eyes had turned black. That doesn't sound like a heart attack. It sounds like arsenic."

Samuel had seen the corpse. He looked down at his desk. "Abigail, innocent people are dying. That isn't supposed to make you feel better or worse, but I can honestly say, Elizabeth Adams's life was worth it. *If,* and that's a big *if,* there was something in the potion, it was an accident."

"A man is dead."

"And an innocent woman would have hanged today had we not intervened."

Abigail slapped her fist into her hand. "I was positive squaw brush was a mild sedative. Positive." She paced the floor. "I can't believe it was deadly."

Samuel watched her pace, unable to remove the burden of her guilt, or his own. He saw the glint of tears in her eyes and felt her pain. "Abigail, I believe the man had a heart attack. These people have never heard of such a thing. They *want* to believe he was poisoned. They *like* to see the devil's hand in all of this. It strengthens their rationalization of what they've done in the past, and what they intend to keep on doing in the future."

"And I gave them a tool!" She whipped around and paced in the other direction. "We saved Elizabeth, and strengthened their hand to kill the hundred poor souls confined in that dungeon."

At last Samuel could watch her pace no longer. He went to her, holding her against him even as she struggled. He knew she wasn't fighting him, she was fighting the situation, her own guilt, and her lack of ability to effect a change in what was happening.

"You did give food to some of the prisoners," he said soothingly as he stroked her back. He could feel her warm, soft skin through the thinness of the boy's shirt, and his desire for her, always so near the surface, fanned into life again.

"And they'll probably pay for that." Looking up at him she saw his love for her. It didn't lessen her guilt, but it gave her strength. "I met the most interesting woman, Brianna March."

"Brianna." Samuel shook his head. "A wonderful woman. She was the schoolteacher, along with her sister, Georgianna. They were quite a pair of beauties in their day, I've been told."

"Neither married?" Abigail found that interesting in a time when marriage was a woman's only safety—and could be her prison, as well.

"They had money. Enough to be sent away for an education. I don't recall where they went, but they came back determined to manage the family farm together. Some of the finest land in the village, and also a large shop in Salem Town. If I'm not mistaken, they still have an interest in several of the ships that make regular runs to the West Indies."

"No wonder Brianna can afford candles."

"Yes, she's faring better than most, but Hawthorne won't establish the formal charges against her. He keeps changing his mind, and I've never been certain if he's accepting money from her family not to bring her to trial, or if he's hoping to force them to come up with a big ransom."

"You think she won't be convicted?" Abigail found that odd.

"If anyone can beat the charges, it's Brianna. The family is politically influential, also. Or they were, until her father died last year."

Abigail digested all of the information. "What about Georgianna?"

"I expect she'll be brought up on some trumped-up charges any day." Samuel had snugged Abigail against him and he felt a warm comfort just holding her. She had gradually relaxed, and they stood, touching as much as possible.

"Why do you say that?"

"The March property is some of the finest. If my theory that the motive for all this is economic gain is correct, that property is crucial to whoever is doing this. It has the best water, and it overlooks the harbor. If I were going to grab land, that's the piece I'd take. As well as yours, Abigail."

"Mine?"

"You and the Marches are neighbors."

"Samuel, is there a way to get some type of ownership map?"

"I don't think those things exist in Salem Village of 1692." He smiled down at her. "Wouldn't you rather have a cheeseburger?"

His humor struck a chord in her and she smiled. "No, I'd like a soft taco with extra-hot salsa, an enormous, fizzy Coke, some amaretto cheesecake, plain, old, hot coffee, my John Prine tape and my water bed."

Samuel squeezed her as he laughed. "And I thought mashed potatoes were supposed to be comfort food."

"Only for the bland of stomach. Now, about that map, maybe we could rough out the parcels. If your economic theory is correct, then we need to find out who the adjoining property owners are. Once we get it plotted out, we may be able to come up with the evidence the governor needs to put a halt to all of this." At the mention of the governor, Abigail had another tremor of uneasiness. Hester and Pearl had been gone nearly a week. There had been no word sent back to her of the success or failure of their venture. If they had arrived at all.

"Let me see if I can find a map of the area. Then we can subdivide it ourselves." Samuel rubbed his jaw with his thumb. "Maps are going to be very hard to come by. I mean, there's no such thing as a copy machine or computer-generated copies."

"Who would likely have one?" Abigail asked.

Samuel's frown deepened. "I've seen one. In Jonathan Appleton's office, or 'chambers,' as he prefers to call them."

"Just down the hall?" Abigail pointed in the general direction.

At the look on her face, Samuel grabbed her hand. "Just down the hall, but don't get any idea about 'borrowing' it. He'd have you drawn and quartered before you were hanged if he caught you touching his personal possessions."

"More than likely." Abigail's voice had a sprightly note in it.

"Abigail, I couldn't do anything to save you."

"Calm yourself, Samuel. I have professional help."

"Who?"

Abigail stood on tiptoe and kissed him on the cheek. "Familiar. The perfect cat burglar."

"No!" He grabbed for her but she had already opened the door and stepped into the hallway. He went charging after her only to run into the guard who had been on duty earlier in the dungeon.

"Shall I catch 'im for you, Goodman Truesdale? Is he making off with your coin?"

Samuel shook his head at Abigail's retreating back. "No, let him be. He's just a boy with no idea of what trouble his actions could cause."

"Ole Appleton will be happy to sentence him to a few days in the stocks if that will tame his spirit."

"I believe that won't be necessary." Samuel returned to his office and shut the door. He couldn't leave until he was certain Appleton wouldn't hold another trial. They would be only too delighted to do so in his absence, for he slowed the process greatly with his questions and insistence on procedure.

Until Hawthorne, Appleton and Grayson left the court, he wasn't going to budge. As for Abigail ... He sighed. He was as lovesick as a schoolboy. He could still remember the scent of her hair on the pillow beside him, like fresh rain. And her skin had been as smooth as a baby's. She was thirty, a crone by 1692 standards. And he himself was an old man of thirty-five. Well into the later years of his life. That made him smile. Thank goodness modern medicine had given him ''a few good years.''

Since his revelation, and his acceptance that he was from the future, he'd been paying strict attention to the life of the people around him. If they could only be made to believe that war with the Indians wasn't necessary, that both cultures could blend and survive, then the entire future of America might be changed. But he'd tried his opinion on a few in the courthouse and found that they looked at him as if he were insane. He'd shut up before he was accused of being a witch's dupe. And there was always the worry that he and Abigail weren't supposed to change the future. He and Abigail both knew the witch trials had stopped, and they both felt that they were there to make sure that historically correct turn of events occurred. But what was that turn?

There had to be a way to make people see right from wrong, but damned if he'd been able to figure out how.

He went to his office window and looked out. The day was almost over. When he got out of the magistrate's building and got his hands on Abigail, he'd ... he laughed out loud. He'd take every stitch of clothes off her and revel in her beauty. He could only wish that she'd be a little more cautious in her full-tilt charge against the enemy.

Dusk was beginning to fall, and he found that he could hardly stand still he was so excited about seeing Abigail. He forced himself to wait at the window. Time would not pass faster if he paced. And he wanted to catch sight of Appleton leaving the premises.

He watched some children in the street, and a dog passing by, its nose to the ground as if it followed an enticing scent. At first he thought he'd imagined a tall, slender woman against the elm tree, but as he looked harder, he recognized Georgianna March. Her back was to the court building, and she was standing as if she waited for someone to meet her.

Her cloak was pulled up around her face, an obvious attempt to hide herself since the day had been unbearably hot. She started to leave, halted, then started again. She walked at a very fast pace, her long legs swallowing the distance.

Samuel had the idea that she might be trying to avoid someone. But he was still surprised when Silas Grayson slipped into the scene.

The farmer-turned-witch-hunter virtually slunk around the corner of the building as he started to follow Georgianna. Samuel leaned forward, his jaw clenched. He saw clearly what was happening.

Silas was following Georgianna so that he could report on her activities. Then a made-up tale of demons and dancing would be put together for Mary Wadsworth or Emily Waters to repeat, and Georgianna would find herself sharing the dungeon with her sister.

"And the March property will be put on the auction block." Samuel spat the words out. "Well, well, Silas, not if I have anything to do with it."

Chapter Thirteen

Abigail clutched the squaw brush in her hand as she climbed out the window of what had once been Elizabeth Adams' home. She stifled a scream as two large, green eyes appeared out of the darkness, followed by sharp claws on her leg.

"Meow!"

"Familiar!" she chided the cat. "You scared ten years off my life."

As she gained her feet in the yard, Familiar began to weave around her legs. Each time she started to move toward home, he nearly tripped her.

"What is it?" she asked in a slightly irritable tone. She wanted to get to the house and brew a cup of tea with the squaw brush. She wasn't going to go another hour without knowing for certain if she'd accidentally killed a man. She was positive the herb was a sedative, not a heart stimulant. Even as she held it in her hand, she knew it was harmless. But she was going to prove it to herself, so at least she could trust herself again.

She had food to prepare to take to the prisoners the next day, and she had to figure out a plan to break into Jonathan Appleton's quarters to find the map of the area. Living in the seventeenth-century was a real pain.

Familiar finally fell into step beside her and they hurried back to her house. Abigail had deliberately not told Samuel about her plans for the evening. She knew he would object—strenuously. And she was determined.

She put the kettle on to heat and prepared the herb. When the water was hot, she poured it over the particles of bark and waited. After it had steeped for five minutes, she took out the bark, added honey, and took a sip.

"Yuck!" She made a face at the cat, who watched her intently. "This is terrible."

Familiar didn't budge. His golden eyes stared unblinkingly at her as she finished the tea. "Now, let's figure out how to rob old Appleton of his map." She yawned and leaned back in her chair.

Try as she might, she couldn't get up the energy to prepare the food for the next day or even finish her chores. "Just a little nap," she whispered as she laid her head down on her arms at the table. "Wake me in an hour, Familiar."

I WAS WONDERING how long it would take her to nod off. Good thing squaw brush is just a sedative or she'd "wake up" in another reality. My concern was the sense that someone had been in Elizabeth's house. I can't believe Elizabeth would come back a third time, risking capture and death. But who else would have been there? Just about anyone, I suppose. Even old Silas Gruesome might have been poking around. At any rate, she's taken her tea and proven herself innocent—and knocked out. I could have told her she didn't poison that guard, but she wouldn't have listened to me. Humans are so stubborn, especially Madame Mysterious. I think she must have been born in Missouri, because she definitely has that "show me" attitude. She needed a little sleep, anyway, and I need some free time.

She didn't bother to bar the door, and it's easy enough to bump open. Ah, out into the free world. I have to be extremely careful not to be seen. I remember a scene from that wonderful old Boris Karloff movie about Frankenstein where townspeople with torches are all chasing the monster. If any of these Puritans catch sight of me, I have the feeling that they'll be after me in exactly the same fashion. And we all know what happened to Frankenstein. It wasn't a pretty sight.

Puff, puff, this running business is for the birds. The good thing about being black, sleek and feline is that I travel light, fast, and unnoticed. Here's the building that passes as a courthouse. I can tell by the lack of noise that it's virtually empty, just the guard at the door. The building is stone, but there's plenty of space around the window to allow for a smart kitty to gain access.

Funny thing about those keys I lifted from Appleton's chambers. Abigail left them in the dungeon, but no one found them, and Appleton didn't mention that they'd been stolen. That in itself creates some unusual implications. I want to check to see if they were returned. If they weren't, someone still has them.

Let's see, here's Lord Apple Dumpling's office. As usual, there is the smell of food lingering in the air. He was here not too long ago and chomping down on, ah, roast beef, potatoes . . . ah, apple pie and . . . some type of alcohol that isn't exactly beer but smells something like it. Part of my ability to reconstruct the menu is my keen olfactory abilities, but the rest is visual. Appleton is obviously a pig. There are splotches of gravy and potatoes on the desk, as well as some apple pie crust. It looks as if he dove into his food with both hands and a trowel.

Now that I've cleared away the food debris, I want to go through this desk. Here's a list of those who've been accused and sentenced. Some ten innocent people. And the list of those in the dungeon is at least seventy-five. Mostly women. I think Abigail might be able to use this. She was also talking about a map. Appleton should have one.

I see it, nailed on the wall. I suppose tape would have been out of the question. The darn thing is just out of my reach, but I believe I can knock it down. If the edges are a little torn, that's too bad. I don't think Abigail and Samuel will be returning it to Apple Butt.

One, two, three, and a giant leap. Yep, it shredded right off the nails and rolled itself into a neat little scroll. There's some interesting scribbling on the back, but I think I'll gather up my map and my list and get out of here while the getting's good. I'm lucky, but not lucky enough to hang around in the chief witch-executioner's lair any longer than I have to.

There is one small thing. An inkwell. And I can't resist leaving Appleton a little memento. If he wants to persecute people and pretend to believe in devils and fiends and familiars, I'll give him food for thought. Lucky the cork is loose in the inkwell. Now I just dab my paw in there and press it down on the very expensive paper on his desk. One little, two little, three little cat paws—four little, five little, six little cat paws... There, that should give the old magistrate something to ponder. A circle of cat prints going nowhere. If he doesn't believe in the devil, he will by the time I finish with him.

WARM FINGERS touched her shoulder, moving up her neck with a gentle massaging motion. Abigail sighed. She clung to her dream images of a wonderful hot bath with jets of water soothing her tired and aching muscles. Samuel was in the tub with her, and they were smiling at each other. She smiled in her sleep and offered her lips for a kiss.

"I hope you're dreaming about me." Samuel spoke softly and then leaned down to stroke her cheek with his lips. Her face was cradled on one arm and he watched as her mouth lifted to him for a kiss. He gladly obliged.

Abigail's eyes opened as he pulled slightly back. "Have I dreamed you?" Her voice was husky with emotion and sleep. "Maybe I've dreamed this whole Salem experience." Her smile was sad. "If that were true, I don't know if I'd want to wake up from this nightmare, because then I'd lose you."

Samuel gathered her into his arms, holding her as tightly as he could. The idea that he might lose her, to the dangers of the present or the future, was too awful to think about. "Whatever the future holds, Abigail, we'll find each other. I promise you that."

She curled her fingers in his hair, feeling again the thick waves that seemed so perfect to her touch. "What are we going to do, Samuel? Things are only going to get worse here. We don't know how to get back home." She laughed to fight back the tears. "I don't even know where home is."

"We'll figure it out. You were so sound asleep, I shouldn't have awakened you." He stroked her hair, his fingers brushing her soft cheek. He'd never met a woman so brave, and yet so vulnerable. At this moment she was tired and discouraged. But he had no doubt that she would rally to the defense of any innocent person.

Abigail's elbow brushed the empty cup on the table, and she remembered the herbal tea she'd drunk. "I didn't kill that guard." Speaking the words out loud made her feel better.

"I know you didn't."

"No, really. I went back to Elizabeth's and got more of the squaw brush and made tea for myself. It's a sedative— nothing more."

Samuel started to scold her for taking such a chance, but he wisely kept his mouth closed. She'd already done it, *and* proven herself innocent. It was something she'd had to do to live with herself.

"I'm going back to the village tonight to get the map," Samuel said. He shook his head as she started to protest. "I have more reason to be in the magistrate's office than you or anyone who might be willing to help us. I can make up an excuse if I'm caught."

"Appleton isn't going to take a lot more from you, Samuel. He's already looking for any excuse to accuse you."

"I know." Samuel looked out the window and gasped. Two large green eyes stared back at him, and it took a second for it to register that the creature was Familiar. "That cat! He's going to give one of us a heart attack."

Abigail went to the door and opened it, watching as Familiar entered with a rolled-up piece of paper in his mouth. "The Salem delivery service," she said as she followed the cat to the table where he deposited his burden.

Samuel was grinning even before he unrolled the map. "And the little devil has even included a list of the accused in scribbled writing. Let's plot this out."

Only the oldest pieces of property were marked on the map, and some had changed hands. Samuel wasn't sure of every piece, but they were able to place enough to begin to see a pattern.

"Everything bordering Salem Town, and all of this strip of cultivated land," Abigail said as she pointed to the map. "You're right, Samuel, it's the most valuable property."

"With a lot of other property thrown in." Samuel's finger moved along the map.

"This is mine." Even as Abigail noted the outline of her parcel of land, she felt strange. It wasn't really hers. Not really. "And here is the March land." It was easy to see that it was the largest holding and the best situated as far as cultivatable fields and access. It also contained the area where the midnight dancers had met around their bonfire.

"You're thinking about the gathering in the woods, aren't you?"

Abigail looked up to see Samuel watching her with concern. "I am. I think we need to figure out who was there, other than Silas."

"And why they're meeting. You don't believe in Satan worshipers any more than you believe in witches."

"No, I don't." Abigail let that sink in. "But it is a very effective tool of intimidation. We don't have to believe, but then, we're not as afraid as the villagers."

"It won't be long before Silas makes his move against Georgianna."

Abigail felt alarm. "How do you know?"

"He followed her home today." He went to the fire and stirred the embers, then moved the kettle onto them to heat. "I followed him, just to see what he was up to."

"And?"

"He stood in the woods, staring at her house. I couldn't see his face, but I could tell that he was watching with a lot of intensity. He wants that property. He wants it so bad he can almost taste it."

Abigail got two clean cups and brewed tea. Her supply of coffee was gone, and the bitter tea the colonists were drinking left a lot to be desired. Still, it was better than nothing. She put a pot of honey on the table for sweetener and sat down. "I think we should let everyone out of their cells."

"A general jailbreak?" The idea had some appeal to Samuel. It would be more justice than the village had seen in a month. At least if they were given their freedom, the accused would stand a chance. They could flee or fight, and he didn't care which.

"I don't know what else to do." Abigail sipped her tea. "We've figured out the motive behind the accusations, but how do Mary Wadsworth and Emily Waters figure in here? They're children, or at least, young adults. They certainly have nothing to gain. In fact, their lives are ruined. Who would marry a witch-finder?"

"I hadn't thought of that." Samuel poured the golden honey in his tea and stirred it with a wooden spoon. "They're obviously pawns, but of whom? Mary's father has been in the forefront of the hunts."

"And Emily's father?"

He shrugged. "I don't know anything about him, except he's a minister." He looked up. "But Tituba might be able to tell you more."

"Tituba." The name sounded familiar on Abigail's tongue. "Hester had come here to talk with Tituba about the islands. She was one of the first accused of witchcraft. But when I went down into the dungeon, I didn't see her."

"She's isolated, and I'm certain she has food." Samuel stared into his cup. "Appleton provides her with rations." He looked up. "I honestly think he's afraid of her."

"I'll talk to her tomorrow when I go down to perform my duties." Abigail gave Samuel a wan smile. "Somehow, I don't think my future abilities are in the janitorial area."

"No, but I know where they are." He put his cup on the table. His gray gaze held hers, the desire kindling between them in an instant.

"You shouldn't stay here." Even as she spoke, Abigail knew that he would stay. They had no guarantees on the future—none that they would even see the future they knew. All they had was the moment, and neither was strong enough to deny themselves.

"If we did what we should and shouldn't do, we'd be hightailing it out of this village and living in the woods with Sanshu and Elizabeth." His rueful smile showed that he had given that idea some serious thought.

"Why us, Samuel?"

"That's one question I have no answer to. Familiar, I understand. It's almost as if he . . . has powers." He shook his head at his own words. "I can't believe I'm saying this, but it's true. And you . . . I see a clear determination in you, a strength of principle that makes you perfect for such a chore. You won't give up. Whether you like it or not, you won't stop until you put an end to this horror, or . . ."

"Or die trying." It sounded like an epitaph to her own ears. "Why? I'm no crusader. In my real life, I've never done anything like this. I know it."

"I've given it some thought, Abigail. Do you suppose we're related to some of these people? Maybe we've been selected because they're our predecessors."

Abigail leaned forward. "You could be right." A note of excitement crept into her voice. "I never paid much attention to any of that, but my grandmother was always talking about how we were some of the original settlers. She never said Salem, specifically. I always assumed it was Plymouth Rock."

Samuel shrugged. "I don't even have that much to go on. As a boy I never spent enough time indoors to listen to anything about family or history. I only wish I had a clearer view of what my future life was about." He gave her a startled look. "The last thing I remember was that we were kneeling in the road, examining Familiar after my car struck him. What if we were run over?"

Abigail laughed softly. "You mean, we're dead? Like angels?"

Her humor touched his and he answered with a chuckle. "Or more appropriately for this time, devils."

"How do we tell if we're immortal? It would certainly make this task we've set ourselves much easier if we knew we couldn't die."

Samuel picked up her hand. His fingers smoothed the soft skin on the back. He turned it over slowly, examining the palm where a blister was slowly developing into a callus. "Farm work?"

"Milking, buckets, firewood, water. This isn't an easy life."

He brought her hand to his lips and kissed it, first on the back, then on the palm. "You're too warm to be immortal," he said. "Too warm and too delightfully human."

"I was afraid you'd say that." But there was no regret in her voice. "You know, Samuel, for all of the horrors around us, I've never been more glad in my entire life to be human. The time that I have with you may be as close to paradise as I ever come."

Abigail rose as she talked and went to him. Easing down onto his lap, she rested her arms on his shoulders. "If I'm here because of heritage, then you're here because you're the man I need to be with me."

The kiss she gave him was long and sweet, building in intensity until both knew that no matter what the cost, they would share the night.

Familiar watched them as they stood, hands clasped, and went into the bedroom. Blinking his green eyes once, he curled on the warm, hand-hooked rug in front the fireplace and closed his eyes.

I DON'T necessarily believe in premonitions, but I have a very bad feeling about this situation. Samuel is right about Abigail. She'll forfeit her life trying to stop these atrocities. I, too, feel that we've been sent back here to do something to help, but we have to have a better understanding of what's behind the accusations here. Abigail is too impatient. And yes, each day, more and more innocent people are being hanged. But I don't want to see Madame Mysterious standing on the gallows with Pilgrim Man beside her. That won't help matters at all.

The problem is that I have such a clear image of that—the two of them standing against the sky. I can see the rope, the wooden gallows, the tree and the people standing around, waiting to see Abigail drop. My only consolation is that many of the witches here have been hanged from trees, not gallows. So maybe it's just an overactive kitty imagination. Only, every time I close my eyes to sleep, I see it again in such clear detail. I hear sirens in my head and "Danger!

Danger! Danger!" fires off in my brain like a twenty-one-
gun salute.

I wish Abigail would stay out of that dungeon. She persists in going back to be sure the prisoners have some food,
and I find her compassion to be almost saintly. But there is
danger there. Grave danger. I feel it in my bones.

I'm going to curl up here and dream about cheeseburg-
ers, shrimp and salmon mousse. The diet here in old Salem
Village is enough to bore the horns off a billy goat. There's
lobster, lobster, lobster. I mean, I'd even settle for some
McNuggets—anything except lobster. Jeez! I'll be glad to
get back to the last few years of the twentieth century where
fast foods, fat and television are the order of the day. What
I wouldn't give for thirty minutes of "Wheel of Fortune."
That's the ticket! I'll dream of Vanna White with a platter
of sizzling burgers just for me. Big money, Vanna, big
money!

SAMUEL OPENED his eyes to the first glow of daylight caught
in the beautiful disarray of Abigail's hair. He knew if he
lived to be a hundred, he would never forget the time they
shared in a corn-shuck bed between clean, linen sheets.
Modern conveniences didn't matter. The only thing that was
important was having her beside him. Curling around her,
he captured her in his arms and kissed her awake.

"The day has begun," he whispered.

Abigail groaned and turned to hide her face against his
chest. "Let's pretend it didn't. My arms ache. My back is
sore. I'm not cut out for this kind of life."

"Of course you are." He patted her bottom. "Cut by a
fine design, I might add."

Abigail gave a false groan. "It's too early and that's a
terrible line."

Samuel kissed the top of her head, his hands moving over
the contours of her body as if he intended to memorize each

inch of her flesh. "It's early, but too late to linger. I have to be at the court."

"And I have to prepare some food and get about my chores." She tilted her head up so she could smile at him. "But I need a promise from you."

"What's that?"

"Tonight, right here, as soon as we finish our duties."

"That's a request I'm more than delighted to honor."

As they began the routine of dressing, Abigail paused. "What will you tell Silas about last night? He'll know you didn't come home."

"That's one reason I have to get to the magistrate's building. I have to tell him that I worked all night." He looked at his clothes. "It appears to be a true statement. But I don't want him to suspect what I actually did."

"Maybe you should simply tell him that you're moving here, as my boarder. That my rates are . . . cheaper, and the service much improved."

Samuel buttoned his coat and gave her a grin. "You are a wicked wench."

"You love it," she answered, giving him a kiss before he hurried out into the gray light of dawn.

Abigail took care of her livestock and filled her wicker basket with food. She was sick of the salted meat, the hard cheese, and dry, crusty bread, but for the prisoners it was a rare treat. She decided to check at the market for apples or some fruit and fresh vegetables. She had no doubt that after weeks of incarceration and starvation many of the prisoners were suffering from scurvy or rickets or whatever the nutritional diseases of the 1600s were.

As she hurried along she saw the tall, erect figure of Georgianna March headed toward her. The woman wore a grim expression, and Abigail felt a twinge of fear for her. No doubt Silas Grayson was already making trouble for her. At least she was still free.

"G'day, Mistress March," she mumbled as she passed her.

"Good day, boy," Georgianna answered in an abstracted way.

Clutching the basket, Abigail hurried on. With the dire prospect of the dungeon ahead of her, Abigail still found that her heart was lighter than the day before when she'd thought that her potion had killed a man. The guard had obviously died of natural causes. Now, the closer she got to the jail, the more excited she became at the prospect of talking with Tituba. Hester had told her that Tituba had been brought from the West Indies as a slave. She'd become the property of Reverend Waters, whose daughter, Emily, had accused the African-American woman of witchcraft.

The story rang a bell in Abigail's memory, but her grasp of history was so scratchy that she couldn't remember the specifics. No matter, she thought as she neared the outside steps that led down to the dungeon, she could satisfy her lack of history with answers directly from the horse's mouth.

The guard gave her little notice as she clanged and banged her pans and brooms, sweeping down the corridor as she doled out food to eager hands.

"Tituba," she whispered at each cell.

There was no answer.

"Tituba," she called, as she wormed her way deeper and deeper into the heart of the old dungeon. The passage was so dark, she had to lean against the harsh stone walls, feeling her way with tentative steps because the floor was so uneven. The damp chill of the place made her heart shrivel and her bones ache. She could only imagine the grim discomfort of the place in the winter. Even the best dressed prisoners would surely freeze.

"Tituba," she called as she rounded a corner.

"Here, child." The voice was soft with an accent that spoke of an island filled with sunshine and kissed by blue waves.

"Tituba." Abigail inched down the corridor, unable to see a thing.

There was the flare of a match and a halo of light escaped from a cell. Tituba had been confined in an area of the prison where there were no other prisoners.

"Come here, girl." Tituba spoke softly.

Abigail went to the bars on the heavy wooden door and peered inside. In the glow of the candle she saw a black woman, her head tied in a white kerchief, staring silently back at her. "I've come to help you, but I need some answers."

"Questions, questions, questions. Dat is all I hear, but none of the answers I tell are good. They want to hear tales of the Dark One." She shook her head. "I know of no such t'ings."

Her accent was that of some faraway exotic place, and Abigail felt a rush of sympathy for the woman. She'd left behind sea and sand and sunshine to come to a land of stark elements, and now she was in prison.

"Tituba, how did all of this witchcraft mess begin?"

Still holding the candle in one hand, Tituba came to the bars of the cell. She grasped the bars with her free hand. "Those little girls begged me for the story. They cry and beg until I gather them beside the fire and spin the tales. We make the cocoa and tell the old stories. But one day the master comes home and hears. He is so angry that I talk of trees that sing and turtles that dance in the moonlight." A tear started down her cheek. "He say I am to be sold, but my husband cannot go. He say Emily is to be spanked and sent to her room without food for a week. He say we are all possessed by the devil to talk of magic. But it was only the story of my land. It has been passed down from the old ones, from mother to daughter, for many years. There is no harm.''

Abigail grasped the woman's hand on the bars. ''There is no harm,'' she agreed.

''Little Emily was afraid of her father. She say I made her listen. She say I cast a spell on her and made her listen. Then she fall on the floor and begin to scream.'' Tituba's voice began to shake. ''She scream and say I send demons to pinch her, and they tie my hands behind my back and bring me here.''

Abigail remembered the story of Tituba at last. It was just as the island woman had told it. Several hysterical girls had charged her with witchcraft to save their own hides from disciplinary action.

Tituba took a deep breath. ''Now they cannot stop the accusations. Those girls...'' She shook her head. ''To avoid the spanking, they have accused innocent people of terrible, terrible t'ings.''

''You will not hang,'' Abigail told her. She remembered that much. ''You will be set free.''

''Mistress! Beware!'' Tituba tried to warn her. ''Behind you!''

Abigail ducked, but she was too slow. A big hand clamped down on her neck and held her tight. ''So, at last, Mistress West, we discover that you are here, talking with the villagers you have corrupted to your evil ways.''

The jolt of fear was so extreme, Abigail thought her heart had stopped. When she realized what had happened, she started to fight, but the grip on her neck was paralyzing. The pain shooting through her was so intense she couldn't even manage a cry.

''She means no harm,'' Tituba pleaded. ''Please, master, she was doing not'ing wrong.''

''Tie her hands.'' Silas Grayson's voice was gleeful. His grip on Abigail still held as another man stepped forward to tie her hands behind her back. With a shove Silas finally released her, pushing her into the wall.

"So, you predict the future, do you?" Silas asked her in the dim light of Tituba's single candle. "Tituba won't hang. Which is more than I can say for you, Abigail West."

Chapter Fourteen

"Run!" Tituba commanded as she held the candle through the bars, the flame catching the sleeve of Silas Grayson's shirt.

Abigail twisted and jerked as Silas released his grip. Without thinking about what she was doing, she lowered her head and rammed into Silas's midriff and then leapt past him on her way down the corridor. Her hands had not been tied securely, and she shook the bonds free as she ran.

Silas careened into the wall, screaming as the flames caught a firm hold on his shirt. From inside the cell, Tituba found her jar of water and threw it on the dancing man.

Abigail didn't bother to look behind her, she simply ran for her life. She ran with no thought other than bursting forth from the dungeon into the crystal air of day.

Propped back in a chair, the guard blocked the final corridor, but Abigail didn't stop to ponder the problem. She ran straight at him, knocking the chair as hard as she could. When the guard went down in a sprawl, she jumped over him and took the steps three at a time.

Wheezing, she pushed open the back door, nearly knocking Walter Edgarton down, and fled into the street.

"Hey!" Walter called after her.

But Abigail didn't stop. She ran as fast as her burning lungs would allow her until she was clear of the village.

At the top of the hill she took cover behind a rock and peeked out to look at the village below. A crowd had begun to gather in front of the magistrate's building, and she could tell by their jerky motions that they were excited. In a moment she saw one of the women lift an arm and point at her. From far below the sound of excited cries came to her as the gathering of people began to move in her direction.

"Damn, damn, double damn!" Abigail panted. She turned away and began to run toward her home. The most she could hope to do was grab Familiar, let the cow and sheep out into the pastures and then beat a hasty retreat into the woods and pray that Sanshu would somehow find her. She couldn't allow herself to think of Samuel. She couldn't warn him—to go near him might jeopardize his life. And she couldn't even tell him goodbye!

The added pressure of emotion only made her lungs burn more, so she turned her mind to other things. Sanshu, Hester, and the fading hope that the governor of Massachusetts would somehow intervene. If worse came to worst, she'd find her way through the woods to Boston on foot! Then the mighty governor had better beware!

She ran into her home and nudged a startled Familiar from his nap beside the fire. In her room she gathered her meager clothes, including the hated dress, and snatched a handful of hard cheese and bread. She also took time to get the ownership map and list of the accused. Those were things she didn't want Silas Grayson to find. There was no time for any other provisions, and she took only a moment for one last look around her home. By the standards of the day, it was extremely elaborate. What would become of it now?

On her way across the pasture to the woods, she opened the barn doors and let the animals out to forage for themselves. As valuable as livestock was, someone would look out for them, and they'd be able to get grass and water until help arrived. It was a bitter thought that Silas Grayson would undoubtedly wind up with Sally and the sheep. "I can only hope she gives him bitter milk," she told Familiar as they both ran to the woods.

She could hear the crowd coming down the road, and she ran across the open expanse of her pasture and ducked into the dense foliage. She was two hundred yards from the open road, but she shifted deeper into the trees. She wasn't safe, not by a long shot, but she didn't want to start out through the woods until she could get her bearings. The thick forest could be deceptive. Many an experienced traveler had become lost, never to find their way out again. Her only real hope was Sanshu and Elizabeth.

"Meow."

"And you, Familiar," she added. The cat did seem to have a keen sense of direction. His company made her feel immensely better, though it was hard to feel safe at all with a mob of people hunting her with the goal of hanging her if they caught her.

The shouts of anger from the villagers intensified as they searched her house and barn and found them both empty. They came out of her buildings and gathered again on the road, where Silas, his arm in a sling, broke them into smaller groups and sent them out in all directions.

"Here comes trouble," Abigail whispered as she saw Earl Wadsworth and two other men striding toward the woods where she was hiding. "We'd better go." She spoke to reinforce her decision. She knew she was leaving Samuel with the very good possibility that she wouldn't see him for quite a while. It was a long journey to Boston. If they made it alive.

"Let's go, Familiar." Abigail stroked the cat's back. Waiting longer would not change the circumstances. Samuel was not going to magically emerge from the trunk of a tree. There was still good daylight in front of her, and many miles to travel.

Familiar stared out into the road as if he, too, expected to see Samuel appear. After several seconds, he stood and went to Abigail

"Meow."

"We'll come back. In triumph," Abigail vowed. Brushing the tears from her cheeks, she turned and started into the deep shadows of the forest.

SAMUEL STOOD perfectly still as Magistrate Appleton paced the confines of his small office and recounted the morning's events—especially how Abigail had used her evil powers to start a fire in Silas Grayson's shirt.

"Fortunately for Silas, his burns were minimal. He was able to smother the flames before he was injured." Appleton stroked his soft cheek with manicured fingernails. "I believe Silas has finally run aground the high priestess of the coven." He walked around Samuel as he talked. "Run her aground, but unfortunately she flew out of his clutches."

"Flew?" Samuel couldn't help his skepticism.

"Flew. That's accurate. Silas and the guard both said she flew like a chimney swift, gliding over everything in her path, straight out the door."

Samuel tried desperately to hide the relief he felt. "Then she escaped?"

Appleton chuckled. "For the moment. But it was all part of our design. She will lead us to the Indians who have induced all of this. They have no true god, so they do not know the dangers of worshiping the Dark One. They have brought this tragedy down on our poor village. It will be as well when every last one of them is dead."

"The Indians?" Samuel was incredulous. "What have they to do with this?"

"Those vile redskins will do anything to drive us off the shores of this country. It is they who have brought evil powers to Abigail West, and she in turn has infected the entire village. I believed it was Elizabeth Adams, but I see clearly now that Mistress Adams was only a serving wench in the grand plan. Abigail West is the Queen of Witches.''

"Don't be a fool." Samuel's voice crackled with scorn. "Surely you don't believe this insanity." But looking into Appleton's eyes, he wasn't so certain. The fat, old fool actually looked afraid. "Abigail is no witch. None of these pathetic creatures locked in the dungeon is a witch. If they were, don't you think they'd fly out of the dungeon as you claim Abigail did?"

Appleton stared at Samuel. "You speak as if you were infected with wickedness." He pointed a finger. "Be warned, Samuel Truesdale. Ye may be an appointee of the governor, but that will not protect ye against the godly people of Salem Village."

"Godly?" Samuel shouted. "This is godly behavior? To starve people into living skeletons? You are a fat, pompous ass."

Appleton walked to the door. "Enough, Truesdale. You no longer have my trust. Nor that of Prosecutor Hawthorne. He has long been suspicious of you. I am writing the governor today to ask that you be replaced as soon as possible."

"Why not request that His Honor, the governor, come to Salem Village to see the trials first-hand?" Samuel's tone held a direct challenge. "I believe when he sees how you mete out justice, you will be the one to be replaced, not me."

"The governor is too busy to take time out for the problems of such a small village." Appleton looked slightly worried.

"Perhaps I shall hand deliver your letter—and my request." Samuel watched the dagger of that threat sink home. Appleton definitely didn't want the governor in Salem Village.

"You are obligated to attend the trials until you are replaced. It is your duty." Appleton had recovered his nerve. He smiled as he turned to give Samuel a full look. "I believe it might be worth the governor's time to come to our small village once Mistress West is captured. Her trial will make history for our village, and for me.''

Before Samuel could respond, Appleton had walked out the door and away.

"Damn you to hell," Samuel whispered after him. The news of Abigail's near capture had almost undone him. He checked the hallway to be sure no one had been left to watch him, then he sneaked out of the building and made for Abigail's house as fast as he could without using the road.

He knew she was gone. He wanted her to be gone. But perhaps she'd left a clue for him where she might be heading. Boston would be the logical choice. And he could follow her. He knew to ask for Hester Prynne. And Abigail had not given up on her plan to get the governor to come to the village.

He thought of all the positive things and did not dwell on the long journey through treacherous forests that Abigail would have to make. With only a cat to guide her. Of course, Sanshu might have come to her assistance. The Indian owed them both a debt, and Sanshu was the kind of man who always repaid his debts. Usually tenfold. "Please, God, let Sanshu have found her," he whispered as he ran.

From the big oak tree in the front yard he could tell that the house was abandoned and partially vandalized. The front door had been beaten down, and the glass windows, a luxury for that age, were broken. Samuel gritted his teeth as he watched Silas Grayson come over the field leading Sally the cow. Several young boys were herding Abigail's sheep toward his pastures.

"So, Silas turns yet another profit off someone else's tragedy," Samuel whispered to himself. It was disgusting.

As soon as Silas had gone down the road, Samuel went into the house. The furniture had been overturned, the household goods either broken or stolen. Items that would be irreplaceable were gone. And nowhere was there a clue of Abigail's whereabouts.

Samuel knew she'd set out for Boston. There was no place else she could go. Still, his heart was heavy as he took in the needless destruction. He took a last look at the bed where only that morning he'd awakened with her, the light of dawn in her hair.

"Abigail," he whispered as he touched the bed that had been tossed and ransacked. "Abigail."

He turned and walked out of the house, his shoulders set rigidly as he walked back to Salem Village and the afternoon portion of the witch trials. He would stay and do his duty. Perhaps Appleton's attempt at dismissing him would finally draw Governor Phips to Salem Village. And Samuel had plenty to tell the governor.

ABIGAIL gave Familiar the last crumb of cheese as she finished the bread and wiped her mouth on the back of her sleeve. Had they only been in the woods two days? That wasn't possible. It had surely been at least a decade. Even Familiar had gotten a leaner, meaner look. And they were going to need it to stay alive.

Abigail pulled the black cat into her arms and held him. He was as tense as a coiled spring and his attention was focused on the same area where she thought she'd seen someone in the shadow of a byre. They were being followed. And it wasn't by the witch-hunters.

Indians.

Abigail tried not to panic at the thought. She'd suspected it for the past four hours. Now she knew it was true. The woods around them were completely quiet. No birdsong. No squirrels barking and fussing at them for invading their domain. Not even the sound of a limb breaking under the foot of a small hedgehog. All was perfectly still. The animals had gone into hiding against the primary predator. Man.

"Familiar," she spoke softly to the cat. "There's nothing you can do. If you try to stop them, they'll kill you." She brushed the cat's forehead with her lips. Moving as swiftly as possible, she removed the pendant from around her neck and looped it several times around the cat. "Be careful, and don't strangle yourself, but take this to Samuel. Get him to find Sanshu." She knew that the Indians watching her were not part of Sanshu's small tribe. If they were friends, they would have shown themselves by now.

Familiar jumped from her lap to the ground, the pendant dangling dangerously from his neck.

"The pendant is important. I don't know how or why, but I know it is. I don't want the Indians to take it from me." She almost lost her nerve at the thought. "Just get it to Samuel and make him understand that only Sanshu can help me now. Go!" She shooed the cat away.

Familiar stared into her eyes. He put one paw on her knee and looked at her, then he turned and ran into the woods.

"Find Samuel," she whispered after him, knowing that he was already gone and could not hear. But saying Samuel's name was her talisman, her good-luck charm. How had she gone from escaping from witch-hunters to falling into the hands of Indians who were angry at the way the white settlers had treated them?

She stood and started to walk to the southwest. She and Familiar had charted a direct route to Boston, and by her calculations, she was better than halfway there. But for the past few hours, they had not been alone in their trek. She tried to remember back to when she'd had the first feeling of someone watching her. She couldn't be exact, but the feeling had grown until she knew she had to send Familiar for help. She wasn't certain what the 1692 Indian attitude toward black cats might be, but she wasn't going the risk the possibility that they both would be captured. Familiar had to get to Samuel.

Behind her she felt the movement of bodies among the trees. There were more than she'd first thought. She wanted to run for it, but she knew she'd never make it beyond a few yards, and the fact that she'd run would prove to the Indians she was terrified of them. It was better to hold her ground. She remembered Hetty, James Fenimore Cooper's heroine. The Indians respected a person who showed no fear.

Right. She stiffened her spine and continued walking as if she wasn't aware they were moving in closer to her.

When she felt the hand on her shoulder, she stopped instantly. She closed her eyes for a brief second, praying for strength, then turned around to confront the brave who had touched her.

With his face streaked with blue and yellow, he stared at her with open curiosity. He didn't ask permission but lifted the cap off her head and stepped back at the tumble of curls that fell to her waist.

He gave a shout of surprise and happiness and then signaled the other braves out of the forest. They made loud exclamations and walked around Abigail, staring and touching her hair.

"I am your friend," she said slowly. She was so afraid, she could feel her knees knocking together. She clamped them tight and continued. "I am going to Boston."

She couldn't understand what they were saying, but she had the feeling that they were discussing what to do with her. The man who had originally touched her had taken a proprietary attitude toward her and was warning the others away. She smiled up at him, wanting him to know that she thanked him for his protection.

He smiled back and gave her arm a playful pinch.

Without any warning he grabbed her arm and thrust her in front of him as he set a brisk pace through the forest.

Every time Abigail tried to stop or talk, he pushed her ahead of him. He was not abusive, but he was determined to keep her moving.

Abigail tried in vain to keep up with the territory. The sun was setting over her left shoulder, so she knew they were headed north. And north was in the opposite direction of Boston. Or nearly opposite.

"I have to go south," she said, pointing over her shoulder. "Boston."

He shook his head and pushed her forward on the trail while the other Indians laughed.

"Where are we going?" she asked.

They didn't bother to answer, if they understood at all. They simply kept up a constant jog that soon required all of Abigail's concentration to keep up.

The sun began to slip down behind the trees, and Abigail felt as if she were going to fall down in her tracks. The Indians kept moving, their moccasined feet creating hardly a sound on the woodland trail they followed.

Abigail knew that attempting to stop and rest would do no good. The Indians hadn't offered to harm her. They simply ignored anything she said or did and pushed her on.

Her awkward shoes were rubbing a blister on her heel, and finally she sat down abruptly in the middle of the path and removed her shoe. "I can't go on any farther," she said, talking to the man who'd apparently decided to assume responsibility for her.

He motioned her to stand.

She shook her head and pointed to her heel. "No. It hurts."

The Indians gathered together for a small conference. They spoke among themselves in low tones, casting looks back at her.

Abigail realized for the first time that if she were really a hindrance to them, there was nothing to stop them from cutting her throat and leaving her behind. Or almost as bad, just going off and leaving her. She'd been too exhausted to pay attention to where they were going or how much ground they'd covered. She was thoroughly and completely lost.

Her benefactor came back to her with something in his hand. In a moment he knelt down, took her foot in his hand and slipped a moccasin on it. He did the same with the other, then motioned for her to stand. When she did, he tied the shoe tighter, giving a snug fit. With a grunt he motioned for her to continue on the trail.

Torn between fear of being left and fear of being killed, Abigail began to walk. At the pressure of his hand on her back, she started to jog. Then she gave up trying to think or rationalize anything—she just kept moving.

When they finally stopped, Abigail was too tired to eat any of the jerky they offered her, too tired to consider the painful blisters on her feet. She curled up with her back to a rock, the Indian who'd taken her as his own at her side, and allowed the tears to fall silently to the ground. Samuel was the last thing she thought of, the last word she whispered to herself as she slept.

REFRACTED LIGHT caught Samuel's eye as he started toward the magistrate's building with his feet dragging and his tired eyes bloodshot. The trials had taken a turn for the worse. Appleton and Hawthorne were railroading the accused in court proceedings that didn't even pretend to dispense justice. So far, in three days, another dozen people had been convicted, and three of them were dead. For the others he'd been able to buy a few days' reprieve from their sentencing with the hopes that Abigail had made it to Boston and would return with the governor. Silas was running around the village insisting that Abigail had set him on fire without benefit of a candle or flame. He was telling everyone that she'd snapped her fingers and a tongue of flame had shot from her hand to his arm. It was ridiculous, but

people believed him. Abigail was developing quite a repu-
tation for herself.

He went to the dock each day at noon to see which ships
were due in and if they were from Boston. He knew Abigail
would sail back into the harbor with the governor at her
side, willing or not. Or else his dismissal would arrive.

He rubbed his eyes as he caught what appeared to be a
prism of some sort on top of the hill that led to Abigail's
house. The rainbow of shattered light brought to mind the
strange pendant Abigail wore around her neck. But then
everything reminded him of Abigail. And every hour increased his worry for her.

She'd escaped the witch-hunters. He knew that for certain. And for the past three days he'd gone into the woods
to hunt for Sanshu to see if he'd had news of Abigail. But
Sanshu, Elizabeth, and the small tribe of Hurons were gone.
The shelters of animal hides they'd used had been taken
down. Only the charred embers of their fires told that they
had ever been in the forest near Salem Village.

Samuel had had to content himself with the hope that
Sanshu and the Indians had begun to migrate south as the
winter approached, and in doing so had taken Abigail with
them to Boston. It wasn't that far. He guessed maybe thirty
miles, maximum. That would be a good two-day journey.
And if she were sailing back, then it might take a total of
four days. She could be back by morning.

The light caught his eye again and he looked up.

The sun was behind him, sending direct rays to the top of
the hill. He wasn't imagining the small black dot that could
be nothing other than Familiar.

Familiar and Abigail's necklace!

He started to run, gaining speed even as he hit the slope
of the hill and fought his way up.

As he gained the crest of the hill, he saw Familiar dart into
the copse of trees where Abigail had once hidden her basket of food for the prisoners.

Was she there, waiting for him? Hiding out? He felt a rush of anticipation that gave him a surge of energy, and he almost flew the last ten yards and into the copse.

Instead of Abigail, Familiar sat upon a rock. Wound around his neck was the necklace, the crystal pendant shimmering even in the soft light of the copse.

"Is she alive?" Samuel forced the question out.

Familiar gave a low meow in reply.

"Is she in danger?"

For answer, Familiar jumped to the ground and went to him, winding around his leg and then heading back to the path.

Samuel didn't have to guess what the cat wanted, he knew. He had a thought for the women and men who would face trial that morning in front of Appleton. But he knew he was ineffective at best in their defense. And he would be worthless, consumed as he was with worry about Abigail.

"Come here," he called to the cat. Very carefully he took the necklace off his throat. "You could have strangled yourself, Familiar." He held it up to the light, then put it around his own neck. As the pendant touched his chest he felt the whisper of Abigail's hand along his cheek.

"She's still alive, and she needs us," he said. With the cat at his side he started to jog in the direction of the woods.

Chapter Fifteen

Familiar circled the area where Sanshu's people had once camped. He prodded the cold fires with his paw, as if he refused to believe the Indians were gone.

"Abigail wanted me to bring Sanshu." Samuel had finally figured out why the cat had insisted on going to the northwest. He was also positive that Abigail had braved the woods with only Familiar at her side. And now she was in some kind of trouble. Familiar had conveyed that much, but the cat had been a little sketchy on the specifics.

Samuel watched the cat as he circled the abandoned camp yet again. He sniffed the dirt, then lifted his nose to the wind. At last he trotted over to Samuel and indicated that he was ready to move along.

"Where to?" Samuel asked.

Familiar trotted toward the west with a determination that indicated he knew where he was going. At a loss for a better plan, Samuel followed. What had Abigail gotten into? Indians were the obvious answer. Scenes from various books and movies drifted into his mind, goading his fear into an accelerated stage. What did he know of the original Americans? Not much. And much of what he did know was inaccurate and biased. Would they hurt Abigail? Were Indians really the savages they were portrayed to be? He'd always believed that the Native Americans had never had a fair shake in the history books. They had committed acts of violence, as had the white settlers, but much of the violence had been provoked by the actions of the white settlers.

He clung—desperately—to the hope that Abigail would not be injured.

Even as he combated those demons, another thought entered his mind. Would one of the braves forcibly take her as his wife? Samuel increased his pace and put his thoughts on hold.

Familiar was moving at a fast clip, dodging through the woods with a natural-born ability. Samuel, on the other hand, had to fight awkward clothing, bad shoes, and an unfamiliarity with forest travel. But his determination made him keep going, and as the hours passed, he was learning to adapt.

Although Salem Village was soon left behind, Samuel could not as easily forget those accused of witchcraft. Perhaps it would have been better to stage a general jailbreak. There were so many ifs. As he pushed on, following Familiar, he came to only one conclusion: Abigail was his heart. He had to save her, and he could not allow himself to consider any other result. Together they would go back to Salem Village and open the dungeon.

The hope of the governor intervening was a vain one. No outside forces were going to halt the witch trials. And as soon as Abigail was safely at his side, he was going to take an action that would put an end to it once and for all, and to hell with the consequences to history.

I DON'T WANT to add to Pilgrim Man's worry, but the Indians who nabbed Abigail are headed north—northwest. That's not exactly the direction I'd choose to go, right into the heartland of Indian territory. I only wish I'd paid more attention to the members of Sanshu's tribe. Huron. Iroquois. Mahican. What tribe are we talking about here? Are

*they an offshoot of Sanshu's tribe? It would be helpful to
know these things.*

*We haven't come across Abigail's trail. Not yet. But I have
the strong sense that she is still alive. No man with breath in
his body and testosterone in his blood is totally immune to
Abigail's charms, and I can only hope that she has figured
out it is her beauty that is keeping her alive. I also hope we
get to her before she becomes the unwitting bride of one of
her captors. This marriage business was carried out with
great expediency in the New World. I mean, people didn't
live long. They had to marry and reproduce, or else where
would the millions of Americans have come from? I don't
think these Indians are keeping Abigail because they think
she has great style in choosing her clothes.*

*I daresay Pilgrim Man is having some of these same
thoughts. The way he's clamped his jaw shut and continues
to trudge through bramble and briar without a complaint
tells me that his only concern is reaching Madame Mysterious.*

*Abigail and I should never have left Salem without him.
But then, on the other hand, I don't think the Indians would
have been interested in taking him along for the hike back
to the village.*

*I only wish Sanshu had been available. He was my big-
gest hope. Now it's up to me and Samuel. One smart cat,
and one smarter-than-average humanoid, which isn't giving him a lot of credit for gray matter. Well, Abigail is
counting on us, and we aren't going to let her down.*

THE COLD WATER made Abigail gasp as she washed her face
in the clear, running stream. As soon as the ripples in the
water stopped, she could see the Indian standing behind her.
She had come to call him Tonto. Not because she thought
that was his name, but it was a familiar name that gave some
comfort, and he smiled when she said it. So far, he made
some type of grunting sound when he looked at her. It did

not bode well for future communications, but Abigail, at the moment, was more concerned with being able to lift one foot in front of the other.

Never before in her life had she been so tired. Or sore. And she was thankful for that, or else she'd be so frightened that she'd probably die on the spot.

Tonto handed her a piece of jerky, which she accepted with a smile and a nod. As long as they were feeding her, they weren't going to kill her. Unless, of course, they were keeping her meaty for the cook pot. Even as she thought it, she knew it was absurd. Native Americans weren't cannibals, except in extreme ritualistic cases. In particular, they didn't eat their white captives because they felt the white people did not have any qualities they wanted to ingest.

Tonto motioned for her to rise, and they set off through the woods again. This time the pace was slower. Abigail didn't know if it was because they were being more cautious, or if they were drawing closer to home and felt more comfortable. She didn't care, at the moment. She wanted only a cool creek to soak her burning feet and a place to lie down. A hard bed of rock would do just fine.

She had lost count of the nights and days they had been traveling. Her mind was as numb as most of her body. The only time she felt exquisite pain was when she thought of Samuel. Had Familiar been able to get to him? Had he understood? Was he looking for her even as she continued on her forced journey away from him? That thought brought fear as well as comfort. Samuel was no woodsman. He wouldn't know how to traverse the dense forest, or how to communicate with the Indians.

She cast a look over her shoulder at Tonto, who watched her with what she had begun to recognize as fascination. She had a bad feeling about what was going to happen when they finally got to their destination. So far, he'd been a perfect gentleman. But it was obvious to her and all the others that she was now Tonto's property. He took care of her and slept near her, guarding or protecting, and she felt sure it was more of the former than the latter.

Her captors slowed their pace even more as they approached a tree-covered knoll. Abigail didn't bother looking up. She was just thankful for the respite to catch her breath as the small party slowed to a near standstill.

When she did look up she was surprised to see several women looking down at her with open curiosity. Two of them held babies. There was no hostility in their faces, merely shock. And they stepped back from her as she walked up the hill, as if they were afraid she might bite.

A lengthy conversation ensued between her captors and the women, and then one of the women motioned for her to follow into a small clearing where structures made of slender trees and hides had been established.

Abigail stopped at the opening of one of the structures. Inside, the Indian woman waited for her with a puzzled look on her face. But Abigail was helpless to move her feet an inch. Hanging from the central pole of the tepee was an animal mask face. The grizzled bear looked back at her with blank eyes.

"The dancers were Indians." Abigail spoke out loud, though she didn't intend to. The sound of her voice broke her paralysis and she stepped forward into the dwelling and examined the mask.

It was intricately made and used the skin and skull of a bear. She could tell by the care that had gone into crafting it that it was a sign of great power to the owner. Carefully she put it back and turned to the Indian woman who was staring at her.

Abigail gave the woman a smile. She had one small element of the puzzle of Salem Village figured out. The masks had been made by Indians, of that she had no doubt. They were not satanic at all. Very possibly they were for some ritual of summer bounty or some paean to the earth. She had no doubt that the masks used by the Salem dancers had been stolen by members of the village. Someone was using the idea of devil dancers as a tool of manipulation.

"Yes," she said as she took the bowl of hot soup the Indian woman gave her. She ate the corn chowder hungrily, hardly noticing the fact that the woman had come close enough to examine her hair.

When she first felt the teeth of a comb being dragged through her unruly curls, she closed her eyes and relished the delightful feel of someone attempting to bring order to her hair. The warm soup had filled her and she was so very, very tired. What a pleasure to close her eyes and relax for a few moments. She felt safe with the Indians. As soon as she figured out a way to talk to them, she felt sure they would set her free. Maybe even help her get back to the village.

As she surrendered to the luxury of someone combing her hair, she thought that her Indian experience had been mostly positive. She'd been treated with firm kindness. Her blistered feet were the only pain she'd suffered, and that was due to poor-fitting shoes and the fact that she wasn't used to wearing moccasins. She had been delayed on her journey, but the Indians didn't know that. They had no concept of what was going on among the villagers. So, all in all, it was a far better experience than she'd anticipated when she'd first realized she was being followed.

The gentle strokes of the comb were combined with the woman's soft singing. Abigail didn't understand a word of what she was saying, but the melody was sweet and the voice pure. With a sigh she gave up any attempt to think at all.

STIFF AND CRAMPED, Samuel awakened with a feeling of panic in his heart. He'd been going deeper and deeper into the Massachusetts wilderness for four days, and still had no clear sign that Abigail was alive. The cat kept up a steady and dogged pace, correcting their course at several points during the day. Samuel knew only that they were traveling west—northwest, a slight change in course from the first day.

There were signs that humans had passed—the remains of a small fire, a bit of tanned deer hide that was snagged. On rare occasion a footprint in the soft, damp soil of the forest floor was evident. They were on a path, and Samuel trusted the cat enough to believe that Familiar knew where they were heading.

But with each hour he felt the pressure of Abigail's safety and the fate of the Salem Villagers who were undoubtedly being tried in his absence. He would not allow himself to entertain thoughts of what might be transpiring under Appleton's eye.

Samuel had grown so hungry that he no longer registered the fact that his body was demanding food. They found enough fresh water to drink along the trail. Food was a handful of berries, or a cache of nuts they found and carried. Familiar had grown lean and hard. He was all whiskers and big green eyes, yet he never slowed. He was one dedicated feline.

Even as he thought about the cat, Samuel caught sight of him ahead. But he had stopped completely and was sniffing the air as if a new scent had arrived on the westerly wind.

"Meow." Familiar looked over his shoulder.

Samuel eased up beside him, trying his best to ascertain what the cat found so fascinating.

At first he thought he was imagining things, but then he was certain he heard the sound of soft singing. Female singing. It was not a language he understood, but it was obviously some type of lullaby. He wasn't at all surprised when a young Indian woman came down a narrow trail that he hadn't noticed before and stopped at a clear stream to collect some water in an earthen bowl. On her back was an infant, and she was singing to the baby.

Samuel watched with fascination. The woman was intent on her chore and taken with her baby that cooed and gur-

gled on her back. When the bowl was full, she stood and
started back up the slight incline.

The village was likely at the top of the hill, which meant
that lookouts were posted somewhere nearby. They should
have discovered Samuel, sleeping within fifty yards of their
settlement.

Samuel eyed the cat. Had Familiar known the Indians
were camping here? Had he come here for help in finding
Abigail? Or was this where she was being held?

Since he had no answer, he decided to stake out the settlement and watch. Familiar assisted in that decision by
scurrying up the slight incline until the temporary village was
in sight, and then climbing a tree for a better vantage point.

"You're one wily cat," Samuel said as he followed the cat
up the big beech tree that provided a comfortable fork to sit
in, the cover of thick foliage, and a great view. Fascinated,
Samuel watched as what appeared to be four women and
two children went about their morning chores.

There were no men apparent in the village, and Samuel
settled into the fork of the tree to relax and wait. If no men
appeared by dusk, he'd approach the women in a friendly
manner to see if he couldn't communicate his dilemma to
them. If he didn't frighten them, surely they would take pity
on a man who was determined to find the woman he loved.

With visions of Abigail's safe return dancing in his head,
he leaned across an enormous branch and drifted into a light
sleep. The tree shifted gently in the small breezes that stirred
the forest and brought the sound of an Indian lullaby to
him. In his sleep he smiled.

He awoke with Familiar's claws digging into the tender
calf of his leg. Startled out of sleep, he nearly fell from his
perch in the tree, but he recovered in time to grab the limb
and hang on.

"You black devil. I can't believe you did that." He bent
to rub his leg. "You nearly caused me to break my neck."

Familiar let out a low hiss and growl, then turned to the village.

Samuel looked, also, and felt his heart stop. Coming out of one of the dwellings was a very distraught Abigail. She was wearing a deerskin dress, bleached and gnawed to the point of being near white. It was beaded with an elaborate network of small red and blue stones, and her hair had been caught in traditional braids.

Samuel could hear her voice but could not determine her words. By the tone, though, he could tell that she was distressed. He could also tell that the Indian woman was completely ignoring her.

When the five males walked into the center of the village in a procession that spoke of some type of ceremony, Samuel knew exactly what was going to transpire. The tallest of the Indians was planning on a marriage with Abigail.

Familiar, too, recognized the formality of the process. A low growl slipped from him as he gave Samuel a glare that ordered him to get busy and do something.

"What do you suggest?" Samuel asked as he began to climb down from the tree.

Familiar leapt past him, jumping from one limb to the next in rapid descent. When he was on the ground he looked up at Samuel, his tail twitching impatiently.

Samuel dropped the last five feet, landing upright and already moving toward the village. There was nothing to do except claim Abigail for his own. He didn't know how that would sit with the Indians, but he couldn't allow the ceremony to take place. The nearer he got, the more he could hear Abigail arguing and resisting. Obviously the male Indians didn't listen to women any more than the Salem Villagers did. It would do all of them a lot of good to spend a summer in 1995 to learn a little political correctness.

Samuel crested the small hill and didn't slow. He ran into the center of the small community yelling, "Halt! This wedding must stop!"

Before he knew what had happened he found three arrows pointed at his heart. The sight of the weapons and the look in the eyes of the Indians, effectively brought him to a screeching standstill.

"Samuel!" Abigail's relief was such that she jerked free of the woman who held her hand and dashed to Samuel's side.

He closed his arms around her. "Abigail," he whispered, fearing that they would draw their last breaths at that moment.

When he did look up he saw red anger in the eyes of the tallest Indian, the one who had wanted to marry Abigail. Not knowing what else to do, he held Abigail with one arm and touched his heart with the other.

The Indian stared at him, undecided which course of action to take. He did not have a bow and arrow, but he held a wicked-looking knife, and it was clutched tightly in his right hand.

"Tonto, please." Abigail shifted so that she was in front of Samuel. She held her hands out to the Indian, then shifted her gaze to appeal to the Indian woman. "Please," she said again. "I love this man. And he loves me."

Tense seconds ticked away as they held each other in a locked gaze.

"We love each other," Abigail tried again, touching her heart and then turning so that she could touch the place on Samuel's chest where his heart would be. She started toward Tonto, but he lifted the knife half an inch higher and the anger in his eyes hardened.

"I don't think he likes the fact that you've chosen me over him," Samuel said in a soft voice to Abigail. "I don't think he likes it at all. I must be a sorry sight in his eyes."

Abigail realized the truth of Samuel's words as she saw the pride and hurt in Tonto's eyes. Swallowing her fear, she stepped toward him. "You are my friend." She lifted a hand up. "Tonto."

She saw him pull his arm back, as if he intended to stab directly into her heart, and she closed her eyes, knowing that she'd made the wrong decision. What a travesty to come all the way back to 1692 to die in a misunderstanding with a man who wanted to marry her.

"Samuel! Abigail! What business brings you here in the deep forest?" Elizabeth Adams's voice rose sharply, then fell into lower tones as she spoke in Huron.

Abigail opened her eyes to see Elizabeth and a very worried Sanshu rushing toward them from the other side of the village.

"So, good sense prevailed and you fled the village?" Elizabeth asked. She had stepped between Abigail and the Indian, and she put a gentling hand on the man's shoulder. Again she spoke in the Native American tongue as Sanshu shifted slightly behind the man so that he could grab him if it proved necessary.

Abigail didn't understand a word of the conversation that passed among Elizabeth, Sanshu, the man she called Tonto, and the Indian woman who looked as if she was about to cry. By the look on Samuel's face, she could tell that he was trying to follow the exchange—without any more success than she had.

Samuel's hand pulled her out of the midst of the controversy and against his side. "I see you decided not to wait for me to propose. I never realized you were mad to marry," he whispered.

Abigail never looked at him. "My grandmother always told me that the early bird gets the worm."

"Your grandmother was full of great wisdom." Samuel felt the need to smile. It was totally inappropriate under the circumstances, but worry about Abigail, hunger, lack of sleep, exhaustion and the ultimate relief of finding Abigail on the precipice of marriage to a man he'd never laid eyes on were all too much.

Reaching behind her, Abigail pinched his thigh. "I thought you were supposed to ride up with the cavalry and save the day. Instead you creep out of the woods looking like a bone the dogs gnawed and buried, then you disrupt a perfectly lovely ceremony."

"Hush," Samuel warned her. "It appears that they've come to some resolution." Even as he spoke, the small group turned to look at them.

"Abigail, Lotuk feels that he found you alone and uncared for, and that has given him the right to take you as his wife," Elizabeth said, glancing once at Sanshu to make sure he was following her translation.

"But—" Abigail didn't get to finish. Elizabeth signaled her to be quiet.

"I have explained to Lotuk that you are already bound to this man, Samuel, and that he has come a great distance to claim his right to you as husband." Sanshu nodded when she looked at him.

"So, the choice is yours. Lotuk wants me to tell you that he is willing to take you as his wife, a high honor for a white woman. You will have the love and respect of his people. He, uh, also feels that you should not necessarily have the right to decide." Elizabeth looked nervously at the warrior. "He did find you alone in the forest, a woman without a man to keep her safe." She swallowed.

"You choose." Sanshu pointed at Abigail. "You will be safe with my people. Like Elizabeth. The life we live is good."

Abigail reached behind her and squeezed Samuel's hand in a gesture that no one noticed. Taking a breath, she stepped forward, staring directly into the eyes of the Indian who had given her food and made sure she hadn't fallen behind.

"You have given me many gifts." She hesitated. "You are a friend to me, Lotuk. But my heart—" she touched her chest and then opened her palm "—belongs to Samuel. I cannot love another man because there is no room in my heart." She closed her fist tight. "But I thank you for your kindness, and I am honored by your offer."

Elizabeth went to the Indian and put her hand on the arm that had held the knife at Abigail's chest. She spoke softly in the language that sounded like water running over rocks. When she finished speaking, Lotuk nodded, then spoke again.

Unable to completely hide her smile, Elizabeth turned back to Samuel. "Lotuk says he accepts Abigail's decision, but that you must marry her right now or he will do what you cannot."

Chapter Sixteen

The ceremony was brief and simple, but Abigail knew that no formal church wedding would ever touch her as deeply. Whether they repeated their vows in their own time in a more traditional ritual or not, she and Samuel were married. At least, in 1692. When—and if—they returned to the future, she had no idea what memories they would have of this time. Would they even recall that they had exchanged vows of marriage? There were no guarantees.

Abigail felt the warmth of Samuel's hand as he held hers. There had been no ring—no need for one in the Indian ceremony. But Abigail didn't feel the lack of some metal symbol. Her love for Samuel was apparent in her eyes, as was his love for her.

The pressure on her fingers increased, and at Samuel's bidding she moved slightly away from the small gathering. After the days of separation, she longed to be alone with him. Even his hand clasping hers made sensual images dance in her head, and the flush of desire began to build.

"Abigail, we have to get moving," he said, looking around for Familiar. The cat had been conspicuously absent from the ceremony. In fact, he'd not made an appearance in the village at all, which was probably for the best since it would be just another thing that would need a lengthy explanation. And Samuel wasn't certain he'd be able to explain Familiar. Not now or ever.

"Are we going to Boston?" Abigail had no desire to return to Salem.

"I'll take you there, but I have to return to the village. God knows what atrocities have been committed in my absence." He spoke with an edge of desperation. His gray eyes went from happy to deeply troubled. "I wish we could simply turn our backs and leave." His gaze trailed from her eyes to her lips, and he reached up to gently touch them. "I want nothing more than to be with you. Just the two of us. This isn't my time or my choice of places to live, but I could find happiness anywhere with you. We could make a life for ourselves, if it wasn't for what's happening to the innocent people in Salem."

Abigail felt the tremendous burden of her task settle back around her shoulders. For the duration of her "capture" by the Indians and the simple beauty of the brief ceremony, she'd been able to forget about Salem, and about everything else. Now it was all back, worse than ever, because she'd had a few moments to taste her dreams, to fantasize about a happy future with Samuel.

"Maybe Elizabeth and Sanshu will take me to Boston." She looked at the two, so obviously in love, and so obviously in a hurry to get back to their own responsibilities.

"No, Elizabeth has told me that she had come to the forest to look for certain herbs for medicines. There are so many sick people in Sanshu's tribe. That's why Lotuk and these others are here alone. They left to avoid the smallpox and to gather medicines for her."

"They have no immunity," Abigail said. "I could help with them. I've been vaccinated." Abigail knew even as she spoke that it was a false offer. Taking care of the sick was not her task. She'd been sent back three hundred years for the witch trials, and she knew it.

"I've been vaccinated, too, but that won't take care of Salem." His tone was grim.

Abigail turned to him. "I hate that place. I hate those people." Tears welled up in her eyes. "I don't want to go back, Samuel. And I don't want you to go. I'm afraid they're going to kill us."

"I know." He couldn't lie and pretend that he was sure of the outcome. He didn't want to go back, either. They were a bleak people with lives centered around their fears. "But we have to go back."

Abigail nodded, finally gaining control of her emotions. "Of course we do. And we'll figure out how to stop it." She forced a smile as she looked up at him.

Elizabeth approached them, her worry apparent in the expression on her face. "I can see by your faces that Salem is the destination you've chosen," she said.

Abigail sighed. "Samuel will go back. I'm going to Boston to try to gain an audience with the governor."

Elizabeth shook her head. "The woman with the scarlet letter on her chest, she made it safely to Boston with her child. Did she not go to seek an audience with the governor?"

"How do you know she's safe?" Abigail was surprised by Elizabeth's revelation. At least she wouldn't have to worry about Hester and Pearl. But why hadn't the governor come?

"Sanshu followed them to be sure they made the journey safely. He knew they were trying to help." Elizabeth picked up Abigail's hand and held it. "Don't go back to Salem. You will swing from the end of a rope as surely as we stand here."

A chill of premonition ran across Abigail's body. That was the image she'd seen so clearly—a gallows and a rope and her.

"Abigail's going to Boston." Samuel spoke with determination.

Still holding Abigail's hand, Elizabeth picked up Samuel's. "They'll hang you just as quickly as her." She looked from one to the other. "Instead of trying the powers of reason on the people of Salem, I have thought of an alternative." The spark of possibility made her eyes shine.

"What?" Samuel and Abigail spoke in unison.

"I left many herbs in my home."

"We know." Abigail rolled her eyes and quickly told Elizabeth of the death of the guard.

"The herb you chose was correct." Elizabeth shook her head. "He must have taken something else. Squaw brush is harmless, even in great quantities."

"What's your plan?" Samuel pushed her to continue. The afternoon was slipping away from them and he wanted to be on the trail. With each hour, more innocent people were being condemned to hang. Now that Abigail was safe, he couldn't stop thinking about the people of Salem.

"You could put the entire village to sleep." She squeezed their hands. "It sounds silly, I know. But it could be done. With enough of the herbs and some cooperation, it could be done. And while the people slumbered, the prisoners could be released from the dungeon."

"And then what? Where would they go? They'd only be recaptured again." Abigail felt the sting of disappointment that Elizabeth's plan wasn't logical.

Elizabeth's eyes began to shine. "Not if an angel of the Lord appeared and told the people of Salem that witches had been cleansed from the village."

Abigail looked at Samuel. The idea was farfetched enough to work. If the townspeople believed that Satan was running amok in Salem, why wouldn't they believe angels were tramping around?

"How would we get everyone in town to use a drug?" Samuel asked.

"That is the most difficult part." Elizabeth's voice gained in excitement. "But if there were a gathering, a meeting, and someone provided some very fine tea or cider as part of the festivities . . ."

Samuel nodded. "Many would drink it."

"Appleton wouldn't pass up free calories," Abigail noted, then saw the curious look Elizabeth shot at her. "Calories is a new word for food," she explained. "He's a glutton. He eats everything."

"Yes, I recall that." Elizabeth's distaste for the man was not hidden.

"It's a very risky plan." Samuel was trying to calculate the odds of getting everyone in the village to drink enough of anything to put them out. It would be hard, but not impossible. Especially if they offered a drink that no one had heard of—which could be anything from lemonade to milk shakes in Salem Village. "But would the people of the town take anything I offered? They think that I'm a sympathizer with the witches." He shook his head in disgust at the foolishness.

"There is someone who will help you." Elizabeth signaled Sanshu to join them.

"Who?" Abigail asked.

"Her sister has been accused, and she will do whatever she can to stop this terrible thing."

"Georgianna March," Abigail said softly.

"Yes." Elizabeth nodded. "She has befriended Sanshu and me in the past. She is the one who helped me gather the herbs, and she even helped me with the sick children of Sanshu's tribe."

"The people of Salem respect Georgianna." For the first time Abigail began to think the plan might actually have a chance. It was farfetched and crazy, but so was what was already happening.

"Are you positive she'll help us?" Samuel had learned to trust no one. "I mean, we could die if she agreed and then changed her mind."

"I'll approach her. We have to have her help, Samuel. I don't have enough herbs." Elizabeth put her arm around Sanshu's waist. "Perhaps if we teach the people of the village to treat each other with more kindness, they'll learn to treat the Indians with kindness and respect."

It was a noble thought, and Samuel didn't want to drown it in the cold water of reality, so he said nothing. "Okay, let's give it a try."

Elizabeth smiled. "Then we have to go back to Salem. We can gather some of the things we'll need along the way."

Samuel moved behind Abigail and gently wrapped his arms around her. "I guess we won't be alone tonight, after all. And I was looking forward to the nuptial bed." He squeezed her against him, feeling the instant desire for her that any contact brought.

Abigail molded her body against his, shifting so that his arms came under her breasts and held her more intimately. "Now that we're married, we don't have time for that foolishness." She could barely suppress her giggle as she waited for his reaction.

Samuel stilled against her for a brief second. Then he bent to whisper in her ear, moving his lips softly in the way he knew she liked. "I'll keep that in mind when we finally get back to 1995. I don't believe an Indian marriage is valid in the eyes of the law, so I suppose we'll have to live together in sin."

Abigail chuckled. He was a hard man to best, even when she thought she'd gained the upper hand. "Touché."

Elizabeth signaled them to follow her, and they said their goodbyes to the Indians who had played captor and host. Abigail took Lotuk's hand. She looked into his eyes as she held his hand, then stood on tiptoe to put a kiss on his cheek. "Thank you," she whispered.

Turning, she took Samuel's arm.

"Exactly what were you thanking him for?" Samuel asked.

Abigail squeezed his arm. "Because he could have hurt me. He could have felt that I was more trouble than I was worth and left me in the woods. He could have done a number of things to me, but he didn't."

Samuel put his arms around her. "Thank goodness for that, Abigail. I don't think I'll ever complain about the danger of city streets when we get home. The truth is, I think we'll go to my apartment, lock the door, have pizzas delivered for three weeks and hide out. Maybe we'll never leave."

Abigail laughed at the picture he presented. "So, you live in an apartment?"

He nodded. "I'm beginning to remember a few more details about my personal life, but not much. Maybe that's the key. Maybe we have to remember before we go back."

"In that case, we're still in trouble. I don't remember anything except Familiar getting hit by your car. Speaking of Familiar, where is he?"

Samuel looked back at the tree where they had both sat watching the Indians. He found the dark shape of the cat, asleep on the limb. "He's there," he said, indicating with his head. "Asleep."

"Familiar missed our marriage." Abigail was amused. "That's not like him."

"I don't think Familiar cares for formal commitment." Samuel looked at her and winked. "It's a guy thing."

ABIGAIL was exhausted. The long trek back to the woods near Salem, the covert stealing of all herbs from Elizabeth's house, the gathering of more herbs, the decision of what beverage to make—it had been one important thing after the next. And now there was only the meeting with Georgianna to plan the date.

They had chosen a small glade in the woods where Sanshu could keep a lookout during the meeting. Abigail, Samuel and Elizabeth found seats on the roots of a big tree as they waited for the schoolteacher to arrive. She came through the trees with the grace of great self-discipline, and she brought a basket of cheese, bread and meat.

As they ate the goodies she had prepared, Abigail, Samuel and Elizabeth listened with horror to the number of additional people who had died at the hands of the witch prosecutions. They had to act as soon as possible. And Georgianna brought news about Samuel—he was now wanted as a witch, along with Abigail.

Brianna was still in jail, as was Tituba and a host of others, but the list of victims grew with each day as the girls, Emily and Mary, continued their accusations and Appleton and Hawthorne continued their prosecutions. Silas Grayson was busier than ever carrying out the edicts of the court, and snooping around Abigail's house to see if she had returned.

Georgianna urged Abigail and Samuel to move as quickly as possible before her sister was next in line for the hangman's noose.

"I think the mulled apples with spices is the best drink we can prepare," Elizabeth said. She had gotten up to pace.

"Why don't we search for the ingredients?" Georgianna said, rising, also. "Abigail, you and Samuel have more knowledge of the official rooms of the court. Would it be possible for you to secure the keys? If we had them in our hands, it would save much time and guarantee the success of our venture."

Samuel hesitated. The magistrate's building could easily be a death trap. But who else could do it? He knew the offices and the desks where the keys were kept. He looked around for Familiar. The cat had disappeared again, a habit that he was developing much to Abigail's annoyance.

He turned his attention back to Georgianna. "I can do that. Abigail can remain with Sanshu and begin to bring the water up to boil the apples."

"Someone should go with you as a lookout. If you're detained, you could throw the keys out the window to the lookout, and then we could free you along with the others." Georgianna looked around the group. "I could do that with no difficulty. No one suspects me."

"But I need your help," Elizabeth said. She looked at Sanshu. Her Indian husband was out of the question.

"That leaves me." Abigail picked up the boy's cap she had carried through all of her escapades. "I know they're looking for me, but I can pass as a boy. It's dangerous, but I can do it."

"No." Samuel stood. "No. I won't have you back in that village."

"There's no other way." Abigail rose, as passionate as he. "I won't let you go down there alone without someone to serve as lookout. You're as wanted as I am."

Elizabeth stepped between them as they glared at each other. "Samuel, it's the best plan. Abigail is fast. She'll be safe."

"It's settled." Abigail tucked her hair under her hat. "We're a great team, Samuel. We can do this." She smiled reassurance at him.

Samuel didn't say anything. His gut instinct told him not to consent, but all along he'd been tormented by the idea that something horrible would happen to Abigail and he wouldn't be able to protect her. Maybe it was his own insecurities that nagged at him. Besides, he had no better plan. They couldn't sit in the woods and wait for someone else to do the dangerous part.

"Okay," he said, nodding his head slowly. "It's the best plan. But I still don't like it. We'll go tonight and get the keys." He looked once again for Familiar. The cat was his ace in the hole, if he was around. Familiar could get into places Samuel couldn't—and the cat could get out.

"That means I have to have everything ready by noon tomorrow," Georgianna said, clasping her hands in front of her. "I think noon would be best. There will be a break in the trials for those attending to find refreshments. I can offer a cup to those who come out of the magistrate's building.''

''Yes.'' Elizabeth nodded. ''We'll begin gathering the last of our ingredients now while Sanshu brings up the water to make the, uh, cider. Let's be off. There's no time for us to waste.''

''Abigail and I will slip down to the village. We need to watch the magistrate's building to be sure there's no one there when we go in.''

''Excellent.'' Georgianna unclasped her hands, then brought them back together and squeezed them. ''Excellent. We must succeed in this venture, or we're all lost.''

ALONE AT LAST. I think there was a great country song about just this topic. I'm referring to Pilgrim Man and Madame Mysterious, of course. They've found a little nook in the copse of trees on the hilltop that overlooks the village. It isn't exactly what I define as secure, but it does provide a cozy little bower for the heavy petting that's going on between them. Lucky for them, I'm sitting lookout. And what an interesting sight Salem Village is these days.

There's old Silas Gruesome down in the square, pointing fingers and taking names. Another list of victims to be accused of witchcraft, no doubt. I wonder why no one has accused him, because he's mean as the very devil.

There's Fattie Appleton, along with that prickly old Hawthorne. The entire trio should be strung up and left for the crows. And throw in that lout Wadsworth. I'm certain he's put his daughter Mary up to the majority of her stunts. There he is, big as life, circling the crowd.

I suppose I shouldn't be so graphic in my vengeance, but those guys are making a profit off the suffering of others, and it scalds me.

Ah, there's Georgianna, back in town. She said she had to go get sugar from the market. There isn't time to find honey, and even though sugar is dear, she was willing to part with her money to buy some. Very generous woman. I suppose her sister's life is at stake here. It's strange, but fortuitous, that Georgianna hasn't been charged.

But it looks like that may be next on Silas Gruesome's agenda. He's stalking her again. He even left his soapbox in the eye of the public to sneak around behind her like some deviant. Hmm. The more I watch, the more I think Silas has the hots for Georgianna.

Uh-oh, she's spotted him. She's one smart cookie. She's acting as if she were glad to see him. Good for her. Don't let him know we have a plan.

Yes, she's sending him back to the square, and she's going on to the market. Excellent. And it seems the trials are ready to resume for the afternoon.

What's that I see over behind the cemetery? Why did I even bother to ask? They're readying the ropes for the hangings. I can only hope they're not today. I don't think Abigail and Samuel will be able to sit by and let people die in front of them. And if they go rushing in like fools where angels fear to tread, they'll end up swinging like yo-yos on the end of a string.

Ah, well, at least they're having a little honeymoon time right now. It does an old feline's heart good to see amour is still such a potent force, even in these primitive times. But then, Samuel and Abigail are from the future.

Well, now it's time for some food. In all of my adventures I've never eaten so poorly. I think I've lost several pounds. All muscle, of course. I never had any fat to lose. Clotilde, that goddess of feline femininity, says that I'm as trim as I was in my salad days. I hope the home fires are banked and burning, because I'm ready to head back to 1995. And Clotilde. And even Eleanor and Dr. Doolittle. That little baby, Jordan Lindsay, would even be a welcome sight. She's just going to have to learn not to drool on my black suit.

Looks like I'm stuck here, watching, until Abigail and Samuel finish up with their personal business. I'll just kick back, watch the village, and dream of home.

CROUCHING LOW beside the base of the building, Abigail kept her hearing tuned to the street. Samuel and Familiar had been inside for less than five minutes, but it seemed like at least five years. Her heart was pounding, and she tried to still it so she could hear better. What if Samuel was caught? Would they kill him on the spot? She put her cold hand to her flushed cheek and tried to calm herself. She had to be alert and calm, ready to save Samuel and the cat if things went bad.

She pulled the cap lower on her forehead, slinking back into the shadows of the building. The streets of Salem Village were empty. Those who had not been accused of witchcraft had taken the dangers to heart. When the sun went down, they were in their homes with the doors barred and the curtains drawn. No one was safe from accusation.

She shifted to the street, checking to be sure no one had silently slipped up behind her. She made her way around the building, keeping to the shadows, keeping her ears open. The village was as silent as a tomb. In the distance, if she concentrated, she thought she even heard the sound of the Atlantic. It was foolishness, of course. There was a storm building, the thick clouds scudding over the stars. Samuel said it was to their benefit, but she only prayed it wouldn't rain while Georgianna was doling out the sedative.

She crept around to the east side of the building, the side where Samuel and Familiar were searching for the keys. They couldn't be certain that Appleton even kept the keys in the same place he once did. They might have to search his entire office. Or that of Hawthorne. It was a daunting thought.

Abigail crept backward into the deeper shadows, her mind on where Samuel and Familiar might be in the building. She shifted, her butt bumping into something solid. Something that shouldn't have been there. Before her brain could register the fact, she felt one hand around her chest, another around her mouth.

Her first thought was that she was going to be raped, and then the reality dawned on her. This was not 1995. This was 1692, and what was about to happen to her was going to be much more deadly.

The hand around her mouth held her nose, clamping down with such force that she couldn't draw a breath at all. She struggled, but she knew she was no match for the tall man who held her. Still struggling, she twisted around to find Earl Wadsworth standing with a rope that he wrapped around her hands. His mouth was twisted in a smirk of satisfaction, but he remained silent.

The man holding her increased the pressure on her nose and mouth. "At last, Mistress West. I've been dreaming of this moment for such a long, long time."

The last thing Abigail heard was Silas Grayson's cruel voice.

Chapter Seventeen

Samuel found the keys in a compartment in Appleton's desk that served as a hidden drawer. The hunt had taken him far longer than he'd anticipated. Just as he palmed the keys, Familiar appeared at his leg in an extremely agitated state. Samuel felt the seed of dread blossom in his chest. Abigail was in danger. He knew it.

He didn't bother closing the desk but ran to the back door and slipped into the night, moving through the shadows like a substantial wraith as he sought Abigail.

Familiar darted into the lead, pausing at a clump of shrubs.

"Be calm," Samuel admonished the cat, though his heart was pounding with dread. He made a circle around the building, his fear accelerating with each step. Abigail was gone. Without a trace. There had been no sound, no indication that she'd been taken. But she'd been spirited away into the night.

Familiar had begun to sniff the ground, and Samuel tried to examine the area, but the night was too dark. The moon was obscured by the building storm, the thick clouds so heavy that no ray of light sifted down from the heavens. Samuel couldn't even see the hand in front of his face, much less marks in the dark earth.

"Meow!" Familiar called from a short distance away.

Sensing that the cat had picked up the trail, Samuel started after him, slipping through the darkness to the back of the building.

At the stairs that led down into the back dungeon entrance, Familiar paused. Quick as a flash, he darted down the steps. To Samuel's surprise, the cat eased the door open and entered.

Wishing for a flashlight, or better yet, an Uzi, Samuel eased into the darkness. He felt as if he'd been swallowed by some large, living beast as the distant sounds of the prison began to come to him, cotton-coated in the darkness.

Soft sighs seemed to whisper from the walls, as if spirits had been trapped unhappily in the stone. But deep in the pit of the building, he heard something else. Something that sounded distinctly like Abigail's voice.

"You low-life creep. Touch me again and I'll kick you so hard you'll sing in the boys' choir."

"She talks like the evil creature she is!"

Samuel recognized Silas Grayson's exultant voice. In the darkness the voice of a second man came to him. He recognized Mary Wadsworth's father, Earl.

"You're a witness, Earl. She's a true child of Satan. Look at her hiss and struggle."

"Aye, Silas. She's as wild as one of those cat creatures. We shall be amply rewarded for catching this one. Especially if we can convince her to confess."

"I trust a dunking in the Mill Pond will prove what I've known all this time. She's a witch. A powerful witch."

"If I was so damn powerful, I'd turn you into a toad. Even better, a wart on a toad's butt."

There was the sound of Abigail's cry of surprise mingled with pain.

Samuel started forward, but Familiar pounced on his leg, stopping him dead in his tracks.

"I'm warning you, Grayson. When I get out of here, I'm going to make you pay. Don't you ever touch me again." Abigail's voice was shaking with fury.

Samuel heard her anger, but he also heard her strength. Whatever they'd done to her had infuriated her more than injured her. And they wouldn't have a chance to do much more, because he was getting her out of there. Familiar was right, though, he needed to have a plan. He couldn't just go charging in there and beat the living daylights out of Grayson and his cohort in crime, Earl Wadsworth. No, that would jeopardize the entire rescue plan for the next day.

"Are you sure her cell is secure, Earl?" Silas asked.

"Aye, them bars will hold, and she's trussed tighter than a hog in November. She won't be going nowhere, that I can assure you."

"Then we should get about our business. Now that the primary witch has been delivered to us, the others should be easy to round up. Our village will be wiped clean of Satan by the end of the week."

"Is it Georgianna March we're after next?" Earl asked.

"Georgianna." Silas chuckled, and it was an unpleasant sound. "Indeed, I feel I must pay her a visit. And soon."

There was the sound of footsteps approaching from the door, and Samuel knew he was trapped. He pushed as far back as possible in the dark recesses of the stone wall. Could he possibly escape detection? He wasn't sure, but there was nowhere else for him to go. He looked down to make sure the cat was safely hidden. To his shock, Familiar streaked out into the corridor and ran as fast as possible.

"Cat! Cat! One of the witches is escaping!" The cry rang out from the exit where the guard had been stationed.

Samuel realized that Familiar had risked his own life to create a diversion so that Samuel would have an opportunity to escape. Just as he stepped out in the corridor and started to run, he felt something hard and heavy against his head. He saw the stone floor rising up at him, and then he fell into the darkness of a black, shifting pit.

ABIGAIL SAT in the dark cell, unable to completely accept what had happened to her. Silas Grayson had appeared out of nowhere. She'd been imprisoned without even knowing what crimes she was charged with, but it wasn't hard to imagine.

"Abigail?"

She heard someone calling her name but didn't have the heart to answer.

"Abigail West?"

She recognized the cultured voice of Brianna March. "I'm here," she finally said.

"I warned you," Brianna said, censure more apparent in her tone than sympathy. "I warned you not to come down here trying to help. Now you're as doomed as we are."

Abigail wanted to refute her charge, but she didn't believe she wasn't doomed. And it was her fault. She'd been careless, crouched in the darkness and never looking behind her. Either that, or someone had tipped off Silas to her presence outside the dungeon.

She thought of Samuel, but that gave her no comfort, only more worry. The last thing she wanted was for Samuel to risk his own life by trying to help her.

From the rest of the cells there was only silence. The prison was dark, but most of the prisoners had a means of figuring out what had happened. With her capture, even the small hope the prisoners might have had was gone. Their plight was indeed hopeless. The hemp strands used to tie her wrists together were cutting into her flesh, and she used her teeth to pick at them, trying to loosen the knots.

"Are ye charged yet?" one male voice called out.

"No," Abigail answered. "Not charged." One knot was loosening.

"Those willful girls have not named ye?" a woman asked.

"No," Abigail answered. "It was Silas Grayson. He's named me as a witch." She had worked one knot free.

There was no response. Determined to free her hands before she lost all feeling in them, Abigail set to work. Using her teeth, she slowly untied knot after knot. Earl Wadsworth had not been kidding when he'd said she was securely tied. But he'd failed to reckon with the fact that, unlike him, she had good teeth.

After half an hour Abigail shook the rope off her hands and rubbed some feeling back into them. There had been no need to leave her tied when the jail was made of stone walls at least two-feet thick. The rope was just another little cruelty in preparation for what was to come next. To stave off those thoughts, Abigail began to explore the dimensions of her prison. It was a tiny cell, but spacious compared to some of the others. She had room to take two steps in each direction. And she could, at least, sit on the floor. Some of the cells were so cramped the people could only stand. As she fumbled around the floor her fingers found the stub of a candle and flint. Instead of lighting it, she put it in the pocket of her trousers to save for later use.

Far down the corridor she heard the opening of a door, and knew the true meaning of the word fear. Had they come to test her? She'd seen Brianna's hands. And heard the horror stories of others examined for signs of witchcraft. It was only a matter of time before her ordeal began.

The sound of slow footsteps echoed off the stone walls, and the silence of the dungeon deepened.

The steps came toward her cell, and the flare of light was so sudden, so powerful, that she pulled back. It took her several seconds to adjust to the light of the lantern, and to see Samuel's stricken face as he held it up. There was a large lump on the side of his head, and blood was crusted around his mouth. Even in the glare of the lantern she could see the discoloration around his eyes.

"Samuel." She reached through the bars. To her horror, he backed away from her.

"Because you used the wiles of Satan to tempt and trick me, I've been allowed to ask you for your confession." Samuel's words were dead. In the lantern light his gray eyes showed all the torment of a man truly condemned to hell. He stepped back, and the light fell on Magistrate Appleton and the prosecutor, Caleb Hawthorne, standing behind him.

"Samuel." Abigail could hear the heartbreak in her own voice. "What have they done to you?"

"Do not call my given name, witch. You defile me, and you shall hang for your crimes."

"I am innocent of any crimes," Abigail said. "You, of all people, should know that."

Samuel was roughly shoved aside, and Appleton stepped up to the cell. "Your beloved has agreed to give testimony against you to save himself. He has broken free of your hold on him, demon. Now you'll face your charges. You've given sustenance to the pawns of Satan. Deny it if you dare!"

"I gave food to hungry people. Even those guilty of crimes should be allowed to eat, and these people aren't guilty. They haven't even been tried. This is America, where a woman is innocent until *proven* guilty."

Appleton almost hissed as he pulled back. "She speaks like a demon. That is proof enough for me."

"I'm no demon." Abigail felt the anger course through her like molten iron. She felt as if she could bend the bars with her bare hands—and what she wanted to do to Appleton and Hawthorne didn't bear thinking about.

Appleton backed up even farther. "She has the tongue of a viper."

"What are her crimes?" Samuel asked. His voice was a monotone.

Abigail looked at him. Was it possible he'd sustained some type of brain damage from being repeatedly struck in the face or head? He wouldn't abandon her. Not unless he couldn't help himself. She felt her anger slipping, and sorrow and fear creeping in. She forced herself to listen to the smarmy tones of the prosecutor.

"The list is incomplete." Hawthorne's voice was rich with satisfaction. He waved a hand in the lantern light. "Consorting with the Dark One, giving sustenance to the accused, tempting our own Goodman Truesdale." His grin was evil.

"I tempt no one. I am guilty of nothing except human kindness. These people are not evil. They are wrongly accused, and *you* are starving them to death for personal gain."

"She is bold," Hawthorne said. "This woman doesn't need a trial, she needs a rope."

"Mary and Emily have not named her." Samuel put forth that fact. "I believe it would be better if the girls made the accusations. That would give her trial the same weight as the others. And the girls are so convincing when they roll and thrash about the floor."

"I will speak with Earl Wadsworth." Hawthorne's smile was mean. "He has great influence with his daughter and her... fantasies."

"Perhaps we have no need for the young women, not if we show she can tempt grown men to do her bidding," Appleton said. "Truesdale, here, has seen her for what she is. Silas Grayson said she tempted him."

"Oh, posh and balderdash! I'm not so desperate I'd tempt that old goat to do anything!" Even the thought of it made Abigail furious. "I've done nothing wrong. You can't prove a single thing against me."

"Silence!" Hawthorne thundered at her. He grabbed Appleton's arm. "She is trying to bring us under her power. Hang her now. Before it is too late."

"She must be tried." Samuel's voice almost cracked, but it didn't. "It is against the laws of England to hang a person without a trial. If you do not give her a trial, it will bring the wrath of the governor down upon us. She has already sent an emissary to the governor to beg his interference. We must use all caution to make certain she is tried within the letter of the law."

Abigail's heart caught a ray of hope. That *sounded* like the Samuel she knew and loved. It was very possible that he'd pretended to accuse her so that he could remain free to save her. It was a masterful ploy—if it worked!

"Shall I torture a confession from her?" Hawthorne's question was laced with desire. "I have a way with convincing witches to tell the truth."

Abigail grabbed the bars and held them to keep from sliding to the floor as her legs turned soft with dread. Many of the other prisoners had been tortured. She felt her stomach roll at the idea of being helpless and in the power of Caleb Hawthorne.

"Leave her." Appleton spoke with firm authority. "We shall try her tomorrow and see what comes of that. If we need a confession, we shall obtain one. And I think we shall let our new colleague, Samuel Truesdale, wring it from her bones." He laughed as he slapped Hawthorne on the shoulder and started away with the lamp. "Come along, Truesdale. I don't trust you enough to leave you down here alone."

Abigail waited for the moment that Samuel would toss her the keys. She knew he was playing along with Appleton and Hawthorne. He had been very convincing, but it was all a game. He would drop the keys and provide a distraction for her to make an escape. Even as he fell in behind Appleton, she kept her hopes up. Not until his steps were merely an echo in the stone corridor did she really believe he'd left her in the dungeon without some word or sign that he intended to come back to help her. What if he really had been damaged?

"Oh, no." She sank down onto the floor and hugged her knees. "What am I going to do now?" she asked the darkness.

STARING INTO Samuel's gray eyes, Abigail did not see a flicker of recognition. The room was jam-packed with spectators as she was led into it, her hands retied—this time tighter than before—with a tether that the guard held.

The noise rose to a deafening roar, but Abigail was numb. Looking at Samuel, she felt as if her heart had already been cut out.

"Abigail West, how do you plead to charges of witchcraft?" Silas Grayson asked the question, his grim face set in lines of smug satisfaction.

For a moment Abigail was tempted to plead guilty and get it over with. She'd seen enough of the previous trials to know that trying to defend herself would only prolong the agony she faced. At least hanging was a quick death. She didn't want to be tortured or examined. But if she could delay the inevitable, maybe Sanshu and Elizabeth and Georgianna would think of some way to save her. And Brianna and the others. Besides, she'd never plead guilty to something she didn't do. Never. She lifted her chin and looked directly into Grayson's eyes, then shifted her gaze to fall on the audience. Wherever she looked, silence fell.

"I am innocent."

"Then I suppose we shall have to put you to the test," Hawthorne said, rubbing his hands together. "I must confess, myself, that no trial in the past has given me such pleasure."

"It has been reported that you have been seen in the company of a black cat." Samuel paced closer to her as he began to talk. "Is this true?"

"Indeed. I have a black cat. His name is Familiar."

The entire audience drew in its breath.

"He's a remarkable creature." Abigail watched the faces of the court with great intensity. Before she died she had to know if these men really believed they were fighting evil, or if they were simply greedy.

"You admit to consorting with a familiar?" Samuel lifted his eyebrows as if he doubted her answer.

"I freely admit that I have a black cat named Familiar."

"And is this cat empowered with any special gifts?"

She saw a flicker of something in Samuel's eyes. What was he driving at?

"Yes. He has special powers."

"And what might these powers be?"

"He, uh, can visit sickness and disease down upon anyone who touches him." Samuel shot a wicked gleam of approval at her that could have passed as a scowl. Abigail continued with more gusto. "Diseases so terrible no one has ever seen the like. Familiar can make a person's skin turn green and putrid and begin to fall from the bone. Why, I've seen him look at a fully grown man and reduce him to a pile of smoldering flesh in hardly more than five minutes."

The audience sat back in their chairs, and even Appleton turned white.

"And does Familiar work at your command?"

Abigail began to enjoy the game. "Indeed, he does. He does everything I tell him."

"So, he is under your direction?"

"Indeed." She nodded emphatically.

"Is this your necklace with which you cast spells?" Samuel withdrew the crystal pendant to the awed exclamations of the audience.

"It is," Abigail said.

Samuel walked toward her and put it around her neck. His fingers gently brushed her hair. "Be strong," he urged her in a whisper. "Fight." Then he stepped back. "And was the necklace a gift?"

"Indeed. From the Dark One himself."

Several members of the audience cried out in horror and held up their hands to block her from their view.

Samuel waited until the room had gotten completely quiet. "And are you a witch?"

"You could say that I have a real witchy twist to my personality." Abigail grinned as she surveyed the room. "I've always been a little hellcat. Now, who would like for me to practice my talents on them?"

Several women in the front row bolted and began to run from the building.

"Be seated!" Appleton thundered at the crowd. "I want witnesses to this woman's confession. Don't you dare attempt to abscond from this trial or you shall be named witch!"

Those who hadn't made it out the front door collapsed into their seats, pulling as far back as they could from Abigail.

"How about you, Applecheeks? Want a little taste of my magic?" Abigail started toward his bench. It took Earl Wadsworth a full thirty seconds before he thought to yank the tether tied to Abigail's hands, pulling her a safe distance away from the magistrate. But the magistrate's fear was not lost on Abigail.

"Hang her!" Hawthorne shouted. "Before she injures us all. Hang her now!"

Appleton made a sweeping motion with his arm. "Take her to the witch tree. We'll be done with her vile threats and the harm she has done the people of Salem."

"And take Brianna March and Tituba with her," Silas Grayson proclaimed. "They are as guilty as she. They are the three primary witches. Perhaps we can cleanse the others charged."

"Take them all," Appleton said just before he stood and ran from the room.

Chapter Eighteen

In the time that Abigail and Samuel had been in the woods, a small platform for the hangings had been erected under a giant elm not far from the village square. Abigail had no choice but to follow Earl Wadsworth as he dragged her through the street. The crowd from the trial formed a rag-tag mob around them as they walked.

Abigail's exhilaration at tweaking the noses of Appleton and Hawthorne vanished in a wave of fear as she realized that she was being taken to be hanged. The trial was over. She had been sentenced to die.

Looking around, she expected to see Georgianna March in the square with her kettle of mulled cider. But there was no sign of the schoolteacher, nor of Elizabeth Adams.

Abigail stumbled, and Wadsworth jerked her forward with a curse. He was afraid of her; she could smell it on him. But he was also going to hang her as quickly as he possibly could. What she'd managed to do in the courtroom simply ensured her death. And Samuel was nowhere to be seen.

Wadsworth virtually dragged her up the steps of the plat-form and, without any words, caught one of three nooses already hanging from the graceful limbs of the tree. He thrust it around Abigail's neck with a gesture that was both rough and fearful.

The hemp was abrasive, and Abigail twisted to avoid contact, but it was impossible. Wadsworth pulled the noose tight, quickly stepping back from her as if contact with her had burned his skin.

Looking over the crowd, Abigail searched for a compassionate face and concentrated on keeping her knees from buckling. She was terrified. She hadn't expected to die. Hadn't planned on it at all. As far as she could see, there was nothing Samuel could do to save her. How had things gone so terribly awry?

A large crowd had gathered around the platform, and they waited eagerly for the execution. But Appleton had ordered that Brianna and Tituba be brought from the dungeon, and the two women, so unused to sunlight and the space to move around freely, were stumbling along at a slow pace.

At the delay in action, the crowd began to chant. "Hang 'er! Hang 'er! Hang 'er!"

Abigail clung to one last hope. Perhaps if she died, she would awaken in 1995, the whole encounter having been a dream. Somehow, though, she knew that her feelings for Samuel were too real to be swept away as dream emotions. The thought of him put some strength into her legs and allowed her to lift her chin as Brianna and Tituba were jerked up beside her on the platform. The remaining nooses were tightened around their necks.

"Have courage," Brianna said softly, standing in the middle. "Don't give them the pleasure of your fear."

"Right." Abigail forced the word out, while Tituba mutely nodded.

On the edge of the crowd Abigail caught sight of Georgianna March. But instead of peddling the cider as she was supposed to be doing, Georgianna was standing with Silas Grayson. So that explained how the plan had fallen apart. Grayson had Georgianna's upper arm in a grasp Abigail could see was clearly painful.

Her observations were interrupted when Wadsworth pushed her forward to the edge of the wooden stand. The platform had not been built as a real gallows. There was no trap door that would drop out from beneath the accused. Looking at the arrangement, Abigail guessed that someone would come up behind her and literally knock her off the platform. It wasn't a pleasant fate to ponder, but she took several deep breaths, waiting for the feel of someone's hand against her back.

Instead she saw Samuel proceeding toward the platform. It took her a moment to realize what he was holding in his hand. A mask! It was the ram's head that she had seen at the midnight bonfire dance. And he was now running toward Silas Grayson as fast as he could!

Sensing something unusual happening on the fringes of the gathering, the crowd slowly turned from Abigail toward Silas, who still held Georgianna's arm. The tall man stood transfixed with terror as Samuel ran at him, brandishing the mask.

"God save me!" Silas cried, then turned and fled.

But Samuel did not pursue him. Instead he halted in front of Georgianna and held the mask out to her. "Your property, Georgianna." His voice was harsh. "The mask you stole from Sanshu's tribe."

Georgianna's smile was tight and victorious as she stepped back from him. "So, Samuel Truesdale, you have fallen under Satan's sway. Fornicating with a witch is a sure way to lose one's soul. Appleton was a fool to believe you'd abandon your precious Abigail."

"Manipulating the fears of a village so that innocent people die is a surer way to burn in hell." Samuel's eyes glittered with pure rage.

From her position on the platform, Abigail could do nothing. She was afraid Samuel was going to strangle the woman with his bare hands. She saw the fury and hatred and contempt that he directed at the tall, slender, school-teacher. What had happened to make him hate her so?

Georgianna didn't flinch an inch. She turned to the platform. "Hang them!" she cried. "Our village must be rid of them. Hang them now!"

Abigail felt the pressure of Earl Wadsworth's hand at her back. All of the childhood prayers she'd been taught jumbled together in her mind, and she clung only to the thought that she was not afraid of death.

"Look!" Earl removed his hand from her back and pointed down the lane that led to the square.

Abigail opened her eyes to see a richly dressed man and woman at the head of a procession that included Hester Prynne and Pearl. Hester was pushing the portly man to walk at a faster pace. It was Governor Phips and his wife! It could be no one else, and as he caught sight of the platform and the three women standing with their hands tied together and nooses around their necks, he bolted forward.

"Halt! Halt this execution immediately. In the name of King George, our sovereign leader, I demand that this be halted."

The crowd spun from Abigail to Samuel, who now held Georgianna March in a viselike grip, and then to the rapid approach of the dignitary.

Georgianna wrenched free of Samuel's grasp and darted into the crowd. She was thin, but she was also spry, and she pushed through the crowd and climbed up on the platform, moving straight to her sister. With a great thrust, she pushed Brianna off the platform. Brianna March's skinny body hit the end of the rope and she was left dangling, her feet kicking the base of the platform as she slowly strangled to death.

"Samuel!" Abigail's cry halted all other noise.

The crowd parted as Samuel ran the remaining few feet. Catching Brianna's struggling body against him, he held her as he climbed back up onto the platform, each inch he gained releasing the pressure on her throat. At the top of the platform, he helped Brianna to stand as he loosened the rope around her neck.

"Hang him, too!" Georgianna pointed a finger at Samuel. "This man has attempted to incite the Indians to attack our village. He is an evil man, a man corrupted by the wiles of a witch."

Samuel didn't even bother to answer. He stepped to Georgianna and gave her a non-too-gentle push into Hawthorne's arms. "Restrain her," he ordered the befuddled Hawthorne.

Appleton sputtered and stepped forward. "These women have been condemned to die. Executioner, do your duty." He jabbed Wadsworth in the ribs.

"Halt." The governor had made great progress through the crowd and was ascending the platform. "Halt. These women have been accused of witchcraft. Have they been tried and duly found to be guilty?"

Standing up taller than Samuel had ever seen him, Appleton stepped forward, dropping a sweeping bow. "Indeed, Your Honor, they have been tried. All have confessed. We have the signed documents in the magistrate's hall, and the deeds they have confessed to are heinous and evil." He motioned to Wadsworth. "Go get the confessions."

"I've signed no confession." Abigail spoke up. "We are innocent, Your Honor."

"Shut up, witch!" Appleton grabbed the noose at her neck. "You'll swing before the hour is out."

"I'll view the confessions," the governor said.

The crowd around the platform grew in size as word of the governor's appearance spread through the small village. In the ten minutes it took Earl Wadsworth to return with the confessions nearly everyone in the village had gathered. With a trembling hand Wadsworth delivered the papers to the governor.

"Oh, my dear," Mrs. Phips said as she stepped to her husband's side, "you know you can't read without your magnifier." She took the pages and began to read them out loud.

The confessions were a documentation of evil deeds that silenced the crowd as they were read. Abigail felt the fear and hatred of the audience grow. And she saw the way the governor's face began to reflect doubts. He had come to stop the witch trials, but as he heard the fake confessions and watched the reaction of the crowd, he was beginning to be swayed!

Abigail stood forward. "Enough! Those are lies. I have confessed to no such activities. Neither has Brianna nor Tituba. This has all been fabricated by Appleton and his cohorts."

"Silence." The governor spoke, his brow beetled in thought. He pulled on the high-stock collar of his shirt. "This is a grave matter that requires much thought. These confessions are signed by the three of you. And they have been made with a sense of pride in the evilness done. I am not so certain that today's executions should be stopped. After all, there are many witnesses to these deeds of witchcraft. Why would an innocent woman be accused of such things?"

Abigail wasn't certain where Familiar came from. She'd hardly given him a thought since her capture. But he streaked through the crowd, darting here and there amid cries and kicks. With what seemed to be wings, he jumped up on the platform and hurled his fifteen-pound body straight into the arms of the governor's wife. Looking up at Mrs. Phips, he licked her on the chin.

Among the spectators, one whispered word passed. "Witch!"

The startled woman held the cat like a child and looked to her horrified husband for guidance. She made one attempt to push the cat aside, but he clung to her heavy dress with claws like hooks.

"Witch!" Samuel pointed his finger at Mrs. Phips as he picked up the whispers of the crowd. "She's a witch and that cat is her wicked familiar!"

"Witch!" Three men in the crowd pointed at Mrs. Phips in horror. Their accusation was punctuated by a tremendous roll of thunder in a sky that was growing darker by the minute. Far in the distance a three-pronged fork of lightning split the sky.

In a matter of seconds the entire audience had surged forward, their fingers pointing at the governor's wife, their eyes wild.

"Hang her before she influences the governor." Samuel only made the suggestion to see it picked up by the crowd.

As the governor's wife began to struggle to get the cat away from her, Familiar dug in and held on. The entire time he proceeded to lick her face.

Abigail watched the scene first with horror, then a growing amusement. When she turned to the governor and saw his face, she felt sudden relief. Never in a million years would he allow his wife to stand trial for witchcraft.

"My wife is no witch," Phips cried, putting his arm around the poor woman's shoulders as she tugged Familiar's claws free one by one. But each time she managed to unhook a paw, Familiar grabbed her dress with another one.

"And Abigail is no witch." Samuel held out his arms and Familiar released his hold and allowed Samuel to take him. "This cat is no familiar. He's merely a very smart cat."

"That's it!" Abigail felt the centuries of history open to her. "It was an accusation of the governor's wife that stopped the witch trials." But in the confusion, no one seemed to hear her.

"This is a trick of Satan." Appleton tried to regain the focus of the crowd. "These women must hang."

The governor, his wife tucked protectively against him, shook his head. "No, there will be no more hangings. I see how easy it is to trick even an educated man into a foolish belief. Were it not for the fact that my wife is married to me, she could as easily hang as these other good women." He nodded to Wadsworth. "There will be no executions in Salem Village today. There has been enough suffering. Enough death. I hereby declare that there shall be no more executions for witchcraft." He eyed Familiar as if he were having second thoughts.

"These women have confessed. They had caused sickness and disease among the people and livestock of my village. I demand that they be executed. I demand—"

"I believe I must go back and examine all of the transcripts on these trials." The governor spoke very slowly and very clearly. "If everything is not in order, Appleton, it will be you standing on this makeshift gallows. Now, do you really want to pursue this witchcraft matter?"

"But, Your Honor, there is evil that must be cast out." Appleton clutched Hawthorne's arm and pushed him forward, Georgianna still in his grasp. "Tell him, Caleb."

"This woman, Abigail West, has admitted her powers...." At the steely look in Phips's eyes, Hawthorne faltered. He turned to Appleton and whispered, "If he reviews each case, there were some discrepancies." He turned back to the governor. "We shall follow your directive, Your Honor."

"Enough of this." The governor finally released his wife and went to Tituba. Taking the rope off her neck, he moved on to Brianna, and then Abigail. He turned to the crowd. "The acts of accusing, of trying, of convicting and of hanging a person for the crime of witchcraft is hereby halted forevermore in the Massachusetts Bay Colony. We shall not delve into this issue again, except to clear the names of those still charged."

"Wait." Abigail looked at Samuel. "This isn't over yet. What about the people who made these accusations and profited from them? They have to be punished."

"What do you mean, 'profited by these executions'?" The governor's interest was definitely piqued.

"We believe that Magistrate Appleton and Prosecutor Caleb Hawthorne, and Silas Grayson . . ."

"And Georgianna March," Samuel added.

"Have all profited from persecuting innocent people. They have confiscated prime lands and used the trials to take them over."

Brianna March pointed at her sister, who was now struggling in Earl Wadsworth's grasp. "I never believed greed would so completely corrupt you, but I know now that it has. As the eldest daughter, the land was mine. I would have shared everything with you. Everything there was. But that was not enough for you, was it, sister? Greed has twisted you into a creature far more evil than a witch. Greed has made you a murderer."

To the silence that followed Brianna's speech, the governor touched his wife's arm. "I believe we'll be staying in Salem Village for longer than we ever intended. We shall have to look into these matters. If our own court officials are so tainted by greed and wickedness, we may have to stay to be certain the evidence is properly heard. Open the dungeon and release those people who have suffered far more than the bounds of decency allow."

He stepped back to allow Samuel to cut the tie that bound Abigail's wrists. As soon as she was free, Samuel gathered her against his chest where a purring Familiar waited.

"Abigail!" Hester ran across the platform and embraced all three as Pearl danced around them.

"Hester! I'd given up hope," Abigail finally managed to say.

"It took forever to convince the governor that he had to come here in the flesh. He cared not to leave the conveniences of the city, and he considers the villagers here little more than savages." She shrugged. "But Pearl and I prevailed."

"Indeed you did." Samuel hugged Abigail again. "I thought for a moment I might really lose you." He kissed her head. "Dear God, what would I have done?"

Abigail felt the tears burn her eyes, and she looked up to see Brianna March standing alone on the platform. A struggling Georgianna was being taken away, along with Appleton and Hawthorne. Several men had gone to find Silas Grayson.

"I should have guessed it was my sister." Brianna still stood proudly erect. "Since we were little girls, she's always plotted against me. But so many innocent people! How could she do this?"

Samuel held Abigail against him as Familiar jumped out of his arms and down to the platform. "I don't know. Even when I found the masks in her home, I didn't want to believe it was her.

"See, when Abigail was captured and they caught me, I decided to pretend to join them. After I finally convinced that fool Appleton that I would prosecute Abigail and get the grandest confession of all, I got away from him and went to Georgianna's, hoping to find her and Sanshu and Elizabeth. On her table I discovered several packets of herbs that Elizabeth had gathered, and I began to suspect that Georgianna was involved in poisoning the guard. She intended to set Abigail up for murder. I looked harder and found those masks."

Abigail was glad of the support of Samuel's strong arm. It was all too much to take in.

"And Silas Grayson?" Brianna asked. "Was he a pawn of my sister's? He's always been in love with her. When they were younger and he tried to court her, it was her rejection that turned him into such a sour and unhappy man. I've always pitied his wife. Sarah has become just like him." She wiped a tear from her face. "We should go down and watch as they empty the dungeon. Before the storm breaks." She eyed the sky, which looked filled with the fury of a natural force. "God's wrath for man's stupidity," she said with a wry smile. "'Tis a fitting end to this day."

"We'll be along in a minute," Abigail said. She wanted a moment alone with Samuel.

The deep rumble of thunder announced that the storm was moving in in earnest. Abigail's thick hair, which had tumbled out of her boy's cap, was caught in a sudden swirl of wind. "Go on, Brianna. We'll follow."

"I'll walk with Mrs. March," Hester announced. She leaned over to hug Abigail, and whispered in her ear, "Along with working to stop the witch trials, I've met a man. William Amston. He has asked to court me, even knowing about little Pearl. And better than that, he is not a coward like Dimmsdale. He's there, waiting at the square."

Following Hester's direction Abigail looked to see a tall, well-muscled man standing alertly, a muzzle loader in his hand.

"If all else failed, we intended to save you by force," Hester said. She kissed Abigail's cheek. "I love you, dear friend." Then she hurried away with Pearl at her side.

Samuel, Abigail and Familiar were left alone on the platform. For a moment they only looked at each other. Then Abigail stepped into the shelter Samuel offered with his arms.

"It's over," she whispered. "At last." She felt completely drained.

"I thought all along it was Silas. I never dreamed it was Georgianna."

"Until you found the masks?" Abigail could feel Samuel's strong heart beating. The pulse was reassuring, and also exciting.

"Yes. The masks and the poison. Even then it took me several minutes to truly believe the implications. Before I trusted my deductions, I went back to Elizabeth and got her help. The herbs I found at Georgianna's weren't the same potion I saw at your house when you so foolishly drank that tea. With that knowledge, I convinced Sanshu and Elizabeth to run for their lives. I knew we were all in the worst danger. We'd let Georgianna into our midst. She knew of our plan."

"She intended to kill all of us." Abigail burrowed closer against him. "Why was Georgianna using the mask? She doesn't believe in witchcraft."

"To frighten Silas. You remember the night of the bonfire?"

"When I thought you were a warlock?" Abigail kissed his chin. "I remember it well. It broke my heart."

"Your wicked imagination broke your heart. Anyway, Silas was out that night. I thought he was going to the bonfire, but he was actually going to Georgianna's. I gather they've been having something of an affair for most of the summer. I believe Georgianna deliberately set it up so Silas would stumble on the bonfire and the dancing figures. That would cinch his belief that witches were around, so she got two tribesmen from Sanshu's tribe to dance with her. They thought it was harmless."

"More of Georgianna's manipulation." Abigail felt a new surge of anger at the woman.

Samuel ran his fingers through Abigail's hair. Everything about her was perfect.

"She was using his fear to control him," Abigail said.

"Exactly."

"Then Silas is as much an innocent victim as the accused."

"I wouldn't go that far. But I do believe that both he and Wadsworth were used, as were the girls who made the accusations. All of this will come out when Governor Phips begins to examine the situation."

"And Appleton and Hawthorne?"

"Greedy men with a streak of cruelty and malice. But perhaps not as evil as we once thought them."

"Oh, Samuel." Abigail crushed herself against him, holding him tight. "It's over. Really over."

"Let's go home." Even as he said the word, he was struck with the reality of that statement. They might return to Abigail's cottage, but they had no way to really go home.

In that bittersweet moment of realization, Abigail turned her lips up to him. "We can't go home, but we have each other. That's more than any benefits of the future."

"I know." He kissed her offered lips, and desire swept all other thoughts from their minds.

WELL, ISN'T THIS COZY? They end up with each other and I get stuck in 1692 with Clotilde waiting for me back in Washington, D.C. Back in the land of filet mignon, Blue Bell ice cream, a sample of Brie and caviar. I have news for these two witch savers—I'm not staying here. They may be satisfied with a corn-shuck mattress and wool underwear, but I'm not spending the winter in this hellhole. And it looks like it's up to me to figure out how to get us out of here.

The witch trials are solved, and I get small notice for my part. It was me who finally figured out how to stop the whole mess. Had I not attached myself to Madame Phips, we'd all be swinging from the witch tree at this time. And what credit do I get? I think it's time to draw a little attention to myself! The libidinous duo should at least give me a few strokes and compliments.

Yeow! Yeow!

ABIGAIL BROKE the kiss with real regret, but Familiar was having a fit. She rushed over to the place where he'd fallen on his side and was writhing on the hanging platform as if he were in terrible pain.

"Samuel!" she called as she tried to get a grip on Familiar to examine him. "What's wrong?" Real panic filtered in her voice.

Samuel knelt beside them. "I don't know. He was fine a minute ago when he saved the day."

"He was brilliant!" Abigail stroked his sleek fur as he began to calm. "Brilliant and wily." She narrowed her eyes at him. "I think this was a ploy for attention."

"And he deserves it." Samuel put his hand on top of Abigail's on top of the cat. "The three of us together, no matter what the future brings."

His words were followed by a deep rumble of thunder that sounded as if the sky were being split apart.

"We'd better hurry home," Abigail said. "I have no desire to go to the dungeon. Let's just slip on home and celebrate alone. With Familiar." She scratched him under the chin. "Our hero."

She bent to capture him and the crystal pendant swung free of her shirt. Familiar's paw reached up to touch the pendant just as a ragged fork of lightning opened the sky with a brilliance so close it blinded Abigail and Samuel.

There was the sense of falling, as if the platform had collapsed beneath them, the smell of something burning, and then blackness.

Epilogue

Samuel felt the harsh asphalt beneath his hands. A large crowd of people was gathered around him, all talking and jabbering as the sound of nearby traffic seemed close enough to run him down. When he looked up, he saw that he was in the middle of a busy street with traffic pouring all around him.

He looked across at the most beautiful woman he'd ever seen. She was helping a huge black cat rise to his feet. The cat staggered a little, then fixed enormous green eyes on the woman.

"Hey, that cat saved your life!" a man in the crowd called out to the woman.

For a moment Samuel thought the man was dressed in some type of Puritan garb, but it had to be the heat of a summer day in Washington, D.C. that was affecting his vision. It was, after all, the summer solstice. The very first day of summer. When he looked again, the man was dressed in a perfectly normal business suit.

"Are you okay?" Samuel asked the woman. She'd stepped right out in front of his car just as he'd been rushing to make an appointment with a client who wanted a new office building designed. If the black cat hadn't darted out of nowhere and pushed the woman to safety, he would have certainly killed or maimed her.

"I'm okay." The woman looked down at the cat. "And I think he is, too. I thought for a minute that he was a goner." She lifted the cat in her arms and stood.

"Let me make sure you're fine," Samuel insisted. He stood, took the woman's elbow and helped her across the remainder of the busy street.

"Hey! Hey! Buddy!" some man was calling to him. "Hey, you! What about your car?"

Samuel looked back over his shoulder. "Move it for me," he said, totally indifferent as to the fate of the car. All he knew was that it was his fate not to let the beautiful woman out of his sight.

Without a word they walked to Cassandra's Tea Room, where the woman went to a back table. Two cups of strong tea were placed in front of them before they could even order.

"Do you come here often?" Samuel was captivated by the woman's odd eyes. One was green and the other gray. And then there were the luminous green eyes of the cat watching him. The whole experience was very disturbing, yet compelling.

"I come here all the time." The woman smiled. "Would you like me to read your tea leaves?"

"Are you a Gypsy?"

"No, an herbalist. I read the leaves for fun. I've been told my grandmother had the second sight."

"I think you've bewitched me," Samuel said.

Abigail put the cat on the table and smoothed his fur. "Then you're one lucky devil, Samuel Truesdale," she said with an impish smile.

Turning to the black cat, she gave him a solemn wink.

I'M NOT CERTAIN Samuel and Abigail are cognizant—yet—of what's just occurred. We spent weeks in 1692 and then return to Washington, D.C., without missing a moment of time. Amazing! All I know is that I woke up in Salem Vil-

lage, a mass of bruises, and now I can tell I'm going to spend the next three days on a pillow in front of the refrigerator, recovering from my cranial attack on the radiator of that car.

Yes, indeedy, Eleanor will smother me with tender concern, and Clotilde will listen to my tales of adventure with breathless delight.

Ah, it's good to be home. I wonder if this tea shop offers anything in the way of an all-beef patty smothered in yellow cheese with a side order of rich cream. I have a real hankering for the kind of food you can only find in America. Modern day America, that is. I've lost three pounds at least—of muscle, of course. There wasn't any fat there to lose.

But I have a feeling I'm going to need sustenance. I can't wait until these love-besotted humanoids begin to remember, and to wonder. It should be real entertaining, especially when Samuel has to admit that those witchy little boots Madame Mysterious is wearing make more than a simple fashion statement. Meow! They don't call me Familiar for nothing!

HARLEQUIN®

I N T R I G U E®

When lovers are fated, not even time can separate them....When a mystery is pending, only time can solve it....

Timeless Love

Harlequin Intrigue is proud to bring you this exciting new program of time travel romantic mysteries!

Be on time next month for the next title in this series:

#346 THE DESPERADO by Patricia Rosemoor

Ryder Smith is a wanted man— by the law in the nineteenth century...and by a woman in the twentieth.

Watch for *The Desperado* (available in November) and for all the upcoming books in TIMELESS LOVE.

HARLEQUIN®

I N T R I G U E®

INNOCENT UNTIL PROVEN GUILTY...
IN A COURT OF LAW

*Whether they're on the right side of the law—or
the wrong side—their emotions are on
trial...and so is their love.*

Harlequin Intrigue is proud to continue its ongoing
"Legal Thriller" program. Stories of secret scandal and
crimes of passion. Of legal eagles who battle the system
and undeniable desire.

Next on the docket is

> #347 CRIME OF PASSION
> by Maggie Ferguson
> November 1995

Look for the "Legal Thriller" flash for the best in
romantic suspense—only from Harlequin Intrigue!

LT-1

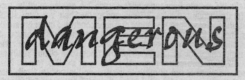